The One I Love

The Rolling Hills Series
Book 3

Chelle Sloan

Cover Design: Kari March Designs

Cover model: Charlie Gaddis

Cover photographer: Golden Czermak, FuriousFotog

Editing: Kiezha Smith Ferrell, Librum Artis Editorial Services

Proofreading: Michele Ficht

*To every woman who has ever been with a guy who made you
feel like less...*

*F*** him. You're the tits.*

Prologue
Shane

~ Seventeen Years Ago ~

As soon as I open the door and take a seat on the front steps, I instantly feel the tightness in my chest ease. There's at least a hundred people inside Simon's house right now. And yes, I know they're all here tonight for me and to send me off to the Army with one last bash, but I wish they'd all leave.

Don't get me wrong; I'm grateful. I know Oliver planned this party for weeks. And though he complained about something every day, the man was in his element with this. But in reality, I would have been just as happy with a bonfire, a case of beer, and my four best friends hanging out until the sun came up. That's how I really wanted to spend my last night before I'm gone for who knows how long. A night with just me, Oliver, Simon, Wes, and Amelia would've been perfect.

"Oh! Shane! I didn't know you were out here."

I flinch at the sound of Emily Babcock's voice. I know she can't help it, but her voice might be the worst sound on the planet. I turn around and see Emily stumbling out of the house. And stumbling is the nice word to say. The girl can barely walk.

"Emily. How about we sit down?"

She nods, but she's so drunk she looks like a bobble head. "Thanks, Shane. You're so nice. You've always been so nice to me."

I don't respond as I guide her—which means carry her—to the porch swing. Sitting her on a moving object might not be the best idea in the world, but it's my only option at this point. "How much have you had to drink tonight?"

She swings her head to look at me, which is when I notice that her hair and makeup are a mess. I can only guess how that happened—or with who.

"Just a little," she says as she pinches her fingers together. "You're hot. You know that?"

I only know that, or that she thinks that, because she tells me every time she's drunk. Which is a lot now that our senior year has come and gone. I think there's been a party every night since we graduated a month ago.

"Thanks, Emily."

She flings her arms over my shoulders, nearly punching me in the process. "Why don't we kiss? We should kiss. You're leaving. I've always wanted to kiss you."

I gently lift her arms off me. "I don't think that's a good idea, Emily."

"Why? Am I not hot enough? Do you think I'm hot?"

Oh, how do I answer this...

"It's not because of that," I say. "It just wouldn't be a good idea."

She lets out a huff. "Why not?"

I came out here to get some air. I didn't come out here to be grilled by a drunk girl who hits on me every chance she gets since freshman year. I'm sure as hell not going to tell her the truth of why it wouldn't be a good idea. No one knows that.

But just as I go to give her some sort of half-assed answer, I feel her head on my lap. I panic for just a second before I realize that she's not trying to suck my dick. She's legitimately passed out.

"Fuck," I groan. I throw my head back in frustration when I hear a familiar laugh.

"I see we've come to the 'Emily finds you and hits on you until she passes out' part of the night."

I look up to see Amelia leaning against the door of the house.

"Something like that."

I gently lift Emily's head off my lap as I stand, doing my best not to move the swing any more than I have to. I quickly take off my flannel shirt and make it into a ball so she has something for her head. Luckily, it's still in the eighties, even though it's well past eleven at night.

"You're really too nice," Amelia says as she goes to sit on the front steps.

I drop down next to her. "Don't say that too loudly. People might catch on."

She gives me a smile that, like always, hits me right in the chest. "You know you won't lose your reputation if people find out you're not the grump and the asshole everyone thinks you are."

"Let's not test that theory. Especially if I'm about to join the Army. I feel like I'll lose my edge if people find out I'm a softie."

That's partially true. I am a softie, but only for the people I care about. And to drunk girls I don't want taken advantage of. And dogs. You can't not care about dogs.

"Your secret, like so many others, is safe with me."

I smile as I look over to Amelia. She knows so many of my secrets. We've been best friends our entire lives. Our moms were best friends, so we grew up together. We went to junior prom together because neither of us had dates. I got in my first fight at school protecting her in fourth grade. She's the only one in the world who knows that I'm scared of squirrels and why I won't eat any white-colored condiments.

Yet there's one secret she doesn't know. And it's a secret I don't think I'll ever tell her.

"Thanks," I say, needing to look away so I don't give myself up. I do this often. She thinks I'm being aloof, but I'm not. It's just me protecting myself so I don't do something stupid like kiss her. Because she's not mine to kiss. "Are you having fun?"

"Surprisingly, I am."

"Why surprisingly?"

She leans back, holding herself up with one hand while the other rubs her stomach. "When you're three months pregnant, still throwing up at random times, and want to go to bed at eight every night, fun isn't exactly in the vocabulary. Or at least, I have a different definition of fun these days that doesn't include beer pong or a game of quarters."

I still can't believe Amelia's pregnant. When she told me, I was in shock. So were the guys when she told them right before graduation. Still, none of us said a word. Not even Simon, who usually can break any tense moment with a well-placed joke or inappropriate statement. But we were all stunned and silent. That is until Amelia broke down and started crying. I still remember the second she fell into my arms and started sobbing, wondering what she was going to do. How was she going to raise a child when she still felt like one? She didn't have a job. She was supposed to go to college next year, but had to defer. She felt like her life was falling apart.

But, like we always do, we assured her we'd be there for

her. Wes started researching everything there was to know about babies and pregnancy, and looked up every doctor, hospital, and midwife in Middle Tennessee. Simon set up bank accounts and called around to every business in Rolling Hills to see who was hiring. I took it upon myself to build her a rocking chair. I figured she could use one when the baby came. And Oliver did what he does best—he planned an event. So last week, four eighteen-year-old guys threw a baby shower for their best friend. The girl who completed our group. The girl who has always been our voice of reason when we were about to do something stupid.

The girl I'm in love with.

"Well, thank you for coming."

She shoots me a look like I'm crazy. "I would have come if I was in the middle of birthing this child."

"I know," I say, a sadness falling over me. "And I'm sorry."

"For what?"

"That I'm not going to be here." I look down to her stomach then back up to her. "I hate that I'm not going to be here for you."

And I do. I've known for a long time that I was going to enlist after high school. That was my path from the beginning. But when Amelia told me the news, I almost withdrew my papers.

"I know," she says, sitting up and taking my hand and holding it between both of hers. "But I'm going to send you pictures. And videos. And I'm sure Simon or Oliver will at some point start making a documentary from it."

I laugh, because that sounds exactly like them.

"And, you know, Paul will be here. He's not going to leave me hanging."

Just the mere mention of Amelia's boyfriend-slash-father of

her child sets my blood boiling. Out of every guy she could have been with, she chose that fucking dickhead.

"Will he, though?" I look back toward the house through the window and see that asshole chest bumping with one of his minions after making a shot in beer pong.

"Shane..."

I hold up my hands in defense. "I know. I'm sorry."

Except I'm not. It's just easier to say that instead of getting into another fight about Paul. It's the only thing we've ever fought about. He's an asshole. A cocky prick who thinks just because he can throw a football and his dad owns the town's car dealership that he's God's gift to mankind. I don't know what Amelia sees in him. And why, out of all the guys at Rolling Hills High School, she had to go for him.

And it wasn't just a little flirtation. The woman tried to join the football team junior year to get his attention. Granted, she was always a tomboy, but trying to play high school football to get a guy is a whole other level.

And it worked. Eventually. They started up right after junior prom. Now, just over a year later, she's pregnant with his baby.

"They want me and Paul to get married."

Her statement takes me by surprise. "Who?"

"My mom. His mom. He's mentioned it a few times."

Married? She can't marry that fucking jackass. "What do you want?"

She shrugs. "I don't know if it matters what I want."

"The fuck it doesn't," I say, turning her slightly so we're facing each other. "Amelia, this is your baby. Your body. Your life. Is marrying Paul what you want to do with it?"

"Don't say it like that."

"Like what? I'm asking a legitimate question. Do you want to marry him?"

She looks up at me with sad eyes. "I don't know what I want."

I take a deep breath, doing my best to calm myself for her. "I know the baby took you by surprise."

"That's an understatement."

"But that doesn't mean you have to get married. Hell, look at Oliver's mom. She raised him alone."

"She adopted him when she was in her thirties. Very different."

"I'm just saying, don't marry him because you feel like you have to. If you want to marry him, do it because you love him. Not because of pressure."

I hate that I suggested an avenue for her to marry him, but as a friend, that's what she needed to hear. Oh God, what if they do get married? Maybe that will be one of the positives of me being away—I won't have to be here for it. Or have to decide whether I'm going to stand up in the service and object. But I wouldn't. I'd never stand in her way like that. And I'd never rock the boat. She's my best friend. A sister to the guys in our group. Our mothers are basically connected at the hip. It would rock so many boats.

"Let's change the subject," she says. "Are you ready?"

"Yeah," I say with a shrug. "I'm packed. We can't take much."

"I'm not talking about that. Are you ready?"

I knew what she meant, but I was trying to deflect. "Can I admit something?"

"Of course."

"I'm scared," I whisper. I can barely admit it to Amelia, let alone some eavesdropping asshole. "I'm fucking scared."

It's weird I never thought about fighting in combat when I decided to enlist. But the country's at war. I don't know where I'm going to end up, but it's possible I'll be shipped overseas.

"That's normal," Amelia says. "I think I'd be more worried about you if you weren't scared."

"What if I don't come back?"

The words fall out of my mouth, though I never meant to say them. It's been the one thing on my mind as the day has come closer and closer.

"What do you mean if you don't come back? You're coming back."

"You don't know that, Amelia." I stand up and begin to pace. "I don't know where I'm going to end up. Those videos and calls you say you're going to make—I don't know if I'm going to be able to get them. What if something happens? What if this is the last time I see you? What if this is the last time I tell Simon to fuck off? What if I never see Wes play a down of football again? What if I'm not here to talk Oliver off the ledge on his wedding day? I'm scared, Amelia. I'm so fucking scared."

I take a deep breath to push the tears back when I see Amelia running over and jumping into my arms. I don't hesitate to catch her as we wrap each other in a hug so tight I don't know if either of us can breathe.

"You're going to come back. You hear me? Because this baby needs its Uncle Shane. *I* need you, Shane. You're not allowed to leave me. I refuse to believe this is the last time we see each other. So you go off and be a hero, then come back and live a very quiet life in Rolling Hills, where the biggest fight you'll have to be a part of is when Simon and Oliver can't decide what to order for breakfast. You got it?"

I huff out a chuckle. "Got it."

We slowly loosen our grip, which allows Amelia to slide down my body. I see tears running down her cheeks, so I take my thumbs and push them away. God, I'm going to miss her. I'm going to miss her smile. Her brown eyes that have always brought me peace. The way she busts my balls to keep me honest. Her laugh. The way she always knows what to say. I'm going to miss her so damn much.

I know I'm not supposed to think like this, but what if this *is* the last time I see her? What if something does happen, and I never tell her how I feel? What if I die and not do the one thing I've wanted to do since I can remember?

Fuck it. What do I have to lose? I know she's with Paul. I know she's going to have his baby. I know that if anyone found out what I'm about to do, my friends would fly to wherever I'm stationed and grill me about it.

I don't care. Because I need to do something stupid.

And I do. I kiss her. I pull her face closer to me and kiss her with everything I have.

For a second, she doesn't move. She stills as our lips meet. But that doesn't last long. Before I know it, she's kissing me back.

Holy shit, Amelia is kissing me back.

Her hands are gripping my biceps as our mouths fumble and we try to find a rhythm. Despite popular belief, I haven't kissed that many girls. How could I when only one girl ever truly interested me? I tried to get her out of my system, but it never worked. Amelia has always been it.

And now that I'm kissing her? I might be doomed for life.

Our tongues connect, and we're finally finding our groove when a loud thump breaks our moment. We jump apart, both gasping for air. When I look back to the porch I see Emily sprawled onto the porch. The drunk fool fell out of the porch swing.

"Where am I? Shane? Where are you?"

Amelia and I look at Emily before turning back to each other. The look of shock and confusion in her face is apparent.

And I know the chivalrous thing is to go check on Emily, but I honestly couldn't care less right now.

"Amelia..."

She shakes her head. "Don't say anything else."

"But..."

"No. Nothing else. That's how we're going to leave this. No talking. No apologies. This is our see you for now. No goodbye. Got it?"

I nod. "Got it."

"Good." She leans up and gives me one more kiss on my cheek. "Be brave, soldier. And make sure you come back to us."

I stand back and watch Amelia walk back toward the house, stopping to help Emily up before she goes back inside. I don't move. I just watch. When she turns back to look at me one more time, my heart about breaks. But at least I know that if something does happen, I kissed the girl of my dreams.

Even if I'm not the guy of hers.

Chapter 1
Amelia

I'm in awe as I watch my future sister-in-law come into the bridal suite in her wedding dress. It's a fitted, lace, floor-length gown with spaghetti straps and a sweetheart neckline. There's just a small amount of sparkle in the dress, which gives her the look of a princess. The diamond necklace and diamond teardrop earrings she's wearing doesn't hurt either.

I expect nothing less from the former beauty queen.

"Is it too much?"

"Why are you asking questions you know the answer to?" That comes from Betsy, her best friend and maid of honor. "You look gorgeous. Jake is going to cry. It's going to be awesome."

"I hope it is," she says, taking another look at herself in the floor-length mirror. "I just want today to be perfect."

Betsy goes up and hugs Whitley from behind. "It will be. Y'all have waited so long for this day. All that's left is to go out and do the damn thing."

I smile as the two share a laugh. I've gotten to know Betsy

pretty well over the past few months. Not only did she move to Rolling Hills because of Whitley, but she's dating Wes, one of my closest friends. She's also his nanny. Though right now I don't know if they are dating. Or if she's nannying. I don't know what happened exactly, but I do know they had a huge fight last week. Wes hasn't said anything to me or the guys. Betsy has been going nonstop with maid of honor and wedding duties. I didn't stand in her way or ask questions. She was a woman on a mission.

"Speaking of, did the cupcakes arrive?"

Betsy nods. "Delivered and currently chilling."

"What about the caterer? I didn't have a chance to talk to Charlie today to make sure that everything was set."

"It's fine," Betsy assures. "I saw her van pulling up a bit ago. Now, can you sit back, take off your event planner hat for the rest of the day, and relax? I mean, that is why you hired a planner instead of doing this all yourself."

"I'm sorry," Whitley says. "Being on the other side of the wedding is more stressful than I thought."

"Here," I say, handing her a glass of champagne. "Sip this. Relax. Everything is under control."

Whitley takes the flute from me and takes a tiny sip. "Remember when I wanted a small wedding?"

This makes both of us laugh. "You really thought you could get away with that?"

"She did," Betsy says. "The daughter of a famous Alabama quarterback, the sister of a professional football coach, and basically Southern royalty, thought she could get away with a fifty-person wedding."

"Really?"

She nods as she takes another sip. "That didn't even include Jake's friends and family. Before we knew it the guest list was at three hundred and I just gave up."

"Wow," I say, unable to fathom the amount of people that are going to be here. "You should have done it like me and eloped."

"You eloped?" Betsy asks.

I nod my head. "Yup. A courthouse wedding on a Wednesday afternoon. Though I don't recommend being eighteen and pregnant while doing it."

"Did you ever have a reception or anything?"

"Never. Our families went out to dinner, but that's it. By the time we did have the money to throw a party, it felt like a waste."

Well, that's what my ex-husband always said. I asked once if we could renew our vows and have the party we never had. Paul vetoed that idea immediately. Hell, once I just brought up in conversation that a nurse I worked with got an upgraded engagement ring from her husband for their anniversary. I never asked for one, but for the next week he made digs about me not liking my ring and how I was ungrateful.

Yet, those weren't even two of the biggest issues or fights Paul and I had when we were married. But I do like to think of them from time to time to remind myself why I'm glad we're divorced.

"I don't know your ex-husband, but he sounds like the worst," Betsy says.

I hold up my champagne flute to Betsy. "I knew I liked you."

We share a smile and each take a sip of bubbly. "This is nice. I've never been in a wedding before."

"Really?" Whitley asks.

"Nope. I didn't have a lot of girlfriends growing up. Then I was pregnant with Luke, so making friends wasn't on the top of my to-do list. The only one of the guys who's been married is Wes and..."

I trail off, hating that I brought up Wes in front of Betsy. "I'm sorry. I didn't mean to."

She shakes her head. And if I'm reading her right, she might push back a tear. "Don't worry."

"Have you talked to him at all?"

She shakes her head. "No."

"I'm sorry."

"Not your fault he's being a jackass."

I laugh. "It's definitely not. I've tried my best for years with all of them, but to no avail."

"You're a saint, Amelia Evans. Those men don't deserve you." Betsy takes a deep breath. "Soon he's going to realize he was ridiculous and in the wrong. Until then I'm going to drown my sorrows in champagne, maybe dance with a Fury player tonight, and pretend to be happy."

"Please, just make sure he doesn't start anything," Whitley says. "The last thing I need is a fight."

She waves her away. "Don't you worry. He's all bark and no bite. Plus, I'll have my wing woman next to me on the dance floor, so it will be no problem."

Betsy looks over to me. Wait. Am I the wing woman? "Excuse me, what?"

"You're going to be on the dance floor next to me."

"I am?"

"You are," Betsy says as she slides next to me. "The way I see it, you're single. I'm not single, but if my man doesn't get his head out of his ass soon, I'm going to be. I can't have the fun tonight I wanted to, so I'm going to play matchmaker and find you a hottie on the Fury. And then if I find one to dance with to drive Wes a little crazy, you'll be there in case something goes down. It's a win-win."

I shake my head. "I can't do that."

"Why not?"

"Because." I stammer for a second, because there are many, many reasons I can't do that, but none seem to be coming to mind right now. "My kids are going to be there."

Yes. The kids. Perfect. I love my kids for many reasons, but using them to get out of shit I don't want to do has to be my favorite.

Betsy narrows her eyes. "So you're telling me you can't dance with a guy because your grown children will be there?"

"Yes. That's exactly it."

"I thought the kids were leaving early to watch Wes's kids?"

I shoot a glance at Whitley, who should be on my side for this. "Yeah, but I don't know what time that's going to be."

"Amelia, even if they are there when it happens, I don't think seeing you having a harmless dance with a man is going to send them to therapy."

She's right. My kids wouldn't care—and they'll be at therapy one day for many different reasons. To be honest, I'm pretty sure they'd dance around me, cheering me on, if they saw me living a little.

"It's just that I don't...I don't date much. I tried it. It's not my thing. And I've never done it in front of my kids."

"Oh," Betsy says. "Well, that's normal. Not wanting your kids to meet someone until it's serious."

I shake my head. "I know. I tried a few years ago. But we either didn't click, or the guys got wind of it and they went into big brother mode and scared them off. At the end of the day, it was more of a hassle than anything. So I've just, I don't know, given up."

"Nope. I refuse that statement," Betsy says. "Now we're definitely doing it. I'm on a mission to get you laid."

"Whoa," I say. "I haven't even agreed to you finding me someone to dance with."

"Fine. We'll start with dancing. But we all know where that can lead."

Betsy wags her eyebrows as I shake my head. "Absolutely not. I can't do that."

"What can't you do?"

I turn toward the door to see my daughter, Mariah, in the doorway of the bridal suite. She looks stunning in her junior bridesmaid's dress, which is the same shade as our pale pink dresses. I have to remind myself she's only thirteen. She looks so grown up.

"Nothing," I say.

"That's a lie," Whitley says. "Mariah, what would you think if your mom danced with a guy tonight?"

"I'd say 'get it, Mom!' As long as he's fine. And knows not to wear brown shoes with black pants."

"See?" Whitley says. "Mariah's seal of approval with standards that should be commended."

I shoot my daughter a look. "You're no help and grounded for a week."

"No, I'm not. But it's cute that you thought you could."

I swear I can discipline my child. "You wouldn't think it would be weird? If you saw me dancing, or maybe flirting, with a guy tonight?"

"Nope," she says, walking over to the mirror to check her makeup. "You and Dad have been divorced for a while. He dates. Why can't you?"

Well, your dad was "dating" before we even split up.

"Don't compare me to him."

"I'm just saying. It's a wedding. Have fun. Luke and I are leaving early to watch the little kids so you don't have to worry about it being weird in front of us. Have fun, Mom. You deserve it."

Betsy claps her hands as she stands up. "There. Settled. I'm setting Amelia up tonight."

I shake my head and try to argue, but the wedding planner enters the suite, telling us it's time to go. We all grab our flowers and make our way toward the ceremony.

I'm not even two steps out the door when I hear the distinct sound of my mother's voice.

"Oh, Amelia, you look beautiful."

I turn around to see my mom, who looks equally beautiful in her mother-of-the-groom dress. "Thanks, Mom."

We give each other a kiss on the cheek. "Isn't today just beautiful?"

"It is. A perfect day."

"Well, almost perfect."

The sad tone she's using used can mean a handful of things. The question is, do I feel like guessing, or just want her to cut to the chase. Due to time restrictions, I'm going to go with the latter.

"What's that, Mom? Why is today not quite perfect?"

She gives me sad eyes. "Because you're here alone."

I could have guessed that. I figured that was the answer, even though I'd hoped she wasn't going to point that out today.

"Mom. How many times do I have to tell you I'm fine?"

"I know," she says with a sigh. "It's just that weddings are so romantic. You should be here with someone."

"Did you bring a date?"

"Oh, Amelia," she says as she waves me off. "Why would I bring a date?"

I love my mother. I really do. But her rationale when it comes to my dating life is so hypocritical it isn't funny. And this isn't new. It's been like this since the day I told her I was pregnant with Luke.

"Because if I have to, then you do as well. Or—hear me out —we could both not have dates and be just fine."

Like me, my mom has been single for years. I don't think she's been in a serious relationship since our dad took off when I was in middle school. Yet that's okay. She's fine. She has her book club, her card club, and of course, bingo with Shane's mom. But me being single? That's a crime against humanity.

"That's not how it works, Amelia."

I just nod, knowing I'm not going to win this fight. "Okay, Mom. I'll keep that in mind for the next wedding."

I give her a kiss on the cheek and quickly walk to where the ceremony is being held. The setting is gorgeous. White and pink flowers are perfectly placed around the old Southern mansion turned elegant venue. People are starting to gather, all dressed their best for the Rolling Hills wedding of the year. Whitley and my brother Jake have been together for nearly five years now. Needless to say, the town, and our families, are ready for this to finally happen.

Whitley makes sure to stay back, her dad meeting us, before we go to our spot at the entrance. I can't help but take a look at the guests in their seats. I know not everyone comes to the ceremony, but it's hard to imagine many more people coming. Somehow, in the sea of people, I see Wes, Oliver, Shane, and Simon.

"I'll be right back," I whisper to Betsy as I hurry over to my crew. I pick up my dress so I don't trip, not trusting myself in the heels I have to wear for today. I really can't wait until I can take them off.

"Look at that, Amelia Evans in heels. I never thought I'd see the day."

"Nice to see you too, Simon." I let go of my dress and take a second and smooth it down. When I look back up, I can't help but feel Shane's stare. "Hey there."

I see him swallow a lump in his throat. "You look beautiful."

My body becomes heated with his compliment. "Thank you. You clean up well yourself. You all do."

It's not that I'm lying when I say that, but I needed to throw the rest of them in there. Because Shane Cunningham is hot every day of the week. Whether it's in his police uniform or casual clothes, the man turns heads. But in a suit? The man is downright delectable.

He's going to have every single woman at this wedding tonight drooling over him. And he's probably not going to even notice.

"Thank you for noticing, Amelia," Simon says as he gives a pull to his jacket. "I was hoping for a better bridesmaid selection."

I look back to where Betsy and Mariah are standing. "Sorry to disappoint. It's just us."

"I mean, I could see what Betsy—"

"Don't you fucking dare," Wes growls.

Simon smiles. "One of these days, fucking with you is going to get old. Today isn't that day."

Wes elbows Simon a little as they sit down. It's then I look over to Oliver, who looks like a lost puppy. I take him aside so I can whisper to him without the guys hearing. "You okay?"

He shakes his head. "Shannon broke up with me."

"Oh no," I say as I rub his arm. "What happened?"

"What do you think?"

"Sweetie, did you propose again?"

He looks away. "I didn't mean to. I swear."

"You never do."

Oliver turns away and goes to sit down, leaving Shane alone.

I love all of the guys. I have a special bond with each of

them. But Shane and I are on a different level. Maybe it's because we've known each other since birth. Maybe it's because the man became my protector in fourth grade and never stopped.

And yes, there was that whole kiss thing. But that was many moons and lifetimes ago. An emotional response to an emotional night. It meant so little that neither one of us have spoken of it since that night.

No. It's not that. The bond Shane and I share is built on years of friendship, respect, and family that's not blood. He's my safe space. My go-to. My person. Which means most of the time I can ignore that the man looks like a Greek god. Today is not one of those days.

"Mom! Uncle Shane!"

I've never been more thankful to hear my daughter's voice. "Hey, sweetie."

"The wedding planner says it's time to head back."

"Oh," I say. "Thanks."

"Wait! We need pictures!" Out of nowhere, my daughter produces her camera. "Hurry. Smile!"

The three of us lean in for a selfie. I don't know how Mariah takes them so effortlessly. I try and it looks like I have six chins and my eyes are crossed.

"Good. Now you two."

I look at Mariah, then Shane, then back to Mariah. "Us?"

"Yeah. Documented proof of Uncle Shane wearing a suit and Mom wearing a dress."

I step next to Shane, who hesitantly puts his arm around my back. "Why is this reminding me of when we went to prom together?"

He chuckles. "Because our moms made us pose for more pictures than I think I've ever taken in my life."

"One, two, three, smile!"

I lean in a little closer to Shane and can't help but be taken aback by his cologne. Why does he smell so good? Does he always smell good? Also, why does his hand resting on my back have heat rays coming from it?

"Got it."

I nod and step away from Shane, instantly missing the touch of his hand. "See you later?"

He nods. "Yeah. See you later."

I turn to walk away but hear Shane's voice before I get too far.

"You really do look beautiful."

This stops me in my tracks. I turn slightly to him. I feel a blush come over me as I see him standing with his hand in his pockets, a shy smile on his face. "Thank you."

Feeling suddenly self-conscious, I quickly walk back to where Betsy and the wedding planner are waiting. But not before I take one more look back to Shane, who is still staring.

"Amelia!"

I turn back around to see Betsy standing next to a very attractive man. "Um...hi."

He smiles. "You must be Amelia."

"I am."

"Amelia, let me introduce you to Anthony Martinez. He's a coach on the Fury."

"Hi," I say, holding out my hand. Wait, am I shaking this guy's hand? What the hell am I doing? Luckily, he doesn't leave me hanging. Because that would have been awkward.

"Nice to meet you, Amelia."

"Likewise."

I can't say anything else because the wedding planner is whisper-yelling to get us all into places and shooing away the people not in the wedding party.

"I guess that's my cue to leave," Anthony says as he takes

my hand and presses a kiss to the top of it. "Save me a dance later?"

I nod, because that's all I can do. I'm not blinking. I'm not breathing. I think I'm blacking out.

"Holy shit, girl," Betsy says as she moves me into place, which partially brings me back to reality. "Am I a matchmaker or what?"

"Oh, Amelia! It's like my prayer was answered!" That comes from my mom just as she begins to walk down the aisle.

"He's cute, Mom. I approve."

"Thanks," I say as Mariah follows the mothers of the bride and groom. I go when I'm told, but I have no idea what I'm doing. All I can think about are the events of the last ten minutes.

Did an attractive man ask me to dance with him? Did he kiss my hand? Is Shane staring at me right now?

That last one really knocks me back to Earth. I know I should be looking around to the guests, smiling pretty and what not, but I can't stop looking at Shane. Because I don't think he's stopped looking at me.

Why is he looking? I know not a lot else is going on, and many people are looking at me, but Shane's stare feels different. I don't know what it is, but it's freaking me out.

When I get to the end of the aisle, I let out a breath and say a thank you to our Lord and Savior Dolly Parton for not letting me trip in these heels. I watch as Betsy comes down the aisle, and because I can't help myself, I look over to see how Wes is holding up. Except I never make it to Wes. I stop on Shane, who's still looking at me.

What the hell is he doing?

And why is it making me feel some sort of way?

Chapter 2
Shane

"Shane?"

"Yeah?"

"I need to fix this."

I take a sip of my drink before telling Wes that yes, in fact, he is a dumbass. "No shit, Sherlock."

He slams his hands on the table at the wedding reception before walking off, thankfully not toward the dance floor where Betsy is dancing with one of the Nashville Fury players. It's nothing suggestive or sexual. Just two people having a good time.

They aren't the only ones. Tons of people are on the dance floor as the song changes from a fast, upbeat one to a slower ballad. I'm not one of those people. I don't dance. I never have. I'm a proponent of not doing things you don't want to do. Like now, I don't want to dance with the few women who have made eyes at me tonight. I don't want to follow Wes as he tries not to punch a hole in the wall. I don't even want to go and stand at the bar and drink with Oliver. No, I'd rather sit at this table, sip my whiskey, and stew as I watch husbands and wives, couples, and even strangers, make their way to the dance floor.

Especially one couple.

Like she knows I'm thinking about her, I see Amelia walk onto the dance floor, hand-in-hand with the guy who has been hitting on her all day. He's about my height, at six-foot-two, and well built, likely one of the many professional football players or coaches in attendance tonight. I wanted to put my fist through his face at the ceremony when I saw him kiss her hand. I almost flipped a table watching them dance earlier.

And now, as I watch him pull her so close there's barely enough room for air between them, I might kill a man.

What is Amelia doing? She doesn't do this. She doesn't dance or date or hang out with men. And why is she laughing like he just told her the world's best joke?

Wait...is he pulling her closer? How can that happen? Wait...is he about to kiss her?

Fuck this shit...

I feel my hand tighten around my rocks glass as I watch this play out. He doesn't kiss her, but their foreheads are touching, and that's just as bad.

I'm shocked I don't break the glass. But holding onto this is the only thing keeping me from racing to the dance floor and pulling her away from him. I know I need to look away, but I can't stop staring at her. It's been like this all day. It's like my eyes are searching for her every second.

I've always thought Amelia was beautiful in her understated way. Her curves are subtle, and she rarely shows them, but today, in her fitted pink dress, every single one is highlighted. My mouth has been watering since the second I saw her walk into the ceremony. She's wearing makeup, which is another rarity, but it's not what makes her beautiful. It's highlighting her already perfect features. Like her eyes. Her brown eyes seem to be sparkling. Her long brown hair is styled in a way I've never seen before, with soft curls hitting at her shoulder.

All those things are different about Amelia, but that's not what I'm being drawn to tonight. No, it's that for the first time in a long time, she looks happy. Free. Like she doesn't have the weight of the world on her shoulders as a single mom to two kids. Or a demanding career. She just looks like a woman who's enjoying her night.

And I'm the bastard who's about to ruin it.

I look around, hoping that one of my friends is here to stop me from doing the stupid thing I'm about to do. Not that they would know what they're stopping me from. None of them know I've been in love with Amelia for decades. That I once kissed her. That since I can remember, I've pushed down feelings for her because I couldn't risk ruining our friendship. Or risk ruining the dynamic of our friend group.

All of those reasons are feeling flimsy as hell right now.

I remember years ago when I decided I was going to kiss her. It was a split-second decision. Like the wire had snapped, and it would be the biggest regret of my life if I didn't kiss her.

That's what I'm feeling right now. I know I need to be stopped. But I also don't want to be.

I look around to see if any are near me. Wes is gone, hopefully trying to figure out how to get Betsy back. Oliver's at the bar hitting on a leggy redhead. My guess is he's three drinks away from proposing. I have no idea where Simon is after he randomly got up from the table and stomped away.

I need to let this go. Or if I'm going to stay, I need to ignore Amelia and the Fury asshole. It's not my place. I'm her friend. That's it. I'm Uncle Shane to her kids. The guy who mows her lawn and shovels her driveway because that's the kind of friend I am.

I kissed her once and it could've ruined everything. The only reason it didn't is because I left for the Army the next day and was gone for the better part of the following eight years. If I do something stupid again, I'll have to face the consequences. And I don't know if I'm ready for that.

Sit still Shane. Breathe. Take another drink of whiskey. Don't look at her. Ignore that her lips are now dangerously close to that fucker's mouth.

Fuck! How can I ignore that? I can't.

I won't.

I'm about to do something stupid again, aren't I?

Fuck...I am.

I can't hold back any longer. Maybe it's the whiskey talking. Maybe it's knowing that Amelia has only dated—or been married to—losers and assholes. Maybe it's still thinking about that kiss from seventeen years ago way too often. But I can't sit by and watch this happen.

Especially now that his hands are starting to drift down lower and lower on her back.

Fuck. That. Shit.

I nearly knock my chair over as I stand up and march to the dance floor. The song ends as soon as I get to Amelia, giving me the perfect opportunity to grab her hand and pull her off the dance floor. I hear her say a quick "Sorry!" as I all but drag her outside.

"Shane?" Amelia asks, clearly confused about what's going on. "What are you doing?"

My hand tightens on hers as I take us to the terrace. There seems to be a dark corner out of sight from the ballroom. I don't know if it's truly private, but it must be better than being in front of every wedding guest who just watched me drag Amelia away like a caveman.

"What the hell, Shane?" she says, pulling her hand away and shaking her arm.

"What were you doing in there?"

Amelia looks at me like I'm crazy, which I might be. "You're going to have to be more specific."

"In there." I point back toward the reception. "Who were you with?"

"Anthony?"

Why is she asking me like I should know?

"I don't know. That fucker who was all over you?"

She rolls her eyes at me, which is warranted. "Oh, my God. Yes, his name is Anthony. And he wasn't all over me."

"Who is he?"

"Why do you care?"

"Humor me."

Amelia lets out a frustrated groan. "Anthony is a Fury coach. We met before the ceremony. He's nice. And polite. And funny. And I thought, you know, because I'm a grown woman, I could dance with a man without being tarred and feathered for it."

"That was dancing?" I say with a bite. "I didn't realize you needed to be that close to dance. Who knew?"

Amelia's eyes are beginning to bulge out of her head. And, because I know her so well, I realize she's five seconds away from ripping me a new asshole. Fine. I'll take it. As long as it means she's away from Coach Grab Ass.

"You're fucking unbelievable!" She starts pacing back and forth, throwing her hands in the air. "Why do you care? Why can't you let me live my life? Are you my keeper tonight? Is that why you've been staring at me all day? If so, I apologize; I didn't know I needed to ask permission to dance with a man who I find nice and attractive. Oh, and have I mentioned that what I do in my private life is none of your business?"

"Nice? Attractive? Really, Amelia? Don't act like you're interested in this guy. You barely know him."

"Are you kidding me?" she screams. "I can't with you. This is always how it is."

"How what is?"

"This! You. Me. The rest of the idiots we call friends. Ever since my divorce—which was *seven years ago*, by the way—whenever I show interest in someone, one of you idiots gets involved and ruins it. Either I get the third degree, or worse, they do. Or you run them off. The others have cooled off over the years, but you? You seem to have made it your personal mission to make sure I die alone."

I take a few slow breaths as I do my best to push down the words that are threatening to come out. "I'm just trying to protect you."

"Protect me? From what? Dating? The outside world? What is it, Shane? Tell me." She takes a few deep breaths to calm down, but it doesn't lower the sound of her voice. "I know you've saved me before. And I'll always be grateful for that. But what are you saving me from now? I'd love to know. Because all I see here is a man, who claims to be my best friend, treating me like I'm a dumb woman who can't make her own choices."

I don't say anything. I can't. She's right. I do all those things. I'm doing them right now. But I can't tell her why I do them, so I don't say anything.

"Of course, the trademark Shane Cunningham silence," she says, her voice growing louder. "Well, since you have nothing to say, let me tell you this: I'm a divorced, single mom of two exhausting teenagers. I rarely get nights to truly let my hair down and forget about my responsibilities. And you know what? I did. I was having fun. I didn't feel guilty for living a little. I was having a lovely evening with a lovely man until you pounded your chest and dragged me away because apparently, fun isn't allowed where you're concerned."

"You can have fun."

This makes her laugh, though I doubt she's finding it very funny. "You really don't get it, do you? You're supposed to be my best friend. Same with Wes and Oliver and Simon, but you more than anyone. You know everything I've been through. Everything *we've* been through. So why? Why can't you let me have this? Why do you insist on being my unofficial bodyguard? Why for one night can't you let me be a single woman who wants to have a good time at a wedding and not worry about work, or my kids, or—"

She doesn't see it coming. She didn't see it coming seventeen years ago, either.

I just grab her and kiss her. I kiss *the hell* out of her. I kiss her the way I've wanted to kiss her for years.

And in that moment, I know that now everything is about to change...

Chapter 3
Amelia

Holy shit, is Shane kissing me?

What in the world is happening right now?

I think that was the same reaction I had when he kissed me all those years ago. I was confused. I froze. I didn't know what to do with my hands. But then my lips decided they wanted to kiss him back, so I did.

The same thing is happening now. My body is still. My mind is racing. My hands are in the air, because they were flailing around just seconds ago when I was giving my Oscar-worthy monologue.

But my lips? Those are moving with his. Because apparently that's what they do when Shane kisses me.

Why is he doing this? I mean, I wondered that when we were eighteen, too, but I eventually chalked that up to an emotional night and an uncertain future. We were young, dumb, and let the night get the best of us.

That's not the case tonight. We're not young. We're not as dumb as we used to be. And back then there was hesitancy in Shane's kiss. That I do remember. Tonight? Right now? There's not a drop of indecision. This man is kissing me because he wants to.

And I'm kissing him back.

My arms soon start moving, looping them around his neck so my fingers can run through his jet-black hair. He brings me in closer, pressing my body up to his rock-hard chest. And his lips? Holy hell. This isn't the same kiss as that eighteen-year-old boy. No, this is the kiss of a man. A man who is trying to kiss me with everything he has in him.

It's...amazing. Real. Raw. Passionate. My body is coming alive with every swipe of his tongue. With every nibble of my lip. I pull him closer, needing more, because now that I know Shane Cunningham can kiss like this, I don't know if I want him to stop.

When Shane kissed me all those years ago, I'll admit, it sent sparks through me. But I didn't think anything of it. Since then, I honestly can say I've never thought about what kind of kisser Shane was. I mean, the man doesn't date. I've never seen him with a woman. And because of that, it was easy to just not think about it.

But considering this man is taking my mouth in a way that I couldn't fight against even if I tried, I'm going to go out on a limb with the assumption this man hasn't been spending every Friday night alone. Because there is no way these lips have been sitting dormant for years.

I push that thought aside, because I don't want to think about Shane kissing another woman right now. All I want to do is bask in the way his hands are cradling my face, holding me to him like he's scared to let me go. I want to revel in the feel of his soft lips kissing me harder than I ever have been in my life. I want to memorize the sensation of his beard against my cheek.

Just as I'm about to give myself permission to truly sink into whatever this is, there is a sound like a glass breaking against the concrete and we both jump back like we've been shocked.

"What was that?" I ask through my short breaths.

Shane looks around but doesn't move away from me to investigate the scene. Some cop he is.

"Probably some drunk."

I nod, not knowing what to say. Because the spell is broken. The moment is gone.

Shane and I stare at each other for what feels like hours. Neither of us says anything. The only sound in the air is our heavy breathing and the rustle of the trees blowing in the soft April breeze of Nashville.

"I'm—"

"That was—"

We both awkwardly laugh at our simultaneous attempts at filling the silence. But I'm glad that happened, because I honestly don't know what I wanted to say. And not just in this moment, but likely the rest of my life.

It was one thing when this happened when we were younger. But this time is different. The kiss felt different. The moment was different. How I feel after feels different. The way he's looking at me right now is different. And the biggest thing —I now have to live with the knowledge that my best friend just gave me the single best kiss of my life.

And I don't know how I feel about that.

"You start," I say, needing to put this on him. I mean, he's the one who kissed me. It's only fair.

Shane nervously puts his hands in his pockets as he looks down at the ground. I know him well enough to know that he's taking his time and trying to figure out what to say. Shane isn't a man of many words. But the words he does say are always pointed and honest. That's one of the things I've always loved about him.

Now you can add kissing to that list...

"I'm sorry. That was a stupid thing to do." His voice is quiet as he slowly looks back up at me. My heart breaks the second his eyes meet mine. Without him saying another word, I can feel the torture and sadness running through his veins. "I shouldn't have done that."

We both take a seat on a nearby bench. Shane leans forward, his elbows resting on his legs as he stares at the ground.

"Which part?" I need to know this. My state of mind is dependent on this answer.

"Everything."

My stomach immediately drops, which shocks me. I didn't expect to have that kind of reaction. Yes, I wanted him to apologize for literally dragging me out of the reception. And I thought I wanted him to apologize for the kiss. Judging by the sudden ache in my gut, maybe I didn't?

I'm so fucking confused. His kiss has confused me. Because how can something that felt so good also make you feel so...confused?

"Okay..."

"I don't know what I was thinking by dragging you out here," Shane says, still not making eye contact with me. "But I know that I was an ass, and I apologize."

"Thank you for that."

And I mean it. He did need to apologize for acting like a jackass. But I need him to address the kiss. Seventeen years ago we both walked away, never to speak of it again. I don't think I can do that again.

I lean forward and tilt my head in his direction, forcing him to look at me. I need to see his eyes when I ask him this next question. "Anything else?"

Shane starts to say something but is interrupted by

someone calling my name in the distance. We both look that way to see Anthony walking toward us.

"There you are," Anthony says. "I didn't know where you went."

"I—" I start to respond with some bullshit excuse but Shane cuts me off.

"I needed her for a second," he says. "One of her kids called her, but she didn't have her phone, so they called me."

I look to Shane, who clearly is a skilled liar along with being a skilled kisser. What else can this man do that I don't know about?

"Everything okay?" Anthony asks.

I nod, still trying to get my bearings. "Yup. Everything's fine."

Anthony extends his hand for me. "Great. Ready to go back inside?"

I look over to Shane, then back to Anthony.

"Go," Shane says with a nod. "We're good out here."

We're good? What in the world is his definition of good? The man just tore me away from the wedding, kissed the hell out of me, apparently regrets it, and is now telling me to go about with my night like nothing happened? That is in no way *good.*

I want to say more, but I don't. Because Shane is saying everything with his eyes.

"I shouldn't have done that."

"I just changed everything."

"Please don't hate me."

"Okay."

I take Anthony's hand as he helps me to stand. He doesn't let go as we begin to walk back into the reception.

"Hey," I say as I stop walking. "Can you give me a minute?"

He nods. "Sure. Want a drink?"

"Please. White wine."

He leans in and gives me a kiss on the cheek. "You got it."

Nothing. That kiss felt like nothing. Granted, it was just a peck on the cheek. But a little something would have been nice.

But no.

Fuck my life...

I watch Anthony walk back into the reception. Until twenty minutes ago, Anthony was perfect. Nice. Handsome. A good dancer. A professional football coach. A lean build that I didn't mind dancing against. He made me laugh and smile. I totally could have seen myself going on a date with him. Maybe even having a little fun tonight. Not fun like Betsy wanted me to have, but, but maybe a little.

But now? All I'm going to think about the rest of the night is Shane's lips against mine and for the first time in years—since the last time he kissed me—my body has felt alive.

I turn around to see Shane staring at me, his gaze nearly knocking me on my ass. It's the same stare he's given me all day. The one that feels like he can see right through me.

I start back in his direction, needing to talk to him more, but he shakes his head, mouthing the word "Go."

That stops me in my tracks. He's right. I need to go back inside. This is my brother's wedding, and I've been gone long enough that people might start wondering where I am. And I have someone who's waiting for another dance.

Too bad I'm now wishing for a different dance partner.

Chapter 4
Amelia

THE ONE NIGHT I WANT A BUSY EMERGENCY ROOM AND we're dead. That might not be the best phrase to use about a place where people could literally die, but if you don't have a slightly twisted humor then you don't belong in an emergency room.

Now, Rolling Hills isn't a big city by any means, but we get our fair share of emergencies on any given night. But tonight, on a night where I want to keep my hands and mind busy to keep it away from the thing that's been living in my head rent free? Nope. Not even a broken bone. Which is why I'm in the supply closet for the tenth time in four hours.

"Girl, what are you doing?"

I turn over my shoulder to see Kendra, my fellow nurse and work wife. "I'm restocking the gloves."

She crosses her arms and tilts her head, clearly giving me the look that she knows exactly what I'm doing. "Because we were out from the time you stocked them thirty minutes ago?"

"We can never be too prepared! We go through hundreds a shift!"

"I don't know who you're foolin' but it isn't me," Kendra says, opening the door wider. "So what we're going to do now is go back to the station. You're going to grab a slice of that wedding cake you brought me, and we're going to talk about why you're being more Type A than normal."

I put down the box of gloves and exit out the door Kendra's holding for me. I do as asked and grab the slices of cake I remembered to take after the reception. I don't know how I remembered. It's safe to say my mind was all over the place last night. And this morning. Basically, the past twenty-four hours have been a blur.

Except the kiss. That kiss is clear as day.

"Girl did you get laid or something?"

This startles me so much I almost drop the cake. "What? No. Of course not. Why would you say that?"

Real cool, Amelia...real cool...

"Sit your ass down woman. We need to chat."

I let out a sigh and do as Kendra says. No point in hiding it.

"I didn't get laid," I say. "But, something happened."

"Girl!" Kendra starts bouncing in her seat. "Did you get some wedding action? I told you to keep an eye on those Fury players. Those men are fine as fuck. And I don't even like men."

I laugh at her enthusiasm, and for a second, the image of Anthony pops in my brain. But just as soon as I picture him, I see Shane coming over to us, tearing me away from him.

"Why does your face look like that?" Kendra asks.

"What? My face doesn't look a way."

"Yes, it does."

"Then please tell me, what does it look like?"

"Like a woman who got fucked but is now overthinking the fuck instead of just leaning into the feeling that is usually accompanied by a few orgasms."

"I told you I didn't get laid."

"Well, then, please tell, because something's going on and you're doing a shit job of hiding it."

I let out a sigh as I try to figure out where to start. "Has something ever happened to you that, until that moment, you didn't know you wanted it? But then you had it and now you want it again, but you're ninety-nine percent sure it's probably the worst decision of your life?"

"Yes," Kendra says. "That's how I figured out I was a lesbian. Now. Spill."

"It...it's Shane. He kissed me."

Kendra's eyes nearly pop out of her head. She looks like a cartoon character I had to watch on repeat when the kids were younger.

"Shane? As in your hot-as-fuck cop friend who I swear if I was into men, I'd let him break my back and then say thank you for the experience? That Shane?"

"Yup. That's the one."

"Girl!" Kendra yells, slapping me on the shoulder. "Details. Now. Every single one. If I find out you left one out, I swear to God I will make you do every enema for a year."

I start at the beginning, because I don't know where else to begin when I recount the tale of how my best friend became my best friend who kissed the hell out of me. I tell her everything. From how he looked at me at the ceremony to how he dragged me off the dance floor, then to the kiss. I didn't think it was that exciting of a story, but Kendra is sitting on the edge of her seat, salivating over every word.

"Wow," she says. "Have you talked to him at all?"

I shake my head. "I saw him this morning. We had to help our friend get his girl back, and he pulled out all the stops. But we barely looked at each other."

Well, I know I barely looked at him. I couldn't. All I could think about was the kiss every time I did. So it was safer to look away. I think he was doing the same thing, because I didn't once get the feeling he was looking my way.

Ugh. This is so bad...

I let my head fall onto the desk, narrowly missing my piece of cake. "What do I do now, Kendra? This changes everything."

She doesn't say anything for a second, which only makes my mind race faster than it already is. I can feel myself spiraling, and that's not something I enjoy.

"I doubt it's everything," Kendra says.

"It is! What if we don't ever talk again? It will be like getting divorced all over again. Or! The other side of the coin is he asks me to date. And that can't happen. So no matter which way we turn, I don't see how things go back to normal."

"Slow down," Kendra says, trying to use her hands to slow my breath. "Those are some big leaps."

"But those are the only possible outcomes as far as I'm concerned."

"Okay, let's role play. But not the fun kind with maid uniforms," Kendra says. "Let's pretend, for just the sake of argument, Shane asks you out on a date. You go. You have a good time. You kiss again. Maybe you break that dry spell you've been in for way too long. Those all seem pretty good to me. So, please, tell me all the things that could go wrong."

I laugh. "Where do I begin? First off, he's my friend. My *best* friend."

"I take offense to that best friend claim."

"You're my work wife. It's different. This is the man who knows every secret of mine. We've been through every phase of life together. He was the first person I told when I was pregnant with Luke. I told him before Paul. He saw me at my lowest during the divorce. Hell, he's the reason I was able to leave him. He's my person. How do you date your person?"

"Easy. You remember he's hot and fuck him every chance you get."

"You're not helping."

"Sorry. Continue."

"And it's not just our friendship I have to worry about, it's the whole group. If we date, or worse, if we break up, Shane and I together would shake up everything. It would throw off the whole dynamic."

"I'm guessing that this friend group is made up of adults that would, after explaining to them what is happening, adjust."

I let out a sigh. "You'd think that. But Oliver will want us to get married immediately. Wes doesn't do well with change, so that will screw with him. And Simon will be Simon, and I don't need any more of that than I already get."

"Okay," Kendra says. "But my point is that they will adjust. They are grown-ass men."

"One would think."

"Fair enough. They are men. But again, what's the big deal? So they freak out a little? It won't be like that forever."

"It's not just them," I continue. "It's about our families. Our mothers are best friends. They took pictures of us together as Mickey and Minnie Mouse on Halloween when we were two. They've been trying to push us together for years. They will be insufferable if this happens. And speaking of families, there's obviously my kids to consider. You know, the kids who call him Uncle Shane...that's a whole other thing."

Kendra gives me a questioning look. "Are they still hoping you and their dad will get back together?"

I shake my head. "Hell no. I think they were more excited than I was the day we left. They knew how unhappy I was. And he's not exactly father of the year."

"Then if they value your happiness, and I'm guessing like Shane, then why would you two dating be a bad thing?"

"Because—" I pause, now realizing I've never told Kendra this. "I haven't been in a serious relationship, or *with* a man, since the divorce."

Kendra rapidly blinks about a hundred times. "Excuse me, what?"

I nod, suddenly feeling embarrassed. "You heard me."

"Amelia, you got divorced seven years ago."

"I know."

I downplayed the sex part to Whitley and Betsy yesterday and just focused on my lack of dating. Which is true. I have tried. Nothing has stuck. And maybe it's my age, or because I haven't had it in forever, but the more you don't have sex, the less you miss it. On the other side of the coin, it's terrifying if you want to ever have it again and realize that you haven't done it in so long you might forget how.

"So you're telling me, in the span of three presidents you've had zero sex?"

"Thanks for putting it in that context, Kendra. I really appreciate that."

"Girl..." Kendra shakes her head and wheels around the nurse's station. "I can't imagine."

I shrug. "You stop missing it after a while."

Kendra suddenly wheels herself next to me, completely invading my personal space. "But..."

"But what?"

"You're thinking about it now, aren't you?"

"No."

She tilts her head. "Thou doth protest too much."

"I'm not protesting. I'm...I'm just..."

Kendra leans in a little closer. "Say it. Say you miss it. Say you want it. Say all the reasons you just gave me were your brain trying to talk you out of this. Say that your friend is sexy as fuck, and he kissed you, and you can't get it out of your head. Say you want him to use that mouth in other ways. Say you want Shane to end the drought. You know you want to."

"I..." I trail off, because I think she's right. "I might."

She throws her head back in defeat. "So close!"

"Did you think I was going to say yes immediately? Without overthinking it six ways from Sunday?"

"A girl can dream."

I'm not going to admit out loud that yes, now that I know what it's like to kiss Shane, I'm curious what more would be like. But I have to be practical. I have to think about things and how they will affect those I love. And myself. Shane and I need to talk and figure things out and be adults. Because all of those reasons I listed weren't excuses. They are realities.

"Amelia?" Kendra asks. "Can I ask you to also keep one thing in mind when you're figuring this out?"

"Sure."

"Don't let your brain talk you out of something your heart wants. Because I know you, Amelia Evans. You will look out for everyone else's wellbeing before your own. And this time, I'm going to need you to say fuck their feelings so you can fuck Shane."

I can't help but laugh at my ridiculous friend. "Just when I thought you were going to be serious and sentimental..."

"You should know better, wifey."

Chapter 5
Shane

The one thing about never wanting a serious relationship, or having more than one night with a woman, is I never had to worry about when to call. Or if I should message them. You don't call someone you meet at a bar or only see once every few months. At the most, it's a quick text. A "what are you doing?" Or a "free tonight?"

Yes, I know that's fuckboy language. Which I didn't know was a thing until I heard two rookies talking about it at the station a few months ago, but it works for me. I've never seriously dated. No one besides Amelia interested me in high school, so I didn't see the point in dating. In my twenties, I was in the Army, so women consisted of the tag chasers hanging out at the bars around base for a quick night of fun. When I moved back to Rolling Hills after my tours, there was only one woman I wanted—and she was married. After her divorce, I could have said something, but I didn't want to rock the boat. I never felt like it was the right time to tell her how I felt. So lowkey flings are it. Or, *were* it.

I don't know what to do, or how to act, now that Amelia and I are in this weird place. We usually talk every day. A quick text, or me popping over to her house, is a normal thing for us. So the fact it's been five days since I've last seen or spoke to her is fucking killing me.

I could text her. Just see how she's doing. But I don't want her to think that I'm using the text as a ploy to bring up the elephant in the room. I also don't want to spook her. I know she needs time to process. That's just how she is.

On the other hand, I feel like the longer I wait, the more the conversation won't happen. And if it does, she'll list all the reasons why kissing was the worst idea possible. Or worse: pretend that it never happened.

"Fuck!" I toss my phone across the room after checking it for the thirtieth time since I got home from work an hour ago. Luckily, it lands softly on my couch. Not so lucky is that as soon as I stand up to go over and get it—just in case I get a message—I hear a knock on the door.

"Shane! Open up! My hands are full, and I can see you in the living room."

I let out a groan as I trudge to the door to let my mom in the house. If her hands are full, that means she brought over food. I might not be in the mood for company, but I don't feel like cooking either. A man can only order takeout so many nights a week. This is Rolling Hills, after all; we have four options for takeout, and none of them make Barb Cunningham's chicken and dumplings.

When I open the door, I have to hold back a laugh. My mom is wearing a gold sequined jacket, her bingo visor, and holding two casserole dishes.

"I hope you didn't dress up just to come see me."

"You think I'd waste my lucky jacket on you? Now move so I can put these in your kitchen."

I do as she says, stepping out of the way as my mom barges past me. "What brings you over, Ma? On bingo night, no less."

"Do you know how many days it's been since I talked to you?"

I laugh under my breath as I head into my kitchen, where Mom is currently putting one of the casseroles in my refrigerator. I'm guessing the other is already in the oven. "I know it's been a while."

"Six days, Shane. Six. Days. Why do I have to go a week without talking to my firstborn?"

"It's not a week, Ma. It's six days."

"Mom Math, Shane. We round up when it's regarding how long it's been since we've talked to our children. Just wait until I finally get a hold of your brother. He's in the doghouse worse than you."

I laugh and make a mental note to text Noah a warning, though I doubt he'll see it. Last I knew he was living in South Carolina, running a chair rental business and learning to surf. But that was eight months ago so who knows where he is, or what he's doing, now.

"I'm sorry, it's just been a crazy week," I say, giving her a kiss on the cheek as I go to get a bottle of water from the refrigerator.

"Must have been. I didn't even get a recap of the wedding."

"Because you were there. I didn't think it warranted a recap."

"It's like you don't know me at all," she says dramatically.

"And it's like you don't know me."

My mom and I couldn't be any more different. She's the life of the party. Always has to know what's going on and has never met a stranger. That she and my dad got married is a total mystery. I take after him. Stoic. Not a talker. I believe I heard him grunt more than anything while I was growing up. But when it came to my mom? The man was in love. She's the only one to whom he showed his softer side.

I can relate.

"Well, you're going to humor me and tell me everything that happened while I was there and after I left."

"Why?"

"Because you're my son, I can still whoop your behind, and I made you a casserole that's currently warming in the oven."

"Fine," I groan. "What do you want to know?"

I see the not-so-subtle mischievous smile forming on her face. That's her 'I want to set you up with a girl' face. "Did you meet anyone? Dance with anyone after I left?"

Yup. The smirk gave it away. "No, Mom. I didn't meet anyone. And you know I don't dance."

And just like that, her smile disappears. "Really, Shane? You were at a wedding with three hundred people, and you couldn't find *one* person to dance with?"

"Well that's not exactly true," I say. "I danced with Oliver. He made me do some dumb line dance."

"Oliver doesn't count and you know it." The angrier she gets, the more I have to hold in my laugh. "I just...I saw so many women without dates. Not *one* interested you?"

Amelia jumps into my mind, and I make a conscious effort to keep my face neutral. There are two people in the world who can read me—one is sitting across the table from me, and the other is the reason I'm in this mind fuck.

"No Mom. No one interested me."

The lie tastes like shit as I say it, but I can't tell her the truth. I'm pretty sure if she found out what happened between Amelia and I, she'd have a heart attack. Or do a cartwheel. Maybe both. It *would* be all over town by the time bingo concluded tonight.

My mom loves Amelia like the daughter she never had. She and Amelia's mom, Tammy, have been best friends since high school, and I know they've plotted ways to possibly set us up. It started when we were kids and has never let up. None of their schemes have ever come to fruition, though one time I did hear them say something about locking us in a room and just seeing what would happen.

"Oh Shane," Mom says sadly, putting her hand on top of mine. "I just want you to be happy."

I cover her hand with my free one. "I know, Mom. I know you do."

My poor mother. All she wants in life is to be a grandma. Unfortunately, she gave birth to a son who has never had a permanent address for more than a year and another who has never had a serious relationship. At this point, I'm pretty sure if I told her I got a woman pregnant she wouldn't even be mad, as long as her future grandchildren call her Gigi.

"One day," she begins. "One day I'm going to come over and you're going to have a smile so big on your face that you can't hide it, and I'm going to know. I'm going to know immediately that you've found your soulmate."

"Don't hold your breath."

"I won't, but I have a feeling I'll know the second it happens."

Normally I wouldn't ask her to elaborate—the woman has a habit of turning a five-minute story into a three-act play—but she's piquing my curiosity. "I'll bite. How will you know?"

"Because you are, and always will be, your father's son." Mom doesn't talk about Dad a lot since he passed away four years ago. I know she misses him. They were the loves of each other's lives. She made him laugh and broke him out of his shell. He kept her grounded and made sure she thought before she acted. They balanced each other out. "The man, like you, was one of few words. He never smiled. Hell, I don't think I ever saw his mouth move."

This makes me laugh. "I can relate."

"Exactly. But, did you know that your daddy had a thing for me for years, and I didn't know?"

Now my attention is really grabbed. "I didn't."

"He did. I didn't have a clue. We went through school together, and I even sat by him in math class. The man never said a word to me. Then, on my twenty-first birthday, I was walking around The Joint telling everyone I was going to try to get twenty-one kisses for my birthday. Tammy was helping me keep score."

I slap a hand to my forehead. "Mom!"

"What? I was young and hot. Don't interrupt. Anyway, your dad overheard me saying this, and before I knew it, the man took me by the arm, pulled me in, and said he was the only man that was going to be kissing me tonight. Then he did. It was my last first kiss and the best birthday present I could have asked for."

"Wow." That's all I can say. I don't know if I'm more shocked by the story or finding out another way I'm a carbon copy of my father.

"Wow exactly." Mom stands up and walks over to the oven, taking the casserole out. "When you know, you'll know."

Mom gives me a kiss on the cheek and heads out the door. But I don't move. I stay right in my chair and replay the story she just told.

The similarities are astounding. The only difference is my mom knew there and then she had found her love. She didn't waiver or second guess.

Now I just need Amelia to realize it as well. Because the

more I wait, the more I know I don't want her to forget. I need to talk to her. I need her to know I kissed her because I couldn't *not* kiss her. I need to tell her how I feel.

I need to make sure that was her last first kiss.

Chapter 6
Amelia

As a single mom, I pride myself on being at every event my children are involved in. I've never missed a sporting event, band concert, or spelling bee. I might skid in on two wheels after praying the whole time I don't get pulled over for a speeding ticket, but I'm there.

Like right now. Mariah's track meet starts in two minutes. Luckily, she doesn't run the first event, so I have time to take a breath, fix my ponytail, and enter the event not looking like a burned-out mom running on fumes and five cups of coffee.

Point is, even though sometimes I might look like I pulled up on the hot mess express, I'm here. It's more than I can say for my ex-husband. Luke is a three-sport varsity athlete, and I can count on one hand how many games he's been to. I don't think he even knows Mariah is running track this season. One reason is because he never calls. The other is because no one ever would think Mariah would do anything athletic related. Hell, when my girlie-girl told me she was running middle school track, I almost fell over. It was the most shocking thing she's ever asked to do.

This girl loves all things makeup, hair products, and clothes —which is the opposite of me. I might have hit copy-paste with her in terms of our looks, but when it comes to our personalities and likes, we are polar opposites. I didn't own makeup until I was in my twenties. She has Diamond Rewards status at Ulta. Hell, she did my makeup for Whitley's wedding. When she was little, she wanted nothing to do with sports. We signed her up for pee-wee softball, and she refused to play outfield because her shoes got dirty. I didn't think this track thing was real, even when I came to her first meet. But there my girl was, in a uniform, bib number across her chest, lining up for the hurdles.

And she's pretty good. Maybe she did get something from her tomboy mom.

I hear the starting gun for the first race, which is my cue to get out of my car and walk into the stadium, grab my sporting event dinner of popcorn and M&Ms from the concession stand, wave to Mariah, and find a place to sit away from the parents I don't like. As I walk past the bleachers and do an initial scan, I see Jessica Mozzaro, Christina Leaftree, and Emily Babcock. That's a hard pass. They decided a long time ago their mission in life was to make mine a living hell. They were the original mean girls. Made fun of me because I was a tomboy. Sent me nasty messages because they could. They were also insanely jealous of my friendship with the guys. Then there's the whole thing that two of them slept with my ex-husband at one point in his life.

Maybe I won't sit. Standing is healthier anyway.

Snacks in hand, I turn to find a place to watch when I run into something very large. And very broad.

And very familiar.

"Amelia."

I'd recognize Shane's deep, smooth voice anywhere.

"Hi, Shane."

I try not to audibly gulp when I look up at him, but it's hard. His stare is paralyzing. His presence is consuming. It took everything in me just to say those two words.

He nods down to the snacks I have in my hand. "Why did you get those?"

I look down at my purchases then back up to him. "Because it's a track meet and this is what I eat at sporting events? It's the dinner of champions."

"I know," he says as he holds up a bag of popcorn and a box of peanut M&Ms.

He bought me snacks? That was...why did he—?

"You didn't have to do that." I mumble the word so low I don't even know if Shane heard me. I duck my head and walk to the fence, but I feel Shane on my heels. I know why he's following me, but does he have to? Doesn't he realize I'm not sure how to navigate this?

"How've you been?"

I turn and give him an incredulous look because fuck the small talk. "What are you doing here?"

My voice has a pinch of anger in it, which I do feel bad about. But why is he here? I know Rolling Hills isn't exactly a hopping place on a Tuesday evening, but I can think of a lot better things to be doing than watching seventh and eighth graders run in a circle.

"Mariah texted me the other day asking if I would come to one of her meets. I was off duty today. I figured it was just as good of a time as any."

"Oh." I didn't realize she did that. Mariah texts Shane all the time. Both of my kids do. "Good. I'm glad. Glad you could make it."

"Me too."

His warm smile makes me nervous all over again so I

quickly turn back to watch the meet and anxiously eat my popcorn. Though I couldn't tell you who was running, even if it were my kid. How can I when Shane's cologne is assaulting my senses in the best and worst way possible? I want to look at him, but I don't. I can't. I want to say something, but words are hard right now. And it doesn't help that he's wearing the leather jacket that makes him look a million times hotter than he already is. Hell, I knew Shane was hot in the jacket before the kiss. Now I'm having sex-on-motorcycle fantasies that are very new—and very confusing.

"So Mariah's running track? That's still weird to say."

I hear his words, but it still takes me a few seconds to respond as I'm still thinking about motorcycle sex. "Yeah. Weird."

I watch Mariah line up at the start, and I'm in awe of her. She looks like a seasoned pro, not someone who just started running a few months ago. She's rotating her neck as she approaches the block and shakes out her legs before getting set. When the starter gun pops, she's off and running. And damn... my girl is fast.

"Go Mariah! Push! Push!"

That's not coming from me. No, it's from Shane. All I can do is smile as I watch this man cheer for my daughter. He's pumping his arm and clapping like he's single-handedly going to help her win this race. I think he's the loudest one right now. And he's not even her dad. Except he is in all the ways it counts.

He's here now. He shows up. She's comfortable texting him and talking to him because he's her constant. When she needs something I can't help her with, it's not her dad, my brother Jake, or her brother she looks to—it's Shane. I'll never forget when she was eight and about to have her one and only dance recital. She came home crying one night because the girls were going to be escorted onto the stage by their dads. She knew Paul wasn't going to show up. So I asked her who she'd like instead. She didn't hesitate. And neither did Shane. He showed up that day with a bouquet of flowers and a tie that matched her costume.

My emotions are about to spill over as I watch him cheer for her. This. This right here is why the kiss has to stay where it belongs—in the past. I might want him, or be curious about the idea of us, and maybe in a perfect world I could let myself be reckless and give into this want, but I can't. I can't risk the possibility this goes south. If it doesn't work out, or if things get weird and Shane and my relationship changes, it would destroy my kids. And no, I don't think Shane would ever cut my kids out of his life in any circumstance, but I know Luke and Mariah. They are fierce protectors when it comes to me. And I don't want that for them. I want them to have their Uncle Shane the way they always have.

So I'm going to do what I've been doing for the past seven years—putting my wants aside for the sake of my children. It might suck, but it's never steered me wrong as a parent.

Even if it was a kiss I can still feel on my lips.

"Look at her go," he says. "Go Mariah! All the way through!"

His words snap me back to the present, where I see Mariah coming to the finish line. Holy shit, is she about to win?

"Go Mariah! Run! Go!"

I'm jumping up and down cheering as my girl crosses the finish line first. Pride rushes through me, then amusement, as she looks back in bewilderment when she realizes she won. I fumble to grab my phone, hating that I didn't record the race while it was going on.

"Mom! Shane!" Mariah comes running over to us, her arms open. "Can you believe it! I won!"

"I know, baby," I say, giving her a hug over the fence. "I'm so proud of you."

"Thanks, Mom." Mariah breaks our hug to move on to Shane. "Did you see? I did what you told me to do. I really concentrated on my start."

"I did, Pipsqueak. You did awesome."

She all but jumps over the fence into his arms, and of course he catches her. And of course, I fight back a tear as I watch the two of them.

How could I ever think about ruining this dynamic? For what? For the chance of maybe Shane being the one? For a few orgasms?

No. I can't. I won't. Because for the hundredth time in their lives, Shane was there for my kids. Not their father. Shane.

And yes, I love him for it. I love him. But I love my kids more.

"Okay, I'm going to go back over there." Mariah gestures toward her team. "Mom, I saw you taking pictures or video or something. You aren't allowed to post anything until I approve and add a filter. See you guys later!"

I laugh as I watch Mariah head back over to rejoin her team. She gives a high-five to a few, even Emily Babcock's daughter, when I see the reason I think my daughter joined the track team.

She just hugged a boy and blushed. And if I'm seeing things clearly, my daughter is giggling.

My daughter doesn't giggle.

"What the fuck is that?"

Apparently, Shane is seeing what I'm seeing. "I'm guessing that's why Mariah is suddenly a track star."

"Like hell it is."

Shane pushes off the fence and begins marching toward the benches where the team members are gathered. I lunge forward and grab his arm. "Shane Cunningham, you will not under any circumstances go over there right now and embarrass her."

He looks at me like I'm crazy. "But you saw that, right? He had his hands all over her!"

"The hug?"

"It was more than a hug."

"Calm down, Shane.

"Amelia! She hugged a boy!"

"I know," I say. "She's thirteen, Shane."

"Exactly. She's *thirteen*."

I laugh and pull him back to where we were standing, though his eyes keep looking back over to the scene of the crime. "If I remember correctly, you were doing more than hugging girls when we were thirteen."

"I know I was. That's why I need to go have a talk with him. Because I know what thirteen-year-old boys think. And it's a lot more than hugging."

I shake my head as we reposition ourselves at the fence. "Stand down, Officer Cunningham. There are worse things that could be happening."

I can't help but chuckle as I realize that my daughter joined track for a boy. I can't even be mad. I tried to join the football team to get a boy to notice me. And it worked. Well, it worked in the sense that after years of pining over him, he asked me out, I lost my virginity to him, got pregnant with Luke, married him at eighteen, then divorced ten years later after one too many close calls with his anger and one too many times ignoring what he was doing on the nights he said he was working.

Maybe I *do* need to have a talk with Mariah...you know... just in case.

"I can't believe Mariah is hugging boys," he grumps.

I smile. "She's not a little girl anymore."

"I refuse to believe that," Shane says. "She'll always be the pipsqueak who used to climb on my shoulders because she wanted to see things."

"And who would cry when you'd put her down."

This makes him smile. "Which is why I never did. I can't stand to see my Pipsqueak cry."

I laugh, remembering all the times Mariah asked Shane for piggyback rides, or to carry her. Yes, her father could have done it. But my girl always wanted Uncle Shane. She's been attached to him since the day he came home from the Army. He was in Afghanistan when she was born, so his welcome home party was the first time he met her. She was four. I swear that was the day my daughter fell in love with him. I think he carried her around that whole party. But he didn't mind. She had him wrapped around her finger from that day and never let go.

Reason nine-hundred-and-forty-six that it's smart for him and I to leave the kiss where it belongs.

"Hey," he says hesitantly. "I don't know what you're doing tonight, but do you want to go get a bite after this?"

I don't look at him right away, because how do I say no? Because I'm not just saying no to dinner, I'm saying no to what he wants to talk about. The conversation we need to have.

"Shane...I—"

"Don't," he says quickly. "Don't say anything else."

"But I—"

He turns toward me, a serious expression on his handsome face. "Don't finish that. Don't put those words into the open. Because once you say them, it will be hard for us to go anywhere but that direction."

"Shane, you need to—"

"No." He cuts me off again, but not harshly. "Just promise

me you'll think about it. Really think about it. Think about what we shared. How it felt. What more it could be. Think about how easily we could fit into each other's lives. Because I have, and I think we could be great."

"Shane, I have thought—"

"I'm not saying you haven't but just take a little more time. Actually, take as much time as you need. I'll be here. I've always been here, and I'm not going anywhere. Just please, promise me, you'll think about it. Toss it around in that over-thinking brain of yours. And then, after you do all that, text me and I'll be there."

Think about it? How can I not? It's all I have been thinking about. But the more I think about it, the more I don't think it's a good idea.

"Shane, I don't want you to get your hopes up."

"Amelia," he says as he steps right beside me, his hand lightly squeezing mine. "I've hoped for you my entire life. I'm not going to give up hoping now."

His words hit me hard as he lets go of my hand. I watch him walk away with my jaw slacked and my mind in a spiral as one word plays on repeat.

His entire life? What does that mean?

But it's something else he said that has me spinning.

Hope...

Because that's what this would be, right? Hoping it works. Hoping it doesn't wreck a lifelong friendship. Hoping that these feelings are real.

Hoping that the risk is worth the reward.

Chapter 7
Shane

I'm never the one to gather the guys and suggest we go out. Most nights I'm content sitting at home, occasionally cracking open a beer, working on my motorcycle, or otherwise just sitting back and relaxing. Especially if it's a Friday night. I don't need the hustle and bustle of a bar. Too many people for my liking.

But the more I sit here alone, the more I think about Amelia. And the more days that pass with no word from her, the more worried I get that this is going to be over before we even had a chance to begin.

I need to get out of my house. I feel like the walls are closing in on me. Which is why I'm about to set the group chat on fire with what I'm about to type.

Shane: Anyone up for a drink? I'm buying.

Wes: Excuse me?

Simon: Who the fuck are you and what have you done with Shane?

Wes: Seriously, are you okay?

Shane: I'm fine. Just don't feel like sitting at home tonight.

Simon: Fuck going out. I'm sending an ambulance. Is Amelia working tonight? We'll need to warn her that you've had a mental break and will need immediate medical care.

Did he have to mention Amelia?

Shane: Are you fuckers in or not?

Wes: I'm in. Betsy and the kids are on the couch watching a movie, so I'm sure I can slip out. I'd rather not watch Harry Potter for the hundredth time.

Simon: I'm in and running up your tab like prohibition is coming back tomorrow and this is our last night of legal fun.

Shane: You're an asshole.

Simon: I think I'll be drinking Johnny Walker Blue...

Shane: I hate you. Oliver? You in? Or are you still ignoring us?

Wes: Oliver, we talked about this. You can't ignore us. We will come knocking down your door.

Simon: Seriously. As your number one best friend, I'm worried about you.

Wes: Are you still ranking the best friends? I thought we squashed that.

Oliver: Sorry, guys. Can't come out tonight. Have one for me, though.

Wes: Why aren't you coming?

Simon: You have a hot date or something?

Oliver: I just can't come.

Wes: He does.

Shane: Please don't propose tonight.

Oliver: No promises.

~

An hour later I'm walking into The Joint, our local bar, and it's everything I usually hate about a Friday night crowd. Busy. Loud. People. But tonight? Tonight, it's just what I need.

I look toward our normal table and see Wes waving me down. I head that way when a voice that sends shivers down my back stops me in my tracks.

"Hey, Shane."

My whole body stiffens when I hear Emily Babcock's voice. I can only compare the timbre of her voice to a combination of nails on a chalkboard and a dying cat. "Hi, Emily."

I might not like people, but I'm not an asshole. Also, as a police officer in town—one of six—it's good business to at least be polite to the people I protect.

Even if that person has been hitting on you since you were fourteen years old and won't take the hint you aren't interested.

"Didn't think I'd see you here tonight," she says, stepping a little closer to me. "What brings you out?"

I nod toward Wes and Simon. "Just meeting the guys."

She looks over to where my friends are sitting and rolls her eyes. "Oh. Simon's there."

"He is."

Shit, now I really have to buy him a drink if he's about to be my way out of this conversation. Women either love or hate Simon. Sometimes both. That's what you get when you're a cocky asshole but also are (apparently) charming. Not that I think he's charming; that's just how Amelia and Betsy have explained it. I've seen it. One time, he hit on a woman, got her number, she slapped him because he was talking to another woman, later ended up dancing with the first woman, then had sex with her in the bar bathroom. The night ended with her slapping him again when he wouldn't take her home.

She rolls her eyes. "Why are you friends with him?"

I ask myself that question every day, but I'm not going to tell her that. "He's a good guy."

"Hmph." Another eye roll. "Well, if you get bored, I'll be over here. I'd love a dance tonight."

All I do is nod my head and walk over to the table. That's the only way I know how to not be an asshole while also not leading her on. But I won't be dancing with her. Or anyone. Not unless Amelia comes in and pulls me onto the dance floor. And I doubt that's happening.

"There he is," Wes says as he passes me a beer. "We were five seconds away from coming to save you."

I tip my beer to him. "Thanks, but Simon's mere presence scared her away."

Simon holds up his drink. And as he promised, it's some sort of scotch that I'm sure isn't bottom shelf. "Happy to help."

The table unintentionally all looks over to Emily, who of course is sitting with Christina and Jessica. They are all shooting daggers at Simon.

"What the hell did you do to her?" Wes asks.

Simon shrugs as we turn our eyes away. "I asked her to stop talking."

"That's it? Kind of rude, but not the worst you've ever said."

"It was during sex. She was riding me, and I asked her if she could quit talking. And screaming. Her screaming is worse than her talking."

"Are you kidding me?" I say, shaking my head in shame for both him and Emily. "You fucked her?"

"Listen, I was drunk, and I couldn't hear her at the bar. I forgot what she sounded like."

"You're something else," Wes says.

Simon proudly leans back against his chair and holds up his drink one more time. "That I am."

I can't help but laugh at my friend's audacity. Then again, it's Simon. He's been this way since he moved here when we were in the fourth grade. And as we approach forty, he hasn't changed a bit. If anything, he's only gotten worse.

"I can't believe you had sex with her," I repeat, because I really can't.

"In my defense, she's had sex with everyone."

"Not me," Wes says.

"Well, we know not you, Mr. Monogamy," Simon says before turning to me. "Didn't she sound like that when you fucked her?"

My eyes grow wide. "I've never slept with Emily."

"Yes, you have," Simon says as he waves me off. "At your going-away party before you went to basic. You were gone for like an hour and so was she. She came back before you and her hair had that clear 'I just gave someone a blow job' look. Then you came back five minutes after with a goofy look on your face."

I start to respond, but I catch myself. Emily's hair looked like that because she was passed out on the porch swing. And if I remember correctly, her hair looked like that when she walked outside. And my goofy look was because I had just kissed Amelia for the first time. I was still high on the moment. But I can't tell them that. I didn't tell them then, and I sure as hell aren't going to tell them now.

"I don't know where she was, but it wasn't with me," I say.

"I call bullshit," Simon says.

"What do you call bullshit on?"

We look up to see Porter, the owner of The Joint and cousin to Wes, standing at our table with a tray of shots. I don't know who ordered them, but I'm not mad about it.

"That Shane didn't hook up with Emily the night of his going-away party."

"He didn't," Porter says as he leans down closer to us. "It was me."

Our table erupts. "Seriously?" Wes asks.

Porter shrugs. "I was a horny eighteen-year-old who was tired of waiting for the girl."

"What girl?" Wes asks.

Porter looks at Simon quickly then shakes his head. "No one. Enjoy the shots. On me."

No one reaches for the glasses as Porter heads back to the bar. "What was that?" I ask. "Did he ever date one of your sisters?"

Simon shakes his head. "Not that I'm aware of. Then again, they don't tell me shit, and they outnumber me. But at least now I know to invite him to the Emily Babcock Regret Club. We meet every other Wednesday. Cheers."

We clink our shot glasses on the table and throw back the drinks. "Man, I was really hoping you fucked her," Simon said with a sigh.

"Why?" I ask. "I wouldn't have come to your fucking club, if that's what you wanted."

"No. It's not that. I just want to *finally* know what your story is."

Now it's my turn to be smug. "And you'll never know."

The guys, especially Simon, have been on me for years to give them any clue about my personal life. I know there's even a bet going around. I don't know the guesses, but I can only imagine the theories. I believe one of them is that I'm a monk.

The real story is that I'm private. So private that if I'm looking for company, or need a night to truly blow off steam, I go out of town. Sometimes up to Brentwood or Franklin. Sometimes I'll just go a few towns over. No one knows me, and I don't know them. It's perfect for the as-needed one-night stand. There are a few women who I've seen on multiple occasions, but the boundaries are clearly drawn. Because that's all I want, if it's not Amelia. I know that's not healthy. I know it's probably not sane. But that's the bed I've chosen to wallow in.

"Why won't you tell us?" Wes asks. "We're your best friends. You should trust us."

I nod because he has a valid point. "It's not that I don't trust you."

"Then what is it!" Simon yells, smacking his hand on the table. "Why won't you fucking tell us!"

"Because I love driving you crazy."

Simon's eyes narrow at me. "Fuck you. I'm going to order another drink. Two of them. Top fucking shelf."

I hear him call me a motherfucker as he walks to the bar, which just makes Wes and I laugh.

"Are you ever going to tell us?"

"One day," I say. "But not until I'm done fucking with him."

Chapter 8
Amelia

"Mariah! Ten-minute warning! And please make sure you bring your phone charger and whatever else you want to take. I'm not going to run it over. I don't care how much you beg!"

I let out a yawn as the bagels pop up from the toaster, scaring me more than I'd like to admit. I reach over for the pot of coffee that just finished brewing, the smell hitting my senses in the best way.

I worked my normal eleven to eleven yesterday, but for some reason, I'm more tired than usual. Maybe it was because I picked up an extra shift last week. Maybe because it's Saturday, and my body wishes it could sleep in. I've also been going nonstop for the past few weeks between work and the kids, so that could be it.

Or maybe it's because I woke up in a sweat last night after a very vivid dream involving Shane, his motorcycle, and me screaming to a deity I don't pray to.

"Yo! Earth to Mom. You awake?"

I shake my head and take a deep breath as Luke comes over

and grabs one of the bagels. My oldest is always the first downstairs and ready to go each morning. Whether it's for school during the week, or baseball practice—this morning's agenda—you can set a watch by him. I don't know where he got that from. It wasn't me. Now Mariah? She inherited my knack for showing up just in the nick of time. She will come down here with two minutes to spare because she needed time to contour. I still don't know what that is, but she insists it's a part of her daily routine.

"Barely," I say as he gives me a kiss on the cheek. I take a sip of my coffee as I watch him pull one of his energy drinks from the refrigerator. "Really? It's seven in the morning and you're already having one of those?"

"What?" He gestures to the cup in my hand that I'm holding onto like it's a rare diamond. "How many cups of that have you had today?"

"You play dirty."

"I learned from the best."

We share a smile as he takes a seat. "Everything go okay last night?"

"Yup," he says. "Nothing to report. I worked on my project for government, and Mariah snapped her friends until her thumbs fell off. I heated up the leftovers for dinner, and we went to bed at a reasonable hour."

"Luke. It was Friday night. You shouldn't have been doing homework. You know I don't mind if a friend comes over to hang out."

He shrugs. "It needed done. I wanted to get on top of it."

"So responsible. One of these nights I'm going to get home from work and you're going to be throwing a rager."

"First of all, no one calls them ragers. Second, you know if that happened it would be Mariah, and I'd be the one trying to clean up."

I stand and walk over to give him a hug, which he doesn't even fight anymore. He knows his efforts are futile. "And that's why I love you."

My schedule has its pros and cons. As a nurse in the emergency room, I work three days a week, but twelve-hour shifts. I used to have to get a sitter, but since Luke got his license last year, he's stepped up. In fairness, both kids have. They came up to me as a united front and said that they were old enough to be responsible for themselves on the nights I had to work. Luke runs Mariah where she needs to go, and they both help keep the house clean. Their grades haven't dropped in the slightest and my house has never looked cleaner.

I know every mom says this, but I have the best kids in the damn world. My daughter is fierce and determined. A leader. She likes what she likes and doesn't hold back. She will tell anyone what's on her mind and what she thinks of you. She also has the biggest heart of anyone I know. That also means that if you break it, you'll pay.

Then there's my son. My gentle, sweet boy. He'll help anyone who asks and will go out of his way to make sure things get done. He's a straight-A student and every teacher he's ever had has told me that they want a million Lukes in class. He's mature for his age. He's helpful, considerate, and responsible. I don't know how I'd navigate life without him. My boy is growing into the best kind of man, and I have everyone *but* his father to thank for that.

"Mariah! I told Wes and Betsy you'd be there at seven-thirty! Hurry up! You don't need perfect makeup to babysit!"

"I'm here, Mom." She might be here physically, but my daughter already has her nose buried in her phone.

"Who could you possibly be texting this early?"

"Gabby got a snap from Connor, and she doesn't know what it means, so we're trying to figure it out. She's going to see him today, and she doesn't know if he's trying to flirt with her or if he's messing with her. He asked her what she was doing. What could that mean?"

"It means eat your bagel so we can get going."

My daughter gives me a teenage huff and sets her phone down. She's a good kid, but the teenage angst phase that we're beginning is about to be my least favorite time of her life.

"Okay. Let's review the day."

Most mornings start like this. If we don't have a morning huddle, we're off our game. This is where we make sure we know where we're going, that they know what my work shift is, and anything big and upcoming that needs reminders. It might not be the most efficient way of staying organized, but it works for us.

"I have baseball practice this morning, then I'm working until four."

I hate that my son has a job in high school, especially when he does so much for me. But when Knox—my brother's best friend—opened his own auto body shop a few years ago, my gearhead kid begged me to work there. The day he turned sixteen, Knox hired him to come in one day a week during the school year and three days a week during the summer.

"And I'll be at Uncle Wes's and Betsy's all day with Emerson. We get to be in charge."

Luke working worried me because I didn't want him to stretch himself too thin. Mariah working as a babysitter worries me because I'm pretty sure one day she's going to organize the masses and either start a riot or a cult, depending on whichever one she can convince to wear better clothes. The only saving grace is that Emerson—Wes's daughter—will be there, who's twelve going on thirty. The two are best friends and couldn't be more different. Between the two of them, they are more than capable of watching Wes's younger children, Hank and Magnolia.

"Sounds good," I say as my phone starts ringing. I can't hold in my groan when I see the name on the screen.

"That's code for Dad's on the phone and she doesn't want us to hear the names she calls him."

I point my finger for them to leave as Luke snickers at Mariah's comment. Though she's not wrong. "Go."

As soon as the kids are out of earshot, I let out a deep breath as I hit answer. "Good morning, Paul."

"Mel."

I hate it when he uses that nickname. He was the only one to ever call me that. At first I thought it was cute. Then I realized after a while he was probably just too lazy to use more than one syllable.

"What do you want?"

Paul never just calls to call. There's always a reason. Or he needs something. He used to call to tell me why he couldn't pay child support that month. Lately it's been why he's going to forfeit his weekend. My guess is he has a new girlfriend, and he can't be bothered with things like being a father.

"I'm going to be in town on Tuesday. I was wondering if I could see the kids."

Well, that's a first. "Wow. An unexpected visit? What do we owe the pleasure?"

"Sarcastic isn't a good look on you Mel," he says. "You always get like this when I ask for one little thing."

I bite my lip so hard that I might break skin. "I wasn't being sarcastic. You haven't seen the kids in months. And now suddenly you want to come visit? Sorry for being shocked."

"Yes. And I shouldn't need a reason to see my kids."

You shouldn't but you usually do...

"Well, Tuesday might be hard," I say. "Mariah has a track

meet, and Luke has a game. They are both at home, so you could theoretically come and watch both."

"That sounds like a pain. What about after if I just take them dinner?"

I swallow a scream. Too hard? Too hard is the weeks where Luke is playing an hour away and Mariah has something at home. Too hard is when I work and I have to beg to switch with someone so I can be there. But yes, going to two events that are in the same complex is just too difficult. But this is classic Paul; things needing to be on his terms or his way.

"It's unexpected, Paul. They are young adults with their own lives and schoolwork. I'll talk to them and we'll let you know. Or, you know, you could come watch them do things they enjoy doing. I'm sure they'd like that."

He lets out a frustrated breath, but doesn't say anything else. Somewhere in his narcissistic body, he knows I'm right. "I'll try. Also, since when does Mariah run track? Or do anything athletic?"

I could answer simply and politely. I would have done that when we were married. Now I don't give a fuck.

"If you ever called your children, you'd know that she wanted to try it this year and she's doing great. She won her race last week and really seems to be enjoying it."

"I don't appreciate the sass."

"I really don't care. In fact, I couldn't give two shits."

"I can't with you."

I bite my tongue, wanting to end this conversation immediately. "Anything else?"

"That's it." His words are clipped. "I'll see you Tuesday."

"Can't wait."

I hang up the phone quickly, needing to have the last word as I let out a big breath. Over the years I've finally built up the confidence to take control of the conversations. I never did that when we were married. Looking back, I hate that mousy, unsure woman I was. The one who fell into the trap of believing the words coming from his mouth. The one who didn't stand up for herself.

But not anymore. At least, I do my best to not be that person. Some days and conversations are harder than others, but I know who I am now, and I know the person I don't want to be again.

"What did Dad want?"

I look up to see Mariah with a concerned look on her beautiful face. Is she a teenage drama queen? Yes. Do I hate that she's out of the boys-are-gross stage? Yes. Am I worried that one day she's going to require bail money? Also yes. But my baby girl has a heart of gold and is a fierce of a protector to those she loves.

"He's going to be in town Tuesday," I say as I straighten myself out. "He says he's coming to your track meet and Luke's game."

She huffs. "I'll believe it when I see it."

"Believe what?" Luke asks as he grabs his keys off the kitchen table.

"Apparently Dad's coming Tuesday to watch us."

"Ha! That's a good one." Luke grabs his bat bag before looking back to me. "Considering I'm still waiting for him to show up to a football game, I won't hold my breath."

"If he does come, do you think this visit will be one where he ignores us or buys us stuff? I could use a new eye shadow palette."

"Let's see if he shows up before you send him your Amazon wish list."

I know I should tell them to not talk about their dad like that. I definitely shouldn't be smiling about it. But deep down I'm proud that my kids are smart and see people for who they are. I'm also not about to try to convince them he's the best dad on the planet. He did this to himself. He showed his colors in many ways over the years. He either love bombs, or berates, or is around all the time, or is gone for months. They are tired of wondering which version of their dad they'll get. And I don't blame them. I wondered that when he was my husband.

The conversation fades as Luke takes off for baseball and Mariah and I head over to Wes and Betsy's. I take a glance over to my daughter, who, of course, is typing something on her phone.

"Still trying to decipher the text code for Gabby?"

She shakes her head. "No. I'm texting Uncle Shane."

"Oh," I say, trying to keep the surprised tone from my voice. "About what?"

"Letting him know that Dad might be coming Tuesday."

I let my head fall back against the seat. "Why would you do that?"

I see a devilish smile form on her face out of the corner of my eye. "Because it's funny to watch Dad squirm when Uncle Shane is around."

She's not wrong. Paul and Shane hate each other. Always have. They did in high school when they played football together. Paul was always questioning me about our friendship. Things escalated when Shane came back from his deployment and things were getting rocky in our marriage. Fights about Shane were a common occurrence. Then there was the day I'll never forget—the day I left. I still remember the look of terror in Paul's eye as Shane pinned him to the floor.

"You know by texting Shane you're just stirring the pot."

She shrugs with a satisfied smile on her face as we pull into Wes and Betsy's. "It's what I'm good at."

We get out of the car to a waiting Emerson and Betsy standing in the driveway. "Morning!"

"Good morning," Betsy says as Mariah and Emerson make their way to the house. "We got donuts and coffee for breakfast."

"Smart idea," I say as she hands me a coffee. "I could kiss you right now."

She waves me off. "Least I could do for letting us borrow Mariah."

Speaking of, she didn't even tell me goodbye. "Mariah! I'll come get you later."

"Okay, Mom!" she says, but stops in the doorway before turning back. "Uncle Shane said he's going to switch his shift so he can be there on Tuesday!"

Mariah and Emerson walk inside, and when I turn back to Betsy, who is nothing but curious. "What is Shane changing his shift for?"

"It's nothing. Her dad called this morning and said he's going to come to her track meet. So my daughter, the shit-stirrer she is, texted Shane to come as well."

"Why would she do that?"

"Their dad isn't exactly the one to always be around. And he hates Shane, and vice versa. My daughter, who is an instigator to her core, woke up today and chose violence."

"Interesting," Betsy says. "And Shane is coming? No questions asked?"

"He is," I say. "Though, in his defense, if my daughter says jump, he asks how high."

"Very interesting."

Betsy's look is more than one of interest. "What?"

"I just find it intriguing that Shane, who most days we can barely get out of his house, is willingly going to middle school sporting events."

"It's for Mariah," I defend. "That's it."

Betsy grabs my hand and gives it a squeeze. "Amelia, I

know we're still getting to know each other, and you're used to the guys, who I love, but are all a little obtuse. I notice things. The guys might just brush off Shane going to your kids' events, but how many have Oliver been to? Or Simon? And I have noticed on more than one occasion that when you're around, Shane is not the same. And he definitely doesn't look at you like you're one of the guys. Oh, and then there was that whole caveman thing at the wedding."

I nearly drop my coffee. "You saw?"

"I saw him march onto the dance floor like a man possessed and drag you away. So either someone was on fire or Shane did *not* like you dancing with another man."

Okay. She didn't see the kiss. But what she saw was enough.

"I can explain."

She shakes her head and gives my hand a squeeze. "There's nothing to explain. All I saw was a man and a woman walk outside. And then a woman who came back a few minutes later looking like her world had been flipped upside down."

Well, shit. Here I thought we were stealthy that night. "It's...I don't know, Betsy. So much happened, and so much could happen, but I also don't want anything to happen and do want everything to happen. Does that make sense?"

"Strangely, it does."

"I also feel weird talking to you because I don't want the guys finding out and I don't want you to lie to Wes. I'm just... I'm so confused."

God, that felt good to say.

"I get that," Betsy says. "And I don't want to put you in an awkward spot. But can I give you one piece of advice?"

"Please."

"I dated a lot of guys before Wes. And if there's one thing I've learned about men, it's that if they want to, they will. If they don't, they can't be bothered. You need to be with a man who will, because you deserve that and so much more."

Betsy gives my hand one more squeeze before she heads inside.

If he wanted to, he would.

I never thought of that before. Paul never wanted to, and he never did. Shane? I think Shane's been doing that for years, and I didn't notice. Or I took it for granted. Probably a little bit of both.

I get back in my car but I don't pull out of the driveway. All I can do is sit and think about everything Shane has done for me and my kids over the years. He comes to their events. He takes my car in to get oil changes because I never remember to. One year Mariah told him she wanted a real Christmas tree because we'd never had one. That man went out the next day and chopped down an eight-foot tree for the family room and another smaller one for her bedroom. He sat down and had the talk with Luke—I know because I accidentally walked in on said talk and Luke wouldn't look at me for a week.

I can't think of four things Paul has done in their lives that I didn't have to force him to do. He used to bitch about changing diapers, and that is literally the bare minimum as a father.

And it just wasn't things with the kids. He never helped around the house. Every chore and project fell on me. Then there were the little things. I can't remember a time when Paul just kissed me because he wanted to. Or brought home flowers just because. Hell, he didn't even do it on our anniversary. Sex was sporadic at best and never ended in anything pleasurable on my end. I never felt beautiful or cherished or loved. I thought I did, but looking back now I know that wasn't the case.

Hell, with one kiss and one night, I felt more loved with Shane than I did for years with Paul. Just one night changed everything. Changed my perspective. Threw my world for a loop.

Shane wanted to kiss me. He wanted to hold me. He wanted to be with me.

He wanted to. And he did.

I grab my phone and pull up my text thread with Shane. I know he asked me not to contact him until I thought about it some more. And I have. There are the cons and the scary things. But there are also the things I can't deny anymore. And we need them all out on the table.

> Amelia: Can you meet me for breakfast at Mona's?

I don't even have to wait more than five seconds for a response.

> Shane: I'll have your coffee and waffles ready. And I'll get you an apple juice just in case you want it. And don't worry, I'll make sure to order extra syrup.

I smile as I head home to change into something presentable.

I know this might be reckless. I know it could blow up in my face.

But I want to.

So I am.

Chapter 9
Amelia

I can tell myself that until I'm blue in the face, but I don't know if it's going to help anything.

I'm nervous. I'm never nervous around Shane. He's the last person in the world I'd ever feel nervous around. But as I walk into Mona's Diner, I think I forget to breathe.

He's looking directly at me, his stare burning into me like it did at the wedding. Then I thought maybe it was because I was all dolled up. Today I'm in leggings, a tank top with a light-weight cardigan, and I might have gone home and swiped a little makeup from Mariah. Better than my normal oversized T-shirt and sweatpants.

Then there's him. A black Henley shirt clinging to his muscular biceps. His hair is slicked back in that way that always looks like he just got out of the shower, and the closer I get, the more I can smell the leather in his cologne.

I thought nothing could smell better than Mona's waffles, but I'm wrong. I was so very, *very*, wrong.

The nerves ramp up to eleventy-million as I approach the booth. If this were any other Saturday morning breakfast, we'd just start shooting the shit, catching up on our lives and families. He'd ask me about Luke and Mariah, and I'd ask if he had heard the crazy story my mom told me about his mom. We'd talk about sports and the guys; specifically, right now what the hell is up with Oliver because that man has dropped off the face of the earth. There wouldn't be an impending talk about us. Or our future. Or if we could actually do this. I definitely wouldn't be staring at his pecs. Or wondering if his cologne would stay on my sheets if he ever stayed the night.

How quickly things can change in just a small amount of time.

"Hey," I say, sliding into the booth.

"Hey, yourself."

Shane's smirk creeps through and it makes me want to giggle like a schoolgirl. Shane Cunningham does *not* smirk. He barely smiles. And when he does, it's because no one is around or he's fucking with Simon. But this? This is making me feel some sort of way.

I smile back and feel my face get flush as Mona, the owner of the diner who refuses to quit waiting tables despite being in her seventies, comes over with my coffee. "Here you go, sweetheart."

"Thanks, Mona."

She looks at me. Then back to Shane. Then back to me. "Something up with you two?"

My eyes go wide. Shit, am I that obvious? Damn my cheeks blushing from a smirk. "What? No. Why would you ask that?"

Her eyes narrow as she gives each of us a onceover. "I've known you two your whole lives. You used to sit next to each other in highchairs while your mamas came in for their weekly lunches. And in all those years, and all those cups of coffee I've poured you, neither of you have ever looked like this."

"Mona, maybe it's time to take a day off," Shane says.

"I don't need a day off. But I do need to know why you have been fiddling with your coffee cup for a half hour and why Amelia over here decided that today was the day she'd get out of her pajamas to come here."

"Hey! I don't come here in my pajamas. It's called loungewear."

She gives me a knowing look. "Amelia, don't piss on my leg and tell me it's raining. Something's up, but I don't have time to figure it out. I'll be back with your food in a minute."

Mona walks away without taking my order, which I couldn't care less about right now. "Well...there you have it. Mona knows, therefore the whole town is going to know by the time the dinner rush hits."

Shane is smiling again. Twice in one day is odd. Twice in a matter of minutes is a freak of nature. He definitely doesn't smile when one of the busiest of town gossips is a few sniffs away from figuring out that something is indeed different.

"Why are you smiling?"

"Because you look beautiful, and I'm glad someone other than me noticed."

I open my mouth to say something, but I almost choke on my words. Because frankly, I don't know how to react to that.

Believing words is hard for me to do. People lie. People can use words as weapons. People can say what they want to make you have a distorted way of thinking. I should know—I was married to one of those persons for ten years.

I look down at my outfit, feeling a little self-conscious, then back up to him. Holy shit, his gaze is just as strong now as it was at the wedding. He really means it, doesn't he?

If he wanted to, he would.

"Thank you," I say. "I heard you talked to Mariah today."

He nods and sets down his cup of coffee. "I did. I hear I'm going to another track meet on Tuesday."

"You know you don't have to," I say. "You can tell her no."

"Pass," he says. "She asked me to come, and I'll be there. Plus, it's been a minute since I've seen the asshat."

He cracks his knuckles as he says that, and I don't know if it's by coincidence or just a reaction to Paul coming up in conversation.

"Just promise me you won't get us kicked off the premises."

"I make no promises."

"Promise."

He lets out a groan. "Fine. I won't."

"Thank you. And, the meet starts at five-thirty this week, which I know is a half-hour later than normal—"

Shane cuts my rambling off. "Amelia."

"Yes?"

"Did you ask me to breakfast to talk about your ex-husband and middle school track?"

I let out a breath and shake my head. "You told me to contact you when I was ready with an answer."

A hush falls over the table. I know he's waiting for me to say something, and the longer I'm quiet the more time seems to stand still.

"Amelia, you have to say something. I'm going crazy over here."

"I know." I swallow the lump in my throat as he leans forward, resting his elbows back on the table. His eyes are burning into me. I swear I can feel it all the way down to my toes. I tilt my head down and stare at the dark abyss in my coffee cup and nod.

"Hey," he says, reaching across the table and tilting my chin up so we're now looking at each other. "Talk to me. No matter what your decision is, we can talk about it."

His words send me back to the night of the wedding after Shane first kissed me, only this time the roles are reversed. And now we don't have adrenaline and liquid courage fueling us. All we have now is a cup of coffee and a cloud of reasons why we shouldn't do this lingering.

"I want this," I begin. "I want to try this. I really do. But I'm scared as hell, Shane. I'm scared about what will happen if this doesn't work out."

He nods and gives my hands a squeeze, but quickly lets go when he realizes what he's done. If people saw us holding hands, it would send the town into a frenzy. "I'm sorry. I shouldn't have done that."

I shake my head. "Don't be. I liked it. I want it. But this is one of the reasons I'm scared. If people saw you holding my hand, you know how the town would react."

"Chaos."

"Exactly. This relationship wouldn't just be us. It would be everyone."

"It's only that if we let it."

I shake my head. "You know that's a lie."

"A man can hope."

"And what if this doesn't work? Then the town would pick sides. And you're a cop and they want to get out of speeding tickets so they'd pick you."

"No they wouldn't."

"They would."

"I'm not worried about that."

"Why?" I ask. "It's a legitimate concern."

Shane leans in closer. "You're worried if this ends badly. I get it. That's the Amelia way. But, what if it's *not* like that?"

"Huh?"

"What if this works? What if this is forever?"

He's right. I haven't even considered that side of things. I'm glass-half-empty. My favorite Winnie the Pooh character is Eeyore because he's relatable.

But it can't be that simple, can it? Just believe it's going to last? That's not how this works. At least, not in my experience. No way that my forever has been my best friend the whole time. No way the man I kissed at the wedding, who was also the boy who played in the creek with me, was always the person I was supposed to be with.

"I haven't thought of that."

He leans over and takes my hand again. I don't even look to see if anyone is looking. I can't. I'm too mesmerized by Shane at this moment.

"I know, and I get why," he says. "But, just for a second, forget the bad things. Forget the scary stuff. Just think about how maybe it's only good things coming."

I try to do as he says, I really do. But as soon as one of those good thing pops into my head, the scary and unknown come right after.

"I want to, Shane. There's just so much we need to consider. For starters, the kids. How are we going to tell them about us?"

"We'll sit them down and talk to them like the young adults they are."

"Okay, but what about the guys? Oliver will have a heart attack out of excitement. Simon would be relentless. Wes would have to deal with them, and then Betsy would have to deal with Wes."

"They're big boys. They can handle it."

"And then there are our mothers! They'll be the worst."

"I'll agree they are the scariest, but they'll also be our biggest cheerleaders."

"Okay Mister I-Have-All-The-Answers, have you considered how hard this will be because of our jobs? My baggage?"

My freakout only makes him smile. "I have. Let's start small. If I asked you on a date, would you say yes?"

"Yes." I shock myself a bit with how fast that came out. "But—"

"Uh-uh. No buts." Shane's thumb starts moving back and forth across my hand. The move is so simple, but also so bold. "Let's take this one situation and one question at a time. That sound good?"

I nod. "Yes. I will go out with you. On one condition, though." I might be slightly swept up in the moment, and the touch of his hand, but I need to say this for my own sanity.

He smiles and lets go of my hand, which I instantly miss. "Name it."

"That this is a test."

"A test?"

"Yes, a test." I sit up a little straighter in the booth, needing him to know this is make or break for me. "Besides the reasons I just listed above, neither of us know what the hell we're doing. I haven't been in a relationship since the divorce, and no one knows what your story is in the dating department."

"I have a story."

"And I can't wait to hear it. But you have to agree this is unchartered territory—in more ways than one—for both of us. Yes?"

"You're right."

"Thank you. So, we need to go in with no expectations and forget that we've already kissed."

His lips form a devilish grin. "Amelia, there is nothing you can say or do that will make me ever, and I mean *ever*, forget that."

Same, but I can't tell him that. Not when I'm trying to

make a point. "You know what I mean. This needs to be a clean slate. As much as you might not want to admit it, there's a lot of ramifications if this happens. And before we rock that boat, we need to make sure this is real and it's not just a fleeting thing."

"It's not."

"Shane," I say sternly. "You don't know that."

"I do."

"Since when are you an optimist?"

He shrugs. "When it comes to the possibility of us? I'm eternal."

He lets go of my hands as we each sit back into the booth, which is a good thing since Mona is approaching with our breakfast. I forgot that I hadn't ordered, yet appearing before me is a stack of Mona's waffles, extra syrup, and an apple juice.

I look down at the plate then back up to Shane. "You ordered for me?"

"I told you I would."

I'm speechless as I look at my breakfast order. I feel the tears starting to build over the simple gesture. It's not exactly like my breakfast order is complex. Shane said he'd do it, and he did. He remembered.

Come to think of it, he always remembers.

Every time we come for breakfast, he always has my order in because he gets here twenty minutes early and I am usually twenty minutes late. He always sits on the side of the booth facing the restaurant because I don't like people looking at me while I'm eating.

If he wanted to, he would.

Shane is the definition of that phrase. And while yes, there might be a million scary reasons to not try, I think the scariest thing of all would be if I wouldn't even give it a shot.

"Shane?"

He looks up from his breakfast, and I can't help but smile at the hopeful glint in his eye.
"Yeah?"
"Let's go on a date."

Chapter 10
Shane

Desperate times call for desperate measures.

That's the only reasoning I can think of that justifies what I'm about to do.

> Shane: You got a minute?

> Simon: Depends on what it's for. I wore a new suit today and I don't want to get shit on it if you need help moving something.

I let out a deep sigh, hating the words I'm about to type.

> Shane: I need your help with something.

I don't even think I've hit send on that message before the text bombing begins.

> Simon: Me? You know this is just me and not the group chat right?

> Simon: Is Oliver still ignoring you? Amelia
> working? Did you call Wes too? Or are you
> really just asking me?
>
> Simon: What's this about? Is it just about
> buying houses or is it something juicy?
>
> Simon: Fuck it. I don't care. I'll be over in ten.

When Amelia finds out that I enlisted Simon's help for our date she's either going to check me into a psych ward or laugh her ass off. Maybe both. That should also show how serious I am about this date, because me asking Simon for help is a once-in-a-blue-moon occurrence.

Don't get me wrong; I love the man like a brother. He's been a part of our group since he and his family moved here in fourth grade. He might be an arrogant son of a bitch, and a pain in the ass most days, but the man is loyal and will move a mountain for you. Hell, Wes was just thinking about moving back to Rolling Hills last year and Simon went and found him a house that wasn't even on the market. We still don't know how that happened. Amelia has joked that if we ever needed someone to bury a body, well, Simon wouldn't do that. God forbid he'd get one of his designer suits dirty. But he would pay the guy to cover it up and drive the getaway car.

Everyone needs a friend like that.

I thought I was going to need to call him the other day if I had come in contact with Amelia's ex. I don't use the word hate a lot, but when it comes to Paul, hate isn't a strong enough word. I know why Amelia married him. Hell, I know why she stayed married to him. But I'll never forget the look in her eye the day she left him. The day I was in the right place at the right time. And for that, the man should always watch his back when I'm around. Because if given the opportunity, I'll end him.

Which is why I almost put Simon on call when I went to Mariah's track meet. Because I'm a man of my word, and I love that girl as if she was my own, I showed up and stayed the whole meet. I even went to watch Luke's game between Mariah's races.

That jackass didn't even bother showing his face. Which I knew he wouldn't. But I was ready.

"Okay! I'm here."

I come out from around the corner of my kitchen into the living room to see Simon bent over, gasping for air.

"Did you run here?"

"Possibly," he says, standing up and taking some long breaths. "But I'm here, and as your number two best friend, I'm ready to give you whatever you need on a subject you've yet to tell me about."

"I thought I was your third-ranking best friend?" I usually don't acknowledge Simon's ridiculous best-friend ranking system, but I need his connections, so today I'll amuse him. And I'm curious to see how I moved up.

"You were," he begins as he unbuttons his jacket before sitting on my couch. "But I dropped Oliver back to last place since he won't return any of my texts. And I even put that hilarious meme in the group chat last week. And nothing! What the fuck, man?"

"Not just you," I say as I sit down across from him. "I've barely talked to him since the wedding."

"Oh, I see. I'm only here because Oliver is possibly dead."

I roll my eyes. "He's not dead. Right now he's at school, because that's what employed teachers do on a Thursday morning in May. But yes, partly."

"You know what? I'm not even mad. His loss is my gain. So, best friend number two, how can I help?"

"That new Italian restaurant in Franklin, don't you know the owner?"

Simon's eyebrow raises. "I do, since I was the real estate agent who found him that property. Why do you ask?"

"How hard is it to get a reservation?"

This makes Simon sit up a little straighter. "Pretty tough. But it's a little easier when you're me. So again, why do you ask, Shane?"

I narrow my eyes because I know he knows—he's just going to make me say it out loud. "Because...I was seeing...if maybe you...."

"Come on, Shane. You can do it. I have faith in you, buddy."

Don't punch him. You need him.

"Can you call the owner and see if you can get a reservation for two for Saturday night?"

The smile forming on Simon's face right now is reminiscent of every villain in every James Bond movie ever made. "Why, yes, Shane. Of course I can."

"Thank—"

"But! Under a few conditions."

My head falls back against the couch. I have to remind myself this is for Amelia. For us. She wanted a test run, and I'm going to give her that.

"What are they?"

"Just a few questions. For starters, who's the woman?"

I let out a groan. "Not telling."

"Well, that's too bad. You would have really liked that restaurant."

"Why are you like this?"

"Part of my charm. Come on. Spill."

He can't know. Even if we were telling our friend group, Simon would be the last person to know. Well, either him or

Oliver. Simon because he's an instigator and Oliver because he'd be too excited to keep it in. Same results, different energy.

But I know he's going to dig in his heels about this, so I need to figure out a way to appease him, while also keeping this a secret.

"This is the first date," I begin. "And we're keeping things quiet until we've been out a few times. But if anything happens, you'll be the first to meet her."

His face turns serious. "The first, you say?"

"Before my mother."

This gets his attention. "Before Barb? The woman who last year ran an ad in the newspaper asking for any single woman to please go out with her son because she wants grandchildren?"

"The very one."

"Damn." Simon finally takes off the black suit jacket and tosses it to the side. "This is for real, isn't it?"

And just like that, Simon the arrogant prick is gone and replaced with the Simon we only see when he wants us to.

"Yeah, man, it is."

"Is this your first date?"

"I already told you it was."

Simon shakes his head. "No, not you and mystery woman, who for now I will call Mary since you won't give me a name. For you. Specifically. When was the last time you went on an *actual* date?"

I sit back and think about the question, because the answer is I don't know. "What do you constitute as a date?"

"A planned outing that wasn't just for sex."

"Then never."

Simon's jaw drops. "Never? Shane, my friend, I am the king of not being in a relationship. I've practically perfected it. But even I have taken the occasional woman out from time to time. How have you never been on an actual date?"

"I don't know," I say with a shrug. "Just never been interested in taking anyone on a date."

That's mostly the truth. If I would have had the balls, I would have asked Amelia out years ago. It just never felt like the right time. I was also pretty sure she was going to shoot me down, and I didn't need to live with that rejection.

"Shane, I need to ask you something," Simon leans closer toward me. "Are you a...virgin?"

I laugh and shake my head. "No. I'm not a virgin."

"Thank God," Simon says. "I wasn't ready to have that talk with you."

I laugh. "Believe me, I wouldn't have called you for that."

"Why not? I must say I've never had a complaint in that department."

"No. Your complaints come the next morning when you ask them to leave."

Simon shrugs. "Some that night. But never during."

We share a laugh as Simon grabs his phone and types something. "There. Sent a text to the restaurant owner. He has you down for two at seven-thirty."

"Perfect. Thanks again."

The two of us stand up and start walking toward the door.

"Hey," Simon says. "I hope it goes well."

"Thanks, man." We come in for a quick back-slapping hug. "I have a feeling it will."

"Can I ask one more thing?"

I let out a groan. "What?"

"Can you please let me come over and pick out what you're going to wear? If left to your own devices it will be jeans and a ratty flannel."

Actually, that wouldn't be a bad idea. And even better because I didn't have to ask him. "Sure. That would be great."

"Good. I can't wait to meet her first. Before everyone else. It's going to be the best day of my life."

I open the door for him. "You're going to hold me to that, huh?"

"You should be grateful I'm not asking you to make me the best man when you two get married."

Chapter 11
Amelia

> Amelia: Get over here. Now.

> Whitley: Is everything okay?

> Amelia: Yet to be determined…

I HAVE NEVER BEEN SO HAPPY MY CHILDREN AREN'T HOME. They don't need to see the destruction that is my bedroom.

Every piece of clothing I own is on my bed. I tried to curl my hair and somehow I now look like Truvy from *Steel Magnolias*. No shame to our Lord and Savior Dolly Parton, but that wasn't the look I was going for tonight. I wanted to be sexy. Beautiful. I wanted Shane to see me and his jaw drop. I wanted to reclaim that feeling I had when he looked at me at the wedding. That feeling from the first time he kissed me.

Yet here I am, standing in a threadbare T-shirt with hair so close to God it could give the Sunday sermon and staring at Mariah's makeup like it's a bomb about to explode. I have an hour until Shane is picking me up and I'm not ready—in so many ways.

"Amelia? Where are you?"

"In my bedroom!"

I've never been so thankful to live within walking distance of my brother and sister-in-law than I do at this moment. And that she's a former beauty queen.

"Oh my…"

I watch Whitley's eyes scan the room in alarm. "I need help."

Whitley walks over to me, clears off a pile of clothes from my bed, leaving us a place to sit. "Okay, what do we need help with? I don't want to assume, but I'm also guessing that you need help with a lot right now."

I look down, more out of shame than anything. "I have a date."

My words come out as a whisper, and I wonder if I even said it out loud.

"Amelia? Did I just hear you right? Did you say you have a date?"

"Yeah. I have a date."

Whitley lets out a squeal that could send every dog in the neighborhood into a frenzy as she wraps her arms around me and tackles me back into the bed. I can't help but laugh as she starts kicking her feet in excitement as she squeezes the life out of me.

"How are you just now telling me this! Why didn't you call me over sooner? Oh my God, this is a huge deal and I am so excited! Are you excited? You must be excited. What time is the date? Who's it with? When was the last time you went on a date? Girl, this is so big!"

"Easy, Tiger," I say as we sit back up. "That's why I called you. The date is in an hour. I thought I could do this alone, but clearly I can't."

"An hour!" Whitley starts ripping through her purse and

pulls out her cell phone. "We need reinforcements. I'll call over Betsy. She can—"

"No!" I grab her wrist to stop her from texting. "You can't ask Betsy to come over."

"Why?"

"Because then she'll find out who I'm going out with, and that can't happen. Even though she'd probably know. Or would guess. But I don't want her to know any more than she already does."

Whitley's eyes double in size. "Are you going out with Wes? Amelia! How—"

"Of course not," I interrupt. "I don't want her to have to lie to Wes if she knows who I'm going out with tonight."

"Amelia...Who are you going out with?"

I wasn't thinking when I called Whitley over that I'd have to tell her. I mean, I wasn't thinking. I was panicking. But I need to tell her. I don't want to *not* tell her then have Shane show up at my door. I can trust Whitley. She's family. She'd understand the need for the secret. At least, I hope she does.

"It's Shane."

She doesn't say anything for a second. But then I watch the realization on her face. And the shock that comes with it.

"Shane! Like Shane, your guy-best-friend Shane? Amelia! He's hot as fuck!"

"Thanks?"

"Yes, thanks. Now, don't get me wrong. I love your brother. He's the most handsome man in the world in my eyes and my soulmate. But Shane? I could put him in Jake's line of work and I think he'd do very well, if you know what I mean."

"No," I say definitively. It's bad enough my brother is a thirst trap on the internet. I don't need my boyfriend being one too.

Boyfriend? Did I just think that? No. Tonight is a test date.

So not that boyfriend is out of the question, but I need to take it one day at a time.

"Okay. Let's get back on track." Whitley starts going through my clothes and holding up different shirts and pants. "Where is he taking you? Or is it a surprise?"

I shake my head. "He wanted to make it a surprise but then I told him I was nervous enough as it was and that I needed as many details as possible. He's taking me to that new Italian restaurant in Franklin and then we're going to go see a band we like."

"Perfect," she says. "Something you two would normally do, just on a bigger scale."

Whitley starts holding up, tossing, and rummaging through the clothes on my bed. Before I know it she has four different outfit options displayed.

"How did you do that?"

She puts one in my arms. "Magic. Now go try this on while I get the makeup ready. It's time to get you ready for the ball, Cinderella."

~

"Holy shit, Whitley. I think you're my fairy godmother."

"Nope. Just an aged-out beauty queen with a knack for layering."

I look at myself in the full-length mirror Whitley brought in from Mariah's bedroom, and I can hardly believe what I'm looking at. I know it's me, but it doesn't look like me. Well, it does, but just a different version.

Whitley picked out a pair of jeans and a flowy white tank top with brown booties. It's May, but a little cool tonight, so she paired it with a long cardigan I would have never thought to wear for a date. I thought I could only wear this on days when I didn't want to leave the house. Knowing I didn't own any jewelry, she raided Mariah's jewelry box for earrings and a necklace. Finally, she fixed my hair and used a straighter to create loose waves and did just enough makeup to make me look like a new woman. Of course, during all of this she grilled me on how things happened for Shane and I to be going out tonight.

Needless to say she was quite happy to find out this all started at her wedding.

I turn back and forth in the mirror, looking at myself in awe. "I don't know how I can thank you."

"Easy," she says as she starts to hang back up the clothes that didn't make the cut. "You can have fun tonight."

I let out a half laugh, half snort. "Easier said than done."

Whitley sits on the bed and pats the now empty spot next to it. "Come here. Let's chat."

"Don't make me freak out or cry. Shane's going to be here any minute."

"I'll do my best." She takes my hand and cups it with both of hers. "Are you freaking out because it's a date? Or because it's a date with Shane?"

"Both."

"That's fair. And what I figured you'd say. Let's break this down in little chunks then. Let's start with that it's a date. Why are you freaking out?"

"Because..." One would think that the more I say this out loud the easier it would be to admit. It's not. "I've been on very few dates since the divorce. None of those became a relationship."

"Okay, so not a lot of dating history..."

"That's one way to put it."

"Listen. Dating sucks."

"Gee. Way to make me feel better."

"Let me finish. Dating sucks when it's a first date with a stranger. The conversation is dull. You feel like you're on a job interview. You're analyzing every little thing he says or does or wears because you are trying to see if he's worth a second date —and he's doing it to you too. Oh, and be ready to talk about all your favorites—colors, food, movies, books, the whole thing."

"Sounds horrible."

"It is. However, you're getting out of that tonight."

I give my head a little shake because she's lost me. "I am?"

Whitley gives me a reassuring smile. "You are. Because it's Shane. Who better to go on a first date with than a man you've known your whole life?"

I didn't think about it like that. "You're right. We know all that stuff about each other, but it's still Shane. Shane!"

"Yes, Shane. So?"

"So..." I look in the mirror one more time. "What if it doesn't go well? What if the wedding was a flash in the pan? What if we go out tonight and it's a dud?"

Whitley gives my hand one more squeeze. "Then you know. You won't have to wonder."

She's right. This is the whole point of the test. I need to stop freaking out, put on my big girl panties, and try to have a good time.

A knock on the door brushes my fledgling positive thoughts away like dry leaves in a wind gust.

"He's here."

Whitley smiles and hands me a purse. Also Mariah's, because I don't own one. "Here. I'll hide until you leave then I'll lock up. Please, go have fun. You, more than anyone I know, deserves it."

"Thank you." I hug Whitley and take one more deep breath for reassurance.

Here goes nothing...

When I open my front door, my mouth goes dry. I don't think I can form words. Shane looks, as Whitley said earlier, hot as fuck. His jeans are dark and fashionable. He's wearing a long, white button-down shirt with the sleeves rolled up. The nurse in me can't stop staring at his veins. The woman in me can't either. His cologne is just as intoxicating as I remember, and the smile on his face is melting me into a puddle.

"Hey, beautiful."

"Hi." I swallow the lump that keeps coming back in my throat.

His smile grows as he holds out his hand for me, which I give him without hesitation.

There. This isn't hard. Shane is holding my hand. We're walking to his truck. He's opening the door and helping me in as I step up into it. When he shuts the door I take a deep breath, letting my nerves try and calm themselves.

Then he gets in the car and shuts the door, and for some reason, right here, right now, this feels very real.

Very, very, real.

Because this is it. This is the moment. The moment that could potentially start it all.

"Hey." His words are soft and soothing. I didn't realize I was outwardly panicking. "It's just me."

I smile as I remember what advice Whitley gave me earlier. "It's just you."

"Exactly," he says. "Just us."

I feel my shoulders start to relax, and my chest become lighter. Yes. I can do this. We can do this. Just relax, have a nice night, and remember at the end of the day that this is Shane. No matter what the outcome is, he'll always be in my life. Nothing will ever change that.

"I wanted to tell you...you look very handsome."

"Thanks." He looks down then back up to me. "You can thank Simon for the jeans."

"Simon? He knows?"

Shane shakes his head. "No, but if this goes well, we have to tell him first."

"What did you do? Also, Whitley knows, so he's not going to technically be the first."

He laughs and lets go of my hand only for the second he needs to put the car into gear. "I'll tell you all about it. Just know that your code name is now Mary."

Chapter 12
Shane

"Would you two like another round?"

I turn my glance to Amelia, who is shaking her head. "I'm good, thank you."

"You sure?" I ask.

"I've had three glasses of wine tonight. I haven't drank this much since…"

She trails off, and both of us can't help but smile.

I look over to the waitress. "We're good. Thanks."

She nods and walks away before I lean into Amelia. "You know if you want another glass of wine, you can. It's your night, beautiful."

She leans in closer as well, making us just inches apart. "Officer Cunningham, are you trying to get me drunk?"

I take her hand in mine. "I would never."

Amelia smiles, her eyes glancing down as she reaches for my hand, which I gladly give to her. She's done this a few times tonight, and each time it's made me feel like I'm on top of the world. I might not have a lot to base this on, but I don't know if a date could go any better than this. Then again, I'm pretty sure the company has everything to do with it.

I'll have to buy Simon a drink—or do what he really wants and promise him future best man rights—for the strings he pulled at the restaurant. Not only was our table semi-private, it was also the only table that had candle light and a bottle of wine chilling when we sat down. The rose on the table was the perfect touch.

Dinner was incredible. And the best part? The conversation flowed like it was just Amelia and me on any other normal day. The only difference was that I held her hand every chance I could. We talked about the kids, our families, and our jobs. Our friends naturally came up—the biggest discussion on if Oliver's going to come back from his vacation to Vegas with a wedding ring. Before we knew it, the check was being delivered, and it was time for stop number two.

"I don't remember the last time we saw this band. I used to love it when they played at The Joint."

I do. "Unless you've snuck out and seen them without me, it was Thanksgiving night, six and a half years ago."

Amelia thinks about it for a second before the recognition sets in. "You're right. How do you remember that? I don't remember what I had for breakfast this morning."

I slide her closer to me, so now we're sitting next to each other at the pub table we snagged just off the main floor. "Because that was the Thanksgiving right after your divorce was finalized. You held it together all day, but after dinner, while everyone was in your kitchen eating pie, you were back in your room breaking down."

She squeezes my hand tighter. "And you found me."

I switch which hand I'm holding so I can put my arm around her. "I found you in your room, and you tried to pretend you weren't crying. You did not hide it well."

"And you sat with me and let me cry. Your shirt was soaked. Then when the tears were gone, you called Oliver and Simon, and you took me to The Joint. You even got Wes down from Nashville."

"Yup. This band was playing, and we got you stupid drunk."

She laughs as she rests her head on my shoulder. "I threw up so much the kids had to stay with my mom the next day."

I chuckle, remembering how many times I had to stop on the way home to let her throw up. "That night, this band played, and you danced and drank and let every problem melt away. It was the night we got Amelia Evans back. And that's why I remember it."

Amelia told us that night she was going to change her last name back to Evans. We asked if she was sure—yes, we hated Paul, but it's her kids' last name. She told us flat out she needed to be separated from him in as many ways as possible, and taking back her name was the biggest way she knew how to do that. We asked her again after she sobered up if she was sure. She said there was nothing she wanted more.

"Thank you."

I look down to see her big brown eyes looking back up at me. I want to lean down and kiss her so badly, but I'm not about to mess up what has been a perfect night. "What for?"

"Tonight. Back then. Every time I seem to find myself in a situation, you happen to appear, like some sort of personal superhero."

"Should I get a cape?"

This makes her smile. "Possibly. I bet you'd look sexy in it."

I know what I thought just a few seconds ago, but I need to kiss this woman more than I need my next breath.

And I do. Nothing big. Nothing deep. Just the briefest touch of our lips together. The second we connect, I feel like

I'm home. I don't know how else to explain it, but that's the feeling that's rushing through my body.

When she pulls away, I'm a little concerned to not see her smiling.

"Everything okay?"

She quickly nods her head. "Is it scary how easy this feels?"

I let out a breath. "Yeah. A little."

"It's just—" She pauses for a second and sits back up so she can look straight at me. "I feel like this has been a whirlwind. One minute you're just Shane, the next you're Shane who I'm holding hands with and smiling at and wanting to kiss all the time."

Now that makes me smile. "All the time?"

"Yes. But that's terrifying. I wasn't looking for anyone. Or to date. I was content with the life I had. Then here you come in, all sweet, with a romantic dinner and small gestures and smelling really, really good—I'm going to need you to never switch your cologne by the way—and making me question everything I thought about us."

"No. Don't question us," I say, bringing her hands to my mouth. "Yes, this is new. Yes, this is different. But it's not just you who is adjusting. I am, too."

"Really?" she asks. "I feel like you're so sure and confident in this. Like you're just taking it all in perfect stride."

I shake my head. "Amelia? Do you know how long I've wanted this?"

She shakes her head.

"Years. So many years that I've lost track."

"Really?"

I nod. "You know that kiss. Our real first kiss?"

This makes her smile. "Yes. Wait...since then?"

"Since then," I repeat. "I kissed you because I didn't know if I was going to come back. I kissed you because I thought not kissing you would be the biggest regret of my life. I wanted to leave knowing that even if something bad happened to me, I knew what it was like to kiss you. Even if it was just once. And for that one second, I got to pretend that you were mine."

This seems to shake her, and I see the tears welling in her eyes. "Shane...I never...why didn't you ever...?"

Here it is. The moment of truth. The moment I tell her everything.

"I never wanted you to know. No one knew. None of the guys knew. Or my brother. No one. Because I was scared. I was scared you'd not feel the same way. I was scared to rock the boat. Like you, I was petrified of what it would do to us. To our families. Our friends. And then there was that whole you were with Paul thing..."

She shakes her head. "Another thing he ruined."

"We'll add it to the list," I joke. "But, yeah, you and me? This isn't a new idea I came up with recently. This is years of admiring you. Loving you from afar. Wanting to be in your life in every way I could. You're it for me."

Her smile hits me straight in the heart. "I don't know what to say."

"Don't say anything." I take her chin in my fingertips, locking our gazes. "I told you that because I wanted you to know that all those scary things like our families and friends? I've worried about them too. I've just had a little more time to game plan and think about the possible outcomes. But this? How easy this is? How I've noticed all night that your hand fits perfectly in mine? That I couldn't prepare for. So yeah, while it's scary this is so easy, it's also a feeling I've never felt."

This makes her smile. "I feel the same way."

"Good. Because we're just getting started."

I lean in to kiss her as the band comes back on stage for their second set. I don't let it linger, even though I want to, and we slowly pull away as an upbeat song from our high school days fills the air. Amelia even gets out of her chair to dance. I just sit back and watch. She turns and looks over her shoulder, the smile on her face the biggest I've seen in years.

I can't help but have a sense of pride that I was a part of that.

I just want her to be happy. That's all I've ever wanted for her. She sacrificed so much over the years; she deserves more than anyone on this planet to be happy. She was a married mother at eighteen. It took her twice as long to get through nursing school because she was raising a child basically alone, even though Paul was there. Hell, she took time off when Mariah was younger because it made more sense for her to stay home. When they got divorced, she pulled herself up by her bootstraps and not only got back into nursing, but built a life for her, Luke, and Mariah. But in doing so, she's made work and kids her entire life. Which I get. I'd do the same thing. But the kids are older. Her job is stable. It's about damn time she starts taking some space for herself. No one has earned it more than her.

And if I get to be a part of that? That's just icing on the cake.

The band has shifted into a slower song, and as soon as I hear the first two notes, I know exactly what song it is. It's the one that has made me think of Amelia every time I've heard it since our junior prom.

"Do you want to dance?"

Amelia looks confused as she looks back at me. "No, that's okay."

Her mouth might have said that, but I know she doesn't mean it. Her body is swaying to the music so subtly I don't even think she realizes she's doing it.

I stand up and walk the short distance around our table and hold out my hand.

"Amelia...dance with me."

"Are you sure?" She looks to the dance floor then back to me before shaking her head. "No. It's okay. You don't have to if you don't want to. I know you don't like to dance so—"

She lets out a small gasp as I take her hand and pull her flush to me. "Amelia. Dance. With. Me."

Her jaw drops a little as I lead her out to the dance floor. It drops even more when I spin her into me, effortlessly placing my hand on her back as we start swaying to the melody.

"Where did you learn to do that?"

"I'm a man of many talents."

This makes her smile. "I'm sure you are."

I bring her in a little closer so I can lean down and whisper in her ear. "And I can't wait to show you."

Amelia rests her head on my shoulder as we let the song and the lyrics run through us. Other couples have gathered around, but I couldn't tell you how many or who is there. Right now, Amelia is in my arms and our bodies are moving together perfectly to the first song we ever danced to.

It's maybe the most perfect moment of my life.

"Do you remember this song?"

She nods against me. "Junior prom. I wasn't going because I was sad Paul never asked me. Then you suggested we go together as friends. Wait! Was that a date?"

I laugh. "No. I was too scared. Friends seemed to be the perfect way for me to ask you without either of us freaking out."

"Okay," she says with relief. "This song...we got to prom and I was bummed I saw Paul dancing with Jessica. But you wouldn't let me be sad. Instead, you took me by the hand, led me to the floor, and we danced to this song."

"You're right," I say as I kiss the top of her head. "Except you left the last part out."

She looks back up to me confused. "No, I didn't. We danced to this song. Then for the rest of the night each of the guys danced with me to make Paul jealous. I remember because Simon decided to give me a lap dance, and that really set Paul off."

"Again, you're right, but you're forgetting one thing. You really don't remember?"

"Shane, I have no idea what you're talking about."

"Think after the dance. When I took you home."

I watch as the wheels turn in her mind. I can always tell when Amelia's racking her brain. It's like you can see the motors running. You can also tell the instant she remembers. Her eyes bulge out of her head. Her mouth forms an O-shape and she blinks so fast she could fly away.

"After the dance..."

I nod at her whispered response. "After the dance I drove you home and the radio was playing. This song came on again and I asked you for one more dance."

"And I told you that you didn't have to because I knew you didn't like to dance."

I push her out from my hold, only so I can spin her back in. "That was one of the few times I've ever lied to you. It wasn't that I didn't like dancing. It was that I only wanted to dance with you."

"What are you saying?"

"Even back then I knew it was you, Amelia," I say as the final words of the song begin to play. "No one interested me. No one made me want to dance. It was you. Only you. I would have danced with you all night. And every time I've heard this song, I've only ever thought of you."

My words stun her for a few seconds, and I wonder if I've

gone too far. That's until she reaches up and takes my face in her hands, pulling me down for a kiss that nearly knocks me on my ass.

Every time we've kissed, it's been me who has initiated it. But this time? It's hitting me in a way I wasn't expecting. There's no hesitation. No teasing. It's all deliberate. Her mouth is seeking mine for something more. Something I'm desperate to give her.

We separate as the song ends, but neither of us step away from each other. I know I couldn't if I tried.

"Let's get out of here," she says.

"Are you sure?"

"Yeah," she says, biting her lip as she leads me off the dance floor. "Let's go do something stupid."

Chapter 13
Amelia

When I married Paul, I remember thinking how sweet it was that I was going to spend the rest of my life with the only man I've ever been with. That he was going to be my first, my last, and my only.

I was an idiot.

I know that now. I don't blame past me for thinking that. I was eighteen, pregnant, and about to walk down a makeshift aisle of the courthouse. Of course I was going to try to find the silver lining in any way I could.

Back then I was naive and hopeful. Now I'm thirty-five, jaded, and nervous as hell as I stand in Shane's living room. I know it was my idea to leave the bar. I wanted it when he picked me up. When he held my hand at the restaurant. When we were dancing like no one was watching.

But now that I'm here? I'm a very different person now. The small amount of liquid courage has gone away, and it's been replaced by fear, insecurity, and the general remembrance of sex. Frankly, I have no idea what the hell I'm doing.

I look around as Shane turns on the lights. I've been to his house dozens, if not hundreds, of times. But something is different tonight. He's always been clean and tidy, so seeing a spotless living room isn't out of the ordinary. He's also always been a minimalist. Shane isn't exactly the kind of guy to have throw pillows or blankets on his couch. The only decorations he's ever had in his living room are three pictures on his mantle —one of him and his mom; another of him and his brother; and a picture of the five of us from his going-away party seventeen years ago.

Except that now that I'm looking, there is a new picture. I take a few steps toward it and smile as soon as I see what it is—a picture of the two of us.

"Is this?"

I look back at Shane, who's walking toward me with two bottles of beer in his hands. He sets them down on the coffee table before he comes up behind me, wrapping his arms around my waist as he brings me closer to him. "Jake and Whitley's wedding."

In all the craziness of that day, and night, I completely forgot that we had taken a picture before the ceremony. "Right before the ceremony."

I feel him nod against me. "I might have asked Mariah to send it to me."

I feel myself smiling, because how can I not? "And you framed it?"

"The next day."

"And you put it on your mantle?"

"Of course. Where else would I put it?"

This man...

The more and more I see him outside the light of just my best friend, the more and more I fall for him. How can I not?

Every day he does something else that takes my breath away. And it's never anything big. It's putting a picture on a mantle, or remembering how I take my coffee. I need to quit fighting this. And I need to get out of my head, because right now, that's the scariest place to be.

I turn to face him and wrap my arms around his neck. His hands tighten around my waist so there isn't an inch between us. His thumbs start gently stroking at the small of my back, which somehow is chasing away the jitters I had just a few minutes ago. They aren't all gone. I don't know if that will happen anytime soon. But somehow being in Shane's arms is calming me in just the way I need.

"Hey," he says as he places a kiss on my forehead. "You know nothing happens tonight that you don't want. Right?"

I chuckle. "Am I that transparent?"

Shane leads me to his couch, where he brings me so close that I'm practically sitting on his lap. "You are. But I also like to think it's because I know you so well."

When you're friends with the guys, there is one topic that's off limits—sex. It's the unspoken rule we've carried since Simon lost his virginity our freshman year. And while I wish I could avoid saying the words that are about to come out of my mouth, I also know that if Shane and I are going to have a chance, I need to be up front with him. Even if it's absolutely mortifying.

"I want this Shane. I want you in every way. The more and more I think about it, the more and more I know I want it."

"I feel like there's a 'but' coming up."

"You do know me well." I look down and start playing with the fabric of his jeans as I try and find my words.

"I...It's been a very—and I mean very—long time since I've been with anyone. I don't want to say the name of that person because I'd rather not talk about him, but yeah, it's been a minute, and there's only been him. And, well, I've never been good at it. And I don't think I was ever doing it right, so I know I'm not going to do it right after a very long, emphasis on very long, hiatus. And I don't want—"

Shane cuts me off by scooping me into his arms and placing me across his lap. His lips find mine—this kiss hard and purposeful—and I'm pretty sure he's doing it to shut me up.

I'm okay with that.

"You're right," he begins. "I don't want to hear about him. As far as I'm concerned, that man has no place when it comes to us."

"I agree."

"However, I know what he did to you. I know what he said to you. How he made you feel. I saw it. It killed me. I wanted to kill him. But now I get to do something better."

I tilt my head, not sure where he's going with this. "What's that?"

"I'm the one who gets to replace those memories. Because Amelia? There isn't a memory I don't want to make with you."

It takes every part of me not to start crying. Because I want that. I want Shane to be the one to make me forget. To make me feel. To help discover this new version of me. To allow me to experience things I've thought were maybe just a fairy tale.

"Shane?"

"Yeah?"

"Kiss me."

He inches closer to me. "Are you sure?"

I nod. "I've never been surer of anything in my entire life."

That's all he needs to hear before he slowly comes to me, his lips finding mine in the most perfect kiss I think has ever existed. His hands softly cup my face, holding me to him as our tongues start working in tandem, sending a mixture of heat and chills through my body. I felt this the night of the wedding, but

I chalked it up to shock and being a little drunk. Now the only thing I'm drunk on is Shane and his kiss.

And I think I'm absolutely addicted.

I open my mouth and our tongues meet, deepening the kiss in the most exquisite way. My hands suddenly have a mind of their own as they start traveling around Shane's muscular back and up his defined arms. He does, as well, and I'm trying to lean into his touch while also enjoying the feel of Shane. I've never wanted to explore a man before. I've never wondered what was underneath the shirt, or what his arms would feel like if I held onto them while he was inside me. But with Shane, I want to know. I want to know everything.

"Amelia..."

I grow bold by the sound of my name on Shane's tongue. It was a mixture of a moan and a plea, and it sounded so damn sexy coming from his mouth. My hands start traveling farther, across his pecs and down his chest until they come to the metal and leather of his belt. I do my best not to break the kiss as I start unfastening it, until his strong hands are on mine stopping me.

"Amelia, what are you doing?"

I hurry and find his eyes because now I'm scared that I misread all of this. I knew I was bad at this, but I didn't realize I was so bad I couldn't even tell when a man didn't want me to take off his pants.

"I'm...did you not want this?"

"Of course I do," he says, cupping my face yet again. "But do you? I don't want to push you too far and too fast. Don't think we have to do this because I want to. I've waited my whole life for tonight. I'd wait another lifetime if that's what you need."

I shake my head as I reach for him. We kiss each other

without hesitation. And for the first time in weeks, I feel confident that what I want is what I also need.

"I want this. I want this so much."

Just as I feel Shane about to lift me in his arms, I hear the sound of a text message from my phone.

"I'm sorry," I say, pulling away to grab it. "With the kids, I never know....it's Mariah."

Shane tenses next to me. "Is she okay?"

I nod. "Yeah. She's staying at Gabby's tonight. They want to order food, and she was asking if she could use my card."

"It's nice that she asked."

I laugh under my breath as I tap out a response to her. "That's only because a few months ago she went rogue and ordered a few hundred dollars' worth of makeup without my permission."

"Holy shit!"

"Yup. So now if I find one transaction I don't know about, she doesn't have her phone for a month."

"Fuck around and find out," Shane says, smiling and sitting back on the couch, his arm casually around me as I wrap up my texting with Mariah. "I can get on board with that."

"This girl is going to either be the death of me or drive me broke. Probably both." I put my phone down and fall back into the couch. "Luke was never like this. Hell, tonight he's having an all-night video game session at a friend's house. To most seventeen-year-olds, that would be code for getting drunk in a field somewhere."

"That's what we'd have done."

"Exactly. But not Luke. He's exactly where he should be. He'd feel bad using my card to buy gas for errands I asked him to run. Mariah? That girl..."

I let my head fall into Shane's shoulder as he gently runs his fingers down my shoulder. "I'm sorry."

"For what?"

"That killed the mood."

"What do you mean?"

I turn to Shane. "That. Mariah. I know we were having a moment, but Mom duty came in. And now it's ruined and—"

Shane scoops me up and brings me across his lap. "And nothing. You're a mom first. Always. No matter what happens between us, Luke and Mariah are your first priority."

"But—"

"No buts."

"Shane—"

"Uh-uh." He shakes his head and lifts me up with ease. "You think the mood is ruined? Oh, Amelia. You have no idea how wrong you are."

Shane carries me to his bedroom, almost running down the hall, and I have to stifle a laugh. The laugh quickly stops as I look up and see the burning look in his eyes as he places me gently on the bed. Have I ever been looked at like this? I'm not sure. I sure as hell know I've never felt my body on fire simply because of how someone looked at me.

"Come here."

Shane doesn't make me wait. He lowers himself to the bed, our mouths coming together again and picking up right where they left off. At least I know we've got this down. I feel his hands on me as he slips off my cardigan and lifts the tank top over my head.

"So beautiful."

His lips continue down my body as his hands reach around to unclasp my bra, leaving me bare and open to him. I'm trying not to feel self-conscious as he gently picks me up just enough to discard the rest of my clothes, but I can't help it when I feel my very soft body against his very hard one.

Here he is, a man who is built like a brick house, with a

jawline that could cut glass and eyes that hypnotize you. And that's before we get to the fact that his kisses make me forget my name. Then there's me. I know my body isn't exactly what men dream of after two kids and a lifestyle that consists of takeout food, coffee, and pizza. But Shane doesn't seem to care. In fact, I think he is setting up camp on my chest, kissing every inch of my breasts, stomach, and hips like it's something to be treasured. Add in the fact that he's tweaking my nipples in conjunction with his tongue tracing a treasure map, and I'm about to come undone again.

"Shane, please..."

I don't even know what I'm asking for. I just know I need more.

Shane softly laughs as I feel his hands slowly coming down my body. By habit, I put my arms over me to cover myself, but he immediately grabs them and pins them above me.

"Don't you dare. Let me look at you."

I do as he says, even though it's a struggle. Shane stands up from the bed, and I stare in awe as he takes off his clothes. The most mesmerizing part? His eyes never stop looking at me. I feel so...exposed. Open. Vulnerable. Yet at the same time, I feel so protected. Like nothing can go wrong as long as Shane is with me. I trust this man implicitly. With my body. With my heart. With everything I have to give.

And even though that's the scariest thought of all, it doesn't frighten me one bit.

"Touch me, Shane," I say. "Please."

He doesn't make me wait. He slips off his pants and joins me back on the bed, kissing me deeply as he lowers himself onto me. I hold onto him with all I have, loving how his warm skin feels against mine. I feel my core starting to throb as our bodies keep connecting, and his hard cock keeps pressing into me.

"So wet for me," Shane says as his hand slips down to my center.

"Yes." It's all I can manage to say. And if his hand keeps going where I think it's going, I'll be lucky to form any coherent words.

My body tenses as he slips a finger inside me, the foreign sensation catching me off guard for just a second. As if Shane can feel my reaction, he kisses me, letting his finger continue to explore while he sets the rest of me at ease the best way he knows how.

"Relax, beautiful," he whispers. "Just relax. I've got you."

And he does. I feel his lips as he takes each of my breasts in his mouth one at a time, lapping and sucking at each one as his fingers continue to work me. I don't know which part to concentrate on, both feel so good. Every time I revel in one more than the other, he does something to draw my attention back. And just when I think I have his pattern figured out, he changes it.

Like now. His mouth is starting to kiss down my stomach and across my hips. I look up and prop myself on my elbows as he repositions himself at the bottom of the bed.

"What are you doing?"

He looks up and smiles the most wicked smile on his face. "I never got to have dessert tonight."

My eyes go wide as I watch him dive into my pussy. My arms give out with the first pass of his tongue. Holy shit, what is this sorcery?

All night I've been doing my best not to compare Shane and Paul. But how can I not right now? I know Paul and I had a very bland and mostly nonexistent sex life. Maybe not at the beginning, but as time passed and Paul disappointed me over and over, it became nothing but an obligation. And by the end, I knew I didn't owe him a thing. In the early years I thought that was normal—the waning interest. I hear married couples talk about it all the time. Or at least, I had convinced myself of that.

But in one night with Shane I'm beginning to realize what I've been missing. I didn't know this was such an...experience. I thought it was an in and out. A thing you did. A box you checked once a month. I didn't realize that it could make you wonder how you're ever going to go without this again, because after just a taste you can't imagine life without it.

"Shane." I moan his name as I grab at his black hair. I pull a little as he slips a finger back in, his tongue flicking at my clit furiously. I feel my body start to tense as the orgasm begins to build, which makes me grab his hair even harder. Shit, that has to be hurting him.

"I'm sorry."

This stops him immediately. "Why are you apologizing?"

"Because...I'm pulling your hair. I didn't mean to."

"Oh, beautiful," he says, sliding back up so he can kiss me. I taste myself on his lips, which gives me a rush I wasn't expecting. "Yank it out for all I care. But don't you ever, and I mean ever, apologize for that. Now, I was in the middle of something."

Shane dips down, throwing my legs over his shoulders as he dives back in. Only this time, he's not gentle. He's not taking his time. The man is on a mission. And I'm pretty sure that mission is to make me scream.

I grab his hair again, knowing I'm pulling harder than before, but I think it's spurring him on. I feel him bring me closer, which seems impossible. His tongue is inside me, and it's a sensation I've never felt before.

"I'm close, Shane. So close."

His fingers find my clit, and with just a few strokes, I'm catapulting out of this bed. Well, at least my soul is. The only reason my body isn't is because Shane is holding me, taking care of me through the high, and the eventual low.

Oh my God. I don't know what that was, but I'm going to need it to happen again.

Shane leaves two small kisses on each of my hip bones as he rolls out of bed. I don't know where he's going, and I don't look. My eyes are growing heavier and heavier as I settle into the softness of Shane's bed. When I feel the warm towel between my legs, I smile but don't look down. I can't. It's like I'm about to fall into the best sleep of my life.

No. I can't. I need to fight this. He needs his. He's given me so much tonight; I can't leave him with nothing. I open my eyes as much as I can as he lies down next to me, which makes it all that much easier to slide down and take his length in my hand and begin to stroke.

"Hey," he says as he reaches down to stop me. "There will be none of that tonight."

I look up at him, clearly confused as to why he'd say that. "But you..."

He shakes his head. "If the next words out of your mouth are about to be 'But you didn't finish,' we're going to stop that right there. This is not a one-for-one. This is not just because you did, I did."

"But—"

He holds a finger to my lips. "But nothing, beautiful. If you don't think watching and feeling you come undone like that wasn't the highlight of my night—of my life—then you don't really understand how crazy I am about you."

I smile. "It was?"

"It was." Shane lifts up the covers, signaling for me to join him. "Come here."

I oblige, nuzzling into his shoulder as he brings me into his arms. I feel him kiss the top of my head as I start drifting off.

I never fall asleep right away. Usually I'm tossing and turning, because I can never turn off my brain.

But not tonight. Tonight I fall right asleep with my body sated and my brain calm for the first time in years.

And it's all because of Shane.

Chapter 14
Shane

I've always been a light sleeper. Chalk it up to years in the Army and growing up with a mom who snored so loud you could hear it a mile away. That's why I'm so startled when I feel something under the covers. And that something is coming very close to my already aching morning cock.

"Amelia? What are you doing?" I slowly open my eyes and see her head resting on my shoulder. I don't think it moved all night. And I'm not complaining about that one bit.

"Just feeling around."

"Are you now?"

She nods as her hand wraps around my dick. "You got to have your fun last night. Now it's my turn."

I don't know where this bold Amelia is coming from, but I like it.

No. I *love* it.

This woman is the epitome of strong. She's overcome so much and battled for everything in her life. Paul made her weak—through no fault of her own, that's just what you get when you're with a narcissistic asshole—and it has taken her years to remember who she was. Her initiating this, and us last night, those are just a few more of the steps to Amelia finally becoming the woman she deserves to be.

Strong. Loved. Cherished. Satisfied.

And I want to help her get to all of that.

"Amelia..." My voice is a low grunt as her hand starts working me. Her touch is gentle, maybe a little tentative, but that doesn't mean it doesn't feel like heaven.

"Do you like it?"

I roll her slightly on top of me, because I need to kiss the nonsense out of this woman's mouth right now. "There will never be anything you do that I don't love."

This makes her smile and gives her a little more confidence, as her hand starts working a little faster. Her grip becomes tighter as she moves back and forth on me. She pulls up the covers before starting to leave a trail of kisses around my chest. It slightly tickles, but feels so good in combination with her hand working me over.

Her lips move lower and lower, soon landing on my pelvic bone. Shit...is she about to?

"Amelia. You don't have to do that."

And she doesn't. Would I like her to? More than I want my next breath. But never would I ask her to do something, or expect her to do something, she doesn't want. But if she wants to? If it's her decision? I'll let her do anything, give her anything she wants. No questions asked.

"I know." Her voice is muffled as she's still under the sheets. "I want to. I want to make you feel as good as you made me feel. But I might need some help."

"Whatever you want, beautiful. Whatever you want."

She nods as she hesitantly licks the tip of my cock. I think it grows another two sizes just from that small touch. I push the sheet farther away so I can look at her. I want to watch her. I want to see her find her confidence and her sexuality. But at the same time, she feels too good. My eyes close, and my head falls back as she slowly takes all of me into her mouth.

Holy fuck...

Blowjobs have always been just okay for me. If a woman wants to give me one, I don't turn it down. But in my experience, they always fall flat. I never came because of it. It was just a means to an eventual end.

But right now with Amelia? I don't think I've ever felt anything better. Her mouth is warm and soft. Her hand is working in tandem with her mouth, feeling all of me at any given moment. With every stroke and every lick, she's getting bolder. Which means I'm getting closer and closer.

"Amelia. You feel so good."

I force my eyes open, not wanting to miss a minute of this. I take her hair in my hand, making sure not to be too forceful as her mouth moves up and down on me. She seems to like this, as her hips begin to writhe, her ass up in the air. I reach over to her, needing to feel her hot center, but she's just out of reach. I do my best to push myself up a bit without stopping Amelia, which gives me just the angle I need to be able to slowly start rubbing her. Holy shit, she's wet. So fucking wet I can't help but let out a groan. Between her mouth, her pussy, and just Amelia being in my bed, I don't know how long I'm going to be able to hold on.

I slowly slide my finger into her, which makes her stop for just a second as she takes in the sudden pressure. "Shane. What are you doing?"

"You don't worry about me. Just keep taking my cock in that beautiful mouth of yours."

I worry for a second that my dirty mouth—the one I've been forcing back since last night—might scare her off. But the glint in her eye is saying otherwise.

I brush a stray piece of hair out of her face and into my hand as Amelia's mouth is back on me. I twist my finger, hitting the spot that makes her back arch, but it only urges her on even more. Her speed picks up, and I swear she's taking me even deeper than she was before. I can't stop staring at her. She's gorgeous. Fierce. Taking what she wants. It's fucking hot as hell.

It's also about to make me come harder than I have in my life.

Feeling it about to hit, I do my best to gently pull her up just as the first shot hits my stomach. I look down and see her brown eyes wide in fascination as she continues to stroke me. It's enough to get me hard all over again. Finally I collapse back into the bed, my cum spilled on me and my breath heavy. I reach down to touch Amelia, needing to feel her right now, but she's not there. When I open my eyes she's crawling back on the bed, a warm wash cloth in her hands.

"I'm sorry I didn't swa—"

I grab her wrist and pull her to me, needing to quickly kiss away whatever nonsense was about to come out of her mouth. "Don't you dare apologize."

"But I—"

Another kiss. Those seem to work. "Amelia, did you like doing that?"

She nods. "I did."

"And did you like watching me finish?"

Her smile gives her away before she can say anything. "I did."

"Then that's all that matters."

I bring her into my arms, and she immediately wraps herself around me. Her fingers start playing with my chest hair as I trace small circles on her back. Perfection. That's the only word I can think of to describe this moment. The only thing that could top this would be sinking into her soft, wet heat, but that would only be the icing on the cake. Just being with Amelia, seeing her open herself up to me, letting me see a side of her that I don't even think she knew she had, is a fucking gift.

"Thank you."

I look down, but her eyes are focused now on her fingers tracing aimlessly on my chest. "For what?"

"Being you. Waiting for me. Being patient with me. Just... thank you."

I roll her on top of me, giving me easier access to kiss her. I try not to deepen it, I know she likely has to leave soon, but it's hard to stop. It's going to be even harder not to do this every time I see her. And not want to do this every night.

"So," she begins. "I think it's safe to say the test went well."

I laugh. It's like she's reading my mind. "I'd call it a success. I guess the question is, what's next?"

I know what my answer is. We tell everyone, and I scream it from the rooftops. But knowing Amelia, and knowing how long it took to get us here, I doubt that's going to be her answer. And while I'd love to do that, this is her show. I'm just lucky to be along for the ride.

"Is it bad that I don't want to tell anyone?"

I swallow a groan, because I was afraid that's what she was going to say. "I figured you'd say that."

She takes my hand in hers and locks our fingers. "It's just that as soon as everyone finds out, this isn't going to be about us. It's going to be about our moms, or our friends, or how you're going to be a bonus dad. I just want time for us. I want to date. I want to send stupid text messages that make me giggle. I don't know, it's...I never got to do this. I've never dated. And I want to date for just a little bit without it involving everyone in my life. Is that bad?"

I shake my head. "Not bad at all. Is it going to kill me not being able to kiss you whenever I want? Yes. Am I going to go mad not being able to hold your hand or touch you when I see you? Likely. But I understand. And I want that, too. I want us, Amelia. And however you want to do this, I'm on board. I'm in. I'm *all* in."

Amelia's mouth finds mine, and we settle into a kiss that says everything.

We're in this.

We're committed.

We're going to make this work.

Just as we let the kiss deepen, I hear a banging on my front door.

"Who the fuck is that?"

Amelia laughs. "Will they go away if you don't answer?"

"Shane! Open the fuck up!" Simon's yelling is only masked by the sound of his fist pounding against my door. "I want Mona's, apparently you changed the lock on your door because my key doesn't work, and I need to hear about your date. Let me in!"

I groan, knowing that he's just going to stay there until I open. "I hate him."

"No, you don't," Amelia says as she rolls off me, leaving a kiss on my chest for good measure. "Go answer the door. I'll get dressed."

I let out a groan as I begrudgingly get out of bed. "Do you have to go?"

"Yeah," she says as she starts slipping on her bra. "I need to pick up Mariah so she isn't suspicious."

"Does she have a meet this week?"

"Yeah. Tuesday again. But it's an hour away."

"So?"

She looks over at me as she puts on her clothes. "So that means you don't have to go."

I walk over to the bed and stand her up, needing her eye-to-eye for this one. "We're a team now. We might be a secret one, but from here on out, it's you and me. And that includes the kids. So if you tell me Mariah has a meet on Tuesday, I'll pick you up from work and we'll go over. Maybe then we can get there early and make out a little."

This makes her laugh. "I never thought I'd hear you use the words *make out*. Oliver's rubbing off on you."

"Don't tell him that."

We smile and share a kiss before the pounding on the door starts again.

"Go," she says, patting me on the back. "I'll hang here until he leaves."

I lean in for one more kiss before I finish getting dressed and leave my bedroom. I make sure to close the door securely before letting Simon in. It's just safer that way.

I open the door and can't even get a word out before he barges in. "What took you so long? And don't tell me you were still in bed, because we all damn well know you get up at a stupidly early hour."

"I slept in today."

"You don't sleep in." But just as the words leave Simon's mouth, his eyes double in size and he looks down the hall to my bedroom. "Holy shit, is she here? Is Mary here?"

I wipe my mouth and shake my head as I figure out how to play this. "She is. Which is why you need to leave."

"Like hell I'm leaving," he says as he makes a show of sitting on my couch and getting comfortable.

"Excuse me?"

"Yup. I'm going to sit right here, maybe watch some TV, and wait for Mary to come out. You said I could meet her first, so here I am. Ready to meet."

Fuck me sideways...

"Can I buy you breakfast instead?"

Simon shakes his head as he flips on the TV. "Absolutely not. You can't bribe me with French toast when I'm about to meet the woman who made you wear dark wash jeans."

"You can't stay here all day."

"You're wrong. I can," he says. "I don't have to work today. My sisters are all staying out of my life for the time being, and I already went to the gym. Mary can't stay in there forever, my man. You might as well accept your fate."

Words like "shit" and "fuck" and "I fucking hate you" are mumbled as I walk toward my bedroom. Except when I open it up, Amelia is gone. I check the closet, my bathroom, and even under the bed, feeling like an idiot but unable to stop myself.

That's when I feel a slight breeze, and it's coming from an open window. When I walk over to it, I see Amelia waving at me as she walks toward her house, which is just around the block.

That's my girl...

"Okay! Where's she at?"

Simon nearly runs me over as he comes into my bedroom, only to find it empty.

"What the fuck, man? Where is she?"

I shrug. "You scared her away."

"Bullshit," he says. "You're lying. You made her up to fuck with me. That's not cool, man. I'm your second-best friend."

I slap him on the back. "Come on. I'll buy you breakfast. You know, to make up for this disappointing morning."

"Fine," he grumbles. "I'm getting two orders of French toast to make up for this emotional damage."

"Whatever you want, Simon. Whatever you want."

Chapter 15
Amelia

Mariah: Is it okay if Luke and I drive to Franklin to go to the mall? I have points expiring and that's like losing money if I don't use them.

Luke: What my sister meant to say is, is it okay if I take her to the makeup store and I run to pick up a few things.

Mariah: For his new girlfriend.

Luke: Shut up, she's not my girlfriend.

Amelia: We'll talk about the girlfriend/not girlfriend later. Both of you can use the debit card. Luke — If you're shopping for yourself, please get something that's not a necessity. Live a little. Mariah — Only get the things you need. And if you could, pick me up a lipstick? One you think would look good on me but not too much, you know?

Mariah: ....

Mariah: You…want me…to get you…lipstick? I don't even care about Luke's girlfriend anymore. This is more interesting.

Luke: You want us to spend your money just for fun? Buy you lipstick? And we don't have to get preapproved spending permission?

Amelia: You're both being dramatic. I've worn lipstick before. And you've bought things before that weren't necessities that weren't cheap.

Mariah: Not on purpose.

Luke: And not when it wasn't our birthdays.

Mariah: Since you're at work, maybe have someone see if you have a fever? Or why you've been in such a good mood the last few days.

Luke: Mom, seriously, are you okay? My psychology class last semester talked about the warning signs for manic episodes. I think we could categorize this as one of them.

Amelia: On second thought, leave the debit card at home.

Mariah: I'LL PICK OUT THE BEST SHADE EVER FOR YOU! Love you to the moon and back!

Luke: Thanks, Mom. We'll be back in a few hours. I'll double-check that my location is on.

Amelia: Love you both.

I laugh as I put my phone down on my desk at the nurse's station.

"I'm seriously about to admit you."

I look over to Kendra, who takes a seat next to me. "First my kids. Now you. I'm fine."

"No, you aren't, but it's okay." Her mouth forms into a knowing grin. "I knew you'd be a little different once you started getting laid, but I'm pretty sure if you keep that smile up for another day I might need to examine you to make sure it's not permanently there."

I shake my head, but my smile doesn't go away. She's right. I have been smiling all week. Most of the time I haven't noticed it. But then I catch a glimpse of myself in the mirror, or Shane will text me something sweet—or flirty—or I'll just think about him, and I feel my smile getting bigger.

I know I'm freaking people out. It's not that I never smiled before, but I know it wasn't like this. If we're going to keep this quiet, I definitely need to work on my face, because I'm about to give everything away. Especially if we're in the same room together, which we haven't been since I snuck out of his window two days ago.

But we have talked. And texted. I know I said that I wanted to have that giggly, honeymoon type feeling, but I didn't think it would actually feel like this. I know I'm a smiling loon right now, but I don't care. I'm happy. And I'm not going to apologize for that.

"So how is it?" Kendra asks as she leans back in her chair. "Clearly it must be good if you've been wearing the shade 'Orgasmic Glow' on your cheeks for the past couple of days."

"We haven't. Yet."

Kendra's eyes go wide. "Yet? Girl. Look at you. No one smiles this big just because a guy held their hand."

"We did more than hold hands," I admit. "We just haven't done that yet. Some things we're taking slow."

Kendra nods. "I can respect that. I don't get it, because two days in lesbian years is two months and we'd be looking at moving in together. But I can respect it."

I laugh. "Thanks. It's good. Granted, we haven't been in front of others yet, so that's going to be tricky, but we'll cross that bridge when we get there."

"Why would it be tricky?"

"We're...not exactly...telling everyone yet."

Kendra stops what she's doing on the computer to look at me. "You're keeping it a secret? Your solution to not having everyone freak out that you're dating is to not tell anyone?"

"Well, putting it like that makes it sound bad," I say. "We just want some time for us. When we tell people—and we have every intention of doing so—it's going to mean a lot of people insert themselves into our relationship. We just want some time for us."

"That makes sense," she says. "Also, I'm flattered that I'm in the know. This must have been what it felt like to know Darth Vader was Luke's father."

I laugh as I hear the doors to the emergency room open, and in an instant, my smile goes from big to physically hurting my face.

"Hey, beautiful."

For years I thought pet names were ridiculous. Just call the person by their name. It's not going to make them love you any less or more.

But I get it now. I totally get it. Because every time Shane Cunningham calls me beautiful, I fall a little bit more.

And when he's calling me beautiful while holding a cup of coffee and wearing his police uniform? I'm a goner.

"Hey."

I stand up and lean over to kiss him, but quickly stop myself.

"Oh, do it," Kendra says as she stands and walks toward one of the rooms. "Ain't no one here that's going to tell on you two."

I smile and turn back to Shane, who meets me for a sweet kiss I feel from my head to my toes.

"I've always liked her," Shane says.

"She's pretty great," I say. "Thank you for the coffee. What do I owe the pleasure?"

"I was in the neighborhood," he says, a sly smirk on his face.

"Really?"

He shakes his head. "Things were slow, and forty-eight hours is just too long to not see you. So I figured I'd pop over for a quick visit."

Well, now my smile is guaranteed to be plastered on my face for the rest of the night.

I walk around the desk so I can stand next to him, which might not have been my best idea. Now there's nothing separating us. And I really want to kiss him again.

"How long is your shift today?"

He looks at his watch, which gives me a perfect glimpse of his muscular forearm.

"I get off at four. You?"

I blink a few times to snap me out of my stare. "Six. I get off at six."

"How about we go get dinner?"

I shake my head. "I wish. But I can't pawn the kids off again. They're going to start getting suspicious."

"Bring them," he says. "Or, I can bring over a pizza. I've done that a hundred times. They won't be suspicious."

I lean in a little closer. "They will if you keep looking at me like that."

"Like what?"

"Like you've seen me naked."

A devious smile I'm starting to love comes out. "Sorry, beautiful. I'll be looking at you like that for the rest of my life."

Before I can say anything, I hear my phone vibrating against my desk. Shane also takes his phone out of his pocket, which can only mean one thing: the group text.

> Oliver: Everyone come to my place for dinner tonight. Six. BYOB.
>
> Wes: What's the occasion?
>
> Oliver: Do I need to have an occasion to invite over my best friends in the world?

"He does need a reason," Shane says.
"Be nice."

> Amelia: You don't, but when you're inviting me and not just the guys that means something is up.

> Simon: Once again, Amelia proves why she is the smartest in the group.
>
> Oliver: Whatever, just everyone come, okay?
>
> Simon: Is it thirty-four? It's thirty-four, isn't it? OLIVER PROPOSED AGAIN!
>
> Oliver: It's not thirty-four.

"Looks like no pizza tonight," I say.
"Guess not. Though I was looking forward to breadsticks. Oh! Maybe he'll make garlic bread?"
"Can't hurt to ask."
I swear the way to a man's heart is really through his stomach.

> Shane: I want garlic bread too.

Simon: Shane, focus.

Shane: I am, on food.

Oliver: Of course there will be garlic bread. Any other requests?

Simon: Yes. You owe me $20 because I was convinced you'd come back from Vegas with thirty-four under your belt. I'm kind of disappointed in you.

We put our phones down as we let Simon take the lead.

"Well," I say. "We knew it was going to happen sooner or later."

He nods. "I didn't think it would be this soon. So the question is, how do we make it through a night with all of our friends without giving away that all I want to do is kiss you?"

"Well, that's easy," I say much more confidently than I feel. "We arrive separately. We don't sit by each other all night. Or across from each other."

"I don't like any of that."

"I know," I say as I tug on his shirt. "But we can do it. Plus, Oliver isn't sending out an SOS just because he wants to catch up. I'm sure whatever it is will make us forget we're even in the same room together."

Shane shakes his head. "Nothing could ever make me do that."

He leans in for a kiss, and I know I'm at work and this is probably unprofessional, but fuck it. It's a Tuesday afternoon, and the only people here right now are me, Kendra, and a construction worker who is dealing with a possible broken arm. So I kiss him back. I put my arms around him and smile as I feel his lips on mine.

"Get a room, you two."

"Gladly," Shane says, pulling apart just enough to get out the word, but not far enough that he can't lean in for one more small kiss. "See you tonight?"

I nod. "Just remember to keep your hands to yourself, Cunningham."

He shakes his head. "No promises."

Chapter 16
Shane

"WHEN ARE WE MEETING MRS. PRICE?"

Part of me is still in disbelief those words just came out of my mouth. The other part of me is wondering how I haven't said those words sooner in the thirty years I've known Oliver.

My best friend has proposed to more women than anyone on the planet. Before he went to Vegas, our last count was at thirty-three. Some of those might have been exaggerated, some were not. The man has loved love and wanted a family for as long as I've known him.

So telling us tonight that he got accidentally married in Las Vegas wasn't shocking. The fact that he barely remembers it? Now that's another story.

"What about Friday?" Oliver says. "I'll bring Izzy to The Joint. Maybe being in public will make it a little less awkward."

"She's meeting your entire friend group in one swoop a week after getting accidentally married in Las Vegas," Wes says. "I don't know if you can avoid awkward."

"What if we bring the kids?" Betsy suggests. "Maybe that will keep some people on their best behavior."

Every person in the room looks over to Simon. "What? Why is everyone looking at me?"

"Because she's talking to you, dumbass," I say. "This is a big night for Oliver, and he doesn't need you being you."

"I'm offended," he says. "How dare you—how dare any of you—think I'd go and do something that would freak out my best friend, or his new wife?"

"Now he's your best friend again?" Wes asks.

"For two men who give me constant shit about friend rankings, you sure do always know the score," Simon stands up and grabs his jacket. "I don't need to take this abuse. I'm out of here. See you Friday. I'm not buying."

"Oh, sit down," Wes says, which Simon does, showboater that he is. "Oliver, it will be fine. I'll bring the kids, and we'll do it early, before the crowd starts piling in."

"And if it goes well, Luke and Mariah can come and pick them up and take them back to the house. That way we can hang out for a bit," Amelia says.

"Yes!" Betsy says. "No matter how it goes, let's do that. We haven't all hung out in forever."

I can't help but look over at Amelia, who happens to be looking at me too. Fuck...she looks beautiful tonight. I mean, she always does. Her beauty is subtle. Delicate curves. Smooth skin. Skin that I now know what it feels like against me. Then there's her smile. It, like always, fills me with a joy I can't describe.

I wish I could touch her. Hold her. Kiss her. Tonight hasn't been bad so far, but twice in a week with our friends? That's going to be pure torture.

Note to self: slyly convince Wes and Betsy to let all the kids crash at their house so she and I can have a night to ourselves.

"Hello! Earth to Shane!"

I give my head a shake and look to Wes. "What?"

"I asked what time you could meet on Friday?"

"Oh. Yeah. I get off at four."

Do I? I'm not entirely sure, but I can deal with that later.

"Perfect," Oliver says as he claps his hands. "This is going to be great. I know she's going to love you guys. Even Simon."

"That's it!" Simon yells, but not in an angry way. In his dramatic, I-like-to-cause-a-scene way. "I can take it from Shane. And Wes. But et tu, Brutus? I'm leaving. And I might show up on Friday, I might not."

"See you Friday, Simon."

"Fuck you, Wes. Fuck all of you!"

We all hold in our laughter until the moment Simon slams Oliver's front door. Then all hell breaks loose.

"I can't stop," Betsy says, holding her stomach.

"He's just too easy to mess with," Amelia says.

"Should I be worried he's going to do something on Friday?" Oliver says in between laughing fits.

"Of course," I say, taking deep breaths to calm myself down. "But it's Simon, so it should be harmless."

Should is the operative word.

"You know what? I don't even care," Oliver says as he sits back. "I'm married. I love my wife. She mostly likes me. What more could a guy ask for?"

We laugh as Oliver goes into more details, the ones he remembers, anyway. Pictures are of course part of it, because no person on the planet takes more pictures than Oliver Price. He showed us some earlier, but these are the rest of the trip. It looks like he and Izzy had a good time. Just a couple enjoying themselves on vacation.

I glance over to Amelia again, who is laughing with Betsy as Oliver goes through fifty different photos of Caesars' Palace. I've thought a lot about Amelia and I over the years, but I've never really thought about things that could happen if we ever got together. I don't know why, but my brain never let me go down the road of what-ifs.

So I never thought about doing things like a vacation. I know just from being her friend that she'd take the beach any day over the mountains. I know she'd want to do every tourist activity possible. I'd also make sure we had time for us. Going to dinners. Dancing under the stars. Making love until the sun comes up.

I want that. Fuck...I want all of that. Now I know why my brain would never let me go down this path—because now that I've imagined it, I want it more than I want anything. I want to show her the world. I want to experience everything I can with her. I don't want another memory to happen without her.

"Shane! For fuck's sake, dude, what's up with you tonight?"

Shit...I really need to stop drifting off. I realize then that everyone is staring at me. Except Amelia. She's trying not to laugh.

"Sorry," I say. "Just a little tired."

I have a feeling Wes is about to call me on something when Oliver's front door comes flying open and Simon marches back inside.

"What the hell, you guys! Not one person is going to follow and try to bring me back?"

We all look at each other, wondering if anyone was even considering that. Judging by the blank stares, the answer is no, we were not.

"Actually, Simon," Amelia says, standing up. "I do need to get going. I have the early shift and should probably get some sleep. Want me to stomp out with you?"

"Thank you, Amelia. You've always been the best out of everyone," he says. "But in protest, I'm going to sit right back down and make these motherfuckers regret their decisions tonight."

"You do that," she says, walking over to Oliver and giving him a kiss on the cheek. My fists start tightening as I watch this unfold. I'm not jealous of the act—Amelia has given Oliver innocent kisses like that our entire lives. And she could give me one. It wouldn't be weird. It has happened before. But right now it's too risky. Because if she does, I'll grab her by the waist, sit her on my lap, and kiss the living hell out of her. And by the look she's giving me right now, she knows exactly what I'm thinking.

"Bye, Shane," she says, giving me a little wave. "Wes. Betsy. I'll call you guys later this week and we can set up the situation for the kids."

"What? No goodbye for me?"

"My apologies, Simon, how could I forget?"

I watch as Amelia goes over and gives Simon a kiss on the cheek. Again. Normal. But I swear to God if that man does one inappropriate thing, or makes one joke, I will end him.

"You're too sweet, Amelia," he says. "What do you think about being my best friend?"

She politely laughs. "I'll take it into consideration."

She waves goodbye, and I don't know if I'm imagining it or not, but I swear her gaze lingers a little longer on me.

"So? What'd I miss?"

We all look at Simon and shake our heads. "You know you could have stayed gone."

He looks at me and just shrugs. "I know. But I didn't have anywhere else to go. Plus, you know I get FOMO."

"You are the best kind of ridiculous, you know that, right?"

Simon smiles over to Betsy. "I do. And remember, I'm here and waiting if that guy fucks up again."

Wes pulls Betsy into him. "Don't you fucking dare."

"Drinks!" Oliver yells in his way to defuse the situation that really isn't a situation. "Who wants another drink?"

"I do!" Betsy yells, popping up from the couch.

The two of them head into the kitchen as Wes and Simon continue to stare each other down. I like to sit back and watch when the two of them do this, because at this point it's not about one being angry at the other. No, this is about who can keep this face up the longest without laughing.

Usually Wes wins.

As soon as I get comfortable, I feel my phone vibrate in my pocket.

Amelia: I think we did it! No one suspected.

> Shane: We were very stealth. Sitting apart was key.

Amelia: Why?

> Shane: Because if I would have been next to you, I don't think I would have been able to keep my hands to myself.

Amelia: Shane...

> Shane: What? I tell the truth. Did you have to wear a T-shirt so tight?

Amelia: It wasn't that tight.

> Shane: Agree to disagree. Also, you looked beautiful tonight. I didn't get to tell you that.

Amelia: Thank you.

> Shane: Was that new lipstick? I've never seen you wear that shade before.

She doesn't respond right away, which is weird. Amelia is an immediate responder. In her words, if she doesn't then, she'll forget. So I start to get worried when it goes on more than a few minutes before she texts me back.

"Is that Mary?"

I look up to Simon, who's giving me a knowing smirk. "Huh?"

"Mary? Are you texting your girlfriend Mary?"

"Excuse me!" Wes yells. "Who is Mary, and when did you get a girlfriend?"

So much for being stealth.

"Don't worry about it," I say, putting away my phone.

"It was!" Simon says as he moves to sit on the literal edge of his seat. "Bring her Friday. That will help ease the awkward."

"I'm not bringing her," I say. "Friday is about Oliver and Izzy."

Wes clears his throat aggressively. "Again, I'd like to ask, who the hell is Mary?"

"Shane's secret girlfriend," Simon says. "He went out with her last week and had me get him reservations and he let me buy him dark wash jeans."

This makes Wes's jaw actually drop. "No fucking way."

"Fucking way," Simon says. "But he won't tell me her name, so I call her Mary."

"Wow," Wes says, shaking his head a bit. "Oliver married? Shane in a relationship? I didn't get the memo that the pigs started flying. Next thing we know, Simon will settle down."

"Whoa! Watch it," Simon says. "Let's not get crazy. Plus, this is about Shane and Mary and us getting to meet her."

I deflect their attempts to get me to bring "Mary" on Friday, all the while laughing my ass off on the inside that she'll be there. I know Amelia wanted to keep this a secret as to not rock the boat. But now I have an added bonus—screwing with Simon.

"Beers all around," Oliver announces as he and Betsy return, which is coincidentally when my phone vibrates again.

Amelia: You noticed I had on new lipstick?

Shane: Of course. It made me want to kiss you even more.

Amelia: When are you leaving?

Shane: Oliver just brought us another beer. Why?

Amelia: Because I want to kiss you.

Shane: What about the kids?

Amelia: I didn't go home yet. I'm sitting at the end of Oliver's street, because I was thirty seconds out of the driveway when I realized I wanted to kiss you and that was before you noticed I had on lipstick.

Shane: Don't go anywhere.

I basically jump off Oliver's couch.
"All right, I'm out of here."
"You're leaving?"
"Yup. Gotta go."
"Yeah, you do," Simon says. "Tell Mary we said hi."
"Will do."
"Yes! Get it, my man! Don't forget to wrap it!"
"Who's Mary?"
Oliver's question is the last thing I hear as I nearly run out the door. I know they're probably having a few jokes at my expense, and having to deal with twenty questions from Oliver, but I don't give two shits right now.
I've got to go kiss my girl.

Chapter 17
Amelia

I don't know the last time I laughed this much. Not even the other night when I almost peed myself at Oliver's when we were digging at Simon. I knew I needed a night out, but I really didn't realize how much I needed time like this.

Luke and Mariah got Wes's kids an hour ago and are set up for the night at his house. The guys are across the bar playing pool. Which leaves me, Betsy, and Izzy to sit here and girl talk. And of course, stare at our men. Well, our men and Simon.

"Who was the first to lose their virginity?"

This question comes from Betsy. This is what we've been doing for the past twenty minutes, playing a game of "guess who" about the guys. Since I know the answer to most of the questions, I've served as keeper of the answers. But some have been hypothetical. Those ones are the funniest.

"I'm going to guess Simon," Betsy says.

"Nah," Izzy says. "Shane."

"Betsy is correct," I say.

"Damnit," Izzy says as she takes a drink. "I wanted to guess Simon, but it felt too easy."

I laugh. "Funny, that's what we said about the girl he lost it to."

I'm not one to bash other women, but when that woman is Christina Leaftree, the rules don't apply. There isn't a man in Rolling Hill she hasn't tried to sleep with. Most of them she did —including my ex-husband while we were married.

"Okay, which one is the most likely to say thank you after sex?"

"Easy. Oliver," I say. "And I'd also like to go back on record that sex questions make me feel weird since these are basically my brothers."

Izzy raises her hand to speak, which makes me laugh. This woman is hilarious. "One, Oliver doesn't say thank you. Then again, we've slept together twice and both of us were drunk so he might have." Izzy says. "Two, you might say they are your brothers, but I think that's bullcrap. Because you don't stare at your brothers like you want to lick them."

"Psh." I wave her off. "I'm not staring."

"Amelia, I realize I've known you for two hours, but my girl, you are not sly."

"And neither is Shane."

My eyes go wide as I look up at the two women sitting across from me. "What are you talking about?"

Each of them covers one of my hands with theirs. "Amelia, we can play this one of two ways," Betsy says. "The first way is you can tell us under the Cone of Sisterhood Silence. Nothing leaves this table."

"Or two," Izzy continues, "we sit here and ignore the elephant in the room that is Shane sending you fuck-me eyes all night. I mean, the guys are oblivious, and we can pretend to be, if that's what you desire."

I look over to Shane again, who is proving their point by also looking at me. We share a smile, and I now realize what

Betsy and Izzy are talking about. We're shit at this. I know more than once tonight I saw Shane staring at me. I know because I was staring at him too. I also have an overwhelming urge to tell him to sneak off with me so I can kiss him. Because kissing Shane Cunningham is quickly becoming my favorite hobby.

"Fine," I say. "But this has to stay here. No one knows. Well, Kendra knows because she's my work wife, but that's it."

"One, how am I just learning you have a work wife? I feel like I need to meet her," Betsy says. "And two, it absolutely stays here. Based on our previous conversation, I know you don't want to put me, and now Izzy, in a weird space with the guys. And I appreciate that. But, even though I'm stupid in love, I will forever be chicks over dicks."

"Same," Izzy says. "Well, I'm not in love. But I am married to one of them. That sounds bad doesn't it?"

I appreciate the moment of levity. "Thanks. Yes. Shane and I are together. But it's a secret. We want some time where it's just us, you know?"

Betsy nods. "You don't have to explain yourself to anyone."

"Thanks," I say. "It's early, but it's good."

"By the look on your face, it's damn good."

I shake my head at Izzy. "It's not like that. Yet."

"Yet being the operative word," Betsy says as she tips her now empty glass to me.

"Okay then, the question must be asked"—Izzy resituates herself so she's now looking back to the guys—"since Amelia here is about to fuck one of them and we can speak for the other two. The question must be asked: which one is the biggest freak in the sheets?"

We look to the guys, but no one says anything. Then, as if we were cued, one name comes out of all of our mouths.

"Simon."

We all start laughing again as Porter brings us another round of drinks.

"Did we order these?" I ask.

"Of course not," Porter says, signaling over to the pool tables where Oliver and Simon are now sword fighting with the pool cues while Wes and Shane look like they want to strangle them. "But I was told tonight was a special occasion, so that means at least one round is on the house."

"Aw, Porter, you big softy," I say.

His eyes narrow. "Don't you say that shit out loud, Amelia Evans. I have a reputation to uphold."

This makes us all laugh. "Apologies. How dare I mess with your grumpy bartender-slash- manwhore persona?"

"Exactly," he says, but throws in a wink at the end. "Wave me down if you need me."

"Will do."

The three of us take our glasses and clink them together. Our conversation continues, but doesn't dwell on Shane and I. We talk about Betsy and Wes and their upcoming summer vacation plans to California. We do our best to get to know Izzy a little more, which I must say, out of all the women Oliver has proposed to in his life, I'm glad she's the one who ended up with a ring on her finger. She's a badass businesswoman. She's fitting right in with Betsy and me. And she gave Simon shit in the first ten minutes. This better work, because Oliver can't do better.

"I'm going to preface this with I know I'm still getting used to this town and people, but who are those women talking to the guys?"

Izzy and I look over to the pool tables, and just as Betsy said, there are three women being very flirtatious with the guys.

The three women who are the bane of my existence.

"That would be Jessica Mozzaro, Christina Leaftree, and Emily Babcock," I say, doing my best to keep my temper even.

"And I take it we don't like them?" Betsy says.

I shrug. "I don't want to tell you what to think of people."

"That's not how this goes," Betsy says. "If you say we hate them, then we hate them. Blind faith. I've hated an actress since I was ten because I read once she didn't like puppies. I later found out she has four and posts pictures with them on Instagram all the time. I still hate her."

"Well, then, we don't like them," I say. "Christina was one of the many women my husband cheated on me with. Jessica slept with him during a break we took during senior year before I got pregnant. I don't know if Emily had sex with Paul, but I wouldn't put it past her. They never liked me in high school—I was a tomboy, and they were the popular mean girls. I think each of them has tried to get with each of the guys, even though they've told them time and time again that they aren't interested. Well, except Simon. But I'm pretty sure he did it either drunk or on a dare. Either way, they've never gotten the hint. Especially Emily. She's had a thing for Shane for years and isn't shy about it."

"Fuck that noise," Izzy says, standing up and...is she taking an earring out?

I grab her arm to pull her back down. "Let's not get you kicked out of The Joint on your first night."

"Fine," Izzy groans. "But just so you know, I don't throw the first punch. I throw the last."

I knew she fit in with us!

We don't go over there, but we can't stop watching. At least that's how I feel. I couldn't tell you what's going on with the other guys because my eyes are glued to Shane, who is currently trying to fend off Emily. Which is no shock. This is what she does. Every time she sees him out, she makes a move.

He always turns her down. I'm not worried about that. I give the girl credit; she's persistent. I'd think if a man turned me down for nearly twenty years I'd give up. But no. Not Emily.

"The fuck she is!"

Betsy said the words, but my brain was thinking it. Because Emily has now cozied up very close to Shane. So close that I can see her fake boobs pressing against him. I see him stiffen, but it doesn't deter her, and she even adds an exaggerated laugh as she throws her head back.

I know for a fact Shane didn't say shit, let alone something funny.

"Are you fucking kidding me?" I say as I bolt up from the table.

Izzy drops her earrings on the table. "Welp, looks like I'm getting kicked out."

I do my best not to stomp my way toward the pool tables, and I know Betsy and Izzy are behind me, so it likely looks like we're a girl gang coming into battle. But at this point I don't care. Let everyone see. Let everyone put the pieces together.

Because the hell if I'm going to let Emily touch Shane in any capacity.

"Hey, guys!" Betsy yells to announce our presence. She immediately throws her arms around Wes.

Izzy slides next to Oliver, placing her arm around him and holding out her other hand to Jessica. "Hi. I'm Izzy. Oliver's wife. Nice to meet you. And you are?"

As much as I want to watch Jessica's face in that moment, my eyes are set on one thing.

"Shane? Can we talk for a minute?"

"Amelia, we're in the middle of something," Emily says with a dismissive tone.

"I'm sure *you* are. I just need Shane for one minute."

Emily's eyes narrow. "I'm sure it can wait."

I shake my head. "Oh, but you're wrong. Shane?"

"Excuse me, Emily." Shane steps out from around her, Emily huffing in annoyance.

He doesn't say anything as the two of us walk out of sight. The bathroom hallway isn't the most private of places, but it's the best I can think of on short notice.

"Amelia, I'm so sor—"

I don't let him finish that sentence. He can't, when I have him pressed against the wall and I'm kissing him harder than I've ever kissed anyone in my entire life.

Because this man is mine. And I need him to know that.

I never thought I was a jealous person. I knew Paul was cheating, and I couldn't muster up the will to care. I used to see Christina around town, knowing damn well she had slept with him, and I still didn't say anything. I was indifferent. But seeing Emily within inches of Shane is making me a little crazy.

"Wow," he says when I pull away. "What was that for?"

"Let's just say I don't like seeing my man being touched by another woman."

His smile is small and sexy, and if I already didn't know I wanted to take him home, I would at this moment.

"Your man, huh?"

"Yeah," I say, tugging him in by the waist of his jeans. "So, I was thinking. I'm going to go tell everyone goodbye. You're going to wait twenty minutes as to not draw suspicion and then you're going to meet me at your place. Got it?"

"Yes, ma'am."

Shane kisses me one more time, but a sudden noise makes us jump away from each other. We look up and see Porter, who is shaking his head and laughing.

"It's about damn time," he says. "Now can you move so I can get into the liquor closet?"

We both laugh and start to walk away, but not before Shane

gives my ass a smack. I turn back to look at him, and the smile on his face is enough to blow my cover. Well, the little cover we have left about this.

"Hey, guys," I say. "I think I'm going to take off."

"Oh no! Really? That's so unexpected and sad," Betsy says a bit dramatically. "Are you sure?"

"Yeah," I say forcing down a laugh. "It was a fun night. Let's do it again soon."

"So fun!" Izzy screams as she walks over to me. She doesn't strike me as a hugger, but she's holding her arms out, so I return the gesture.

"I hope you have the best orgasm of your life tonight," she whispers to me. "And don't worry, your secret is safe with us. We'll make sure the guys are nice and distracted for Shane's escape."

I might love this woman more than Oliver does. "Thank you."

I wave to everyone else as I leave the bar, making sure to give Emily and her crew the side eye as I walk out. They each give me a scathing look. I could return one of my own, but I instead try to kill them with kindness. I dramatically wave and even mouth a "goodbye" to them as I walk out of the bar.

"You know he's never going to be with you."

I know I shouldn't engage. I should keep walking. She wants me to respond.

In high school I never did. I took the mean shit they said about me and pretended I didn't hear it. That only made them chirp at me worse. But back then I didn't because I thought they were right. I thought I was an ugly duckling. That I had no business being friends with Shane, Wes, Oliver, and Simon, let alone date someone like Paul.

But now I know that's not the case. I might not be a beauty

queen like Whitley or Betsy, or a powerful businesswoman like Izzy, but I know my worth.

And I know the man she wants is coming home with me tonight. Not her.

"That's funny, Emily," I say, slowly turning to their table. "Because I'm on my way out the door. And in about twenty minutes, you're going to watch Shane leave too. You can use your imagination about where he's going, but I'll give you a hint —it's not your place. Have a great night."

I turn on my heel and "accidentally" bump into their table, causing their drinks to spill on their laps.

Oops. My bad.

I don't say I'm sorry or even acknowledge their shock as I walk out of the bar with my head held high.

Fuck, that felt good...

I don't even care if that's how our secret gets out. I'd do it again in a heartbeat.

For years those three made my life hell. I don't know how they did it, but they always made me feel inferior. Even in adulthood. I just always felt like somehow they were better than me.

But no more of that. Not anymore. That Amelia is gone. Tonight proved that they have nothing over me.

I have friends. I have family. I have a man who has eyes for only me. And starting tonight, I'm taking what I want and not letting anyone bully me into thinking it's anything less than what I deserve.

I turn on the car but grab my phone first, firing a quick text to Shane.

> Amelia: Don't wait too long. I'll be the woman naked in your bed.

I toss it on the passenger seat as I pull out of The Joint. I don't know what switch in me flipped, but as I make my way down the back roads to Shane's house, I feel like a different person.

I feel stronger.

I feel confident.

I'm taking what I want.

And tonight, I want Shane.

Chapter 18
Shane

Speed limits? Those don't exist right now.

I've never driven so fast in my life. I've run three stop signs, blew a red light, and might have run over a squirrel before I nearly flipped my truck pulling into my driveway. Just the thought of Amelia in my bed—naked, no less—was worth every speeding ticket I should write myself.

The second I put the car in park the gravity of the night comes down on me. Tonight's the night. Amelia didn't say it word for word, but I saw the look in her eye. It's one you don't mistake. She was determined. Sexy. Brazen. She was a version of Amelia I want to see all the time.

And she said I was hers.

That's what did me in. It's all I could think about as I waited the twenty agonizing minutes to leave the bar. It's all I could think about—that and her text—as I broke every traffic law to get home.

Don't fuck this up, Cunningham. Don't you dare fuck this up...

That's the speech I give myself as I get out of my truck and enter my house. I might not have fantasized about things like vacations or mundane relationship milestones when it came to Amelia, but I did dream about this night. I dreamed what it would be like to feel her under me. To kiss every inch of her body. To hear and feel her come apart in my arms. I know I've gotten to experience some of that already, but tonight is going to be a night I'll remember for the rest of my life.

She's been my dream girl for as long as I can remember. She was what got me through my time in the Army. I remember the night I kissed her before I went to basic, thinking that I needed to do it in case I never saw her again. Not kissing her would have been the biggest regret of my life.

Now my biggest regret will be if I don't make this perfect for her. Because she deserves every bit of that and more.

I turn off the light in my kitchen as I make my way down the hall to my bedroom. I can see the faintest hint of a light coming from under the door. When I open it, I see my bedside lamp on, but my bed empty.

"Amelia?"

I take a step into the room as I take off my watch and place it on my dresser. Only then do I notice the light coming from under my bathroom door.

"Beautiful? You okay?"

Amelia opens the door, and I think my legs give out. I know what she said in the text, but I never in a million years expected her to be naked for me when I got home.

But here she is. Standing in front of me, gloriously naked, looking like a goddamn goddess.

And all mine.

"Come here." She takes a step toward me, and it's all I need to reach out and pull her in. The fact I can't feel her naked body against me is a crime, and I'll rectify that in a second. Right now I just need to kiss her.

There's nothing rushed about this. It doesn't feel like we're on the clock. It's just her, me, and the rhythm we've developed. I never knew this could happen with someone. I didn't know kissing could be as natural as breathing. But with Amelia, it is. In just our short time together, I already know where she's going to put her hands. I know how she's going to move her mouth. I know that when I let my hands slide down to her ass, she grabs onto my hair a little harder. Some might think knowing all of that might be boring. Not me. To me this means we were always meant to be. That finding each other was always part of the plan.

I scoop her into my arms and take the few steps needed to set her down on my bed. I stand back up to undress, and while I don't expect Amelia to lay back and watch me strip, I am surprised when she sits back up.

"What are you doing?"

She looks up at me with a sparkle in her eye. "You."

My cock springs to life with that one word. Before I know it, Amelia has worked my belt off and pushed my pants and boxer briefs down. I step out of them and suck in a breath when I feel her hand wrapped around me. But that's nothing compared to my body clenching when she puts me in her hot mouth.

"Fuck, Amelia," I groan, taking her hair in my hands as she starts sucking me.

Before when she did this, I knew she was trying to figure herself out. Test her own limits and seeing where her comfort level was. But now? This isn't that same Amelia. This woman is claiming me.

She didn't need to do that. I'm hers. I always have been.

I take a moment to look down at her. Yes, this feels fucking amazing. But it's more than that. Seeing Amelia this unhinged, this sexy, this wanton, is the image I want to carry with me the rest of my life.

My hips start thrusting into her, and I don't know how long I'm going to be able to hold on. She feels too good. But I don't want to finish like this. No, tonight I need to be inside her.

I pull out of her mouth, rip my shirt over my head, and as she gasps for air, I fall into the bed with her. I do my best to keep my weight off her, which is hard when she begins wrapping her legs around me. Her hands are gliding up and down on my back as our kiss deepens. I start moving my lips down her neck before landing on her waiting nipple, which is all but begging me to take it in my mouth. As my mouth works that, I let my fingers trail down her smooth stomach until I land at her hot center.

"So wet already," I groan before switching my mouth to the other side. I coat my finger in her wetness, loving how ready she is—and we've just started.

"I want you, Shane," Amelia says as she claws at my back. "I want this so much."

I release her nipple with a pop and I quickly roll over to my bedside table to grab a condom. I go to my knees and rip it open, quickly sheathing myself. When I look back to Amelia, I'm overwhelmed with emotion. She's laying on the bed, her eyes hooded as she watches me. Her body is subtly twisting on the bed as she seeks relief. Relief she only wants from me.

Don't worry, beautiful, I'll take care of it. I'll take care of you...

"I'm ready, Shane."

I knew I wanted to hear a certain three magical words from Amelia. I just didn't realize it was those three.

"Hey," she says, tipping my chin up so I'm looking her in the eye. "Talk to me."

I shake my head, not because I don't want to talk to her, but because I need to get my head right. "It just hit me."

"What?"

"That this is happening."

She smiles that beautiful smile and strokes the side of my face. "Yes, it is."

Another three words that puts my body at ease. I kiss her one more time before sitting back on my knees, lining myself up to enter her. I slowly push in and nearly scream as I feel her pussy slowly opening for me. Holy fuck, she's tight. She's tight and perfect and I was right; this is better than every fantasy.

"Shit, Amelia," I say, slowly starting to move in and out as she becomes accustomed to me.

"Slow, please, Shane," she says, her face in a mixture of pleasure and pain. "You feel so good. Just slow..."

I do as she asks. I brace myself over top of her, slowly moving in and out, letting her set the pace. We can stay like this all night for all I care. Her body fused with mine, kissing her skin as she claws at my back? I don't know what heaven is like, but I'm pretty sure this is damn close.

Amelia slowly starts opening for me, her body urging me to go a little faster. I do my best to read her, trying to anticipate what she needs. The only problem with that is my own head is getting in the way. More specifically, my emotions.

I tried my best to mentally prepare, but I should have known nothing could have braced me for this. I'm suddenly remembering every single time I realized I was in love with Amelia. Junior prom. On the porch the night we kissed. Seeing her the first day I came back to Rolling Hills when I was discharged. The night of the wedding, when everything changed. And those were only the major milestone moments. That's not counting every little moment, and every little instance, when she made me feel that no other woman would ever compare to her. And now that we're here? I was right. No other woman compares. None ever had. None ever will.

"More, Shane."

Her words bring me back, and I do as she demands. I sit back up, ready to pick up the pace, when she does something that shocks me—she starts playing with her nipples.

Holy fuck, that might be what sends me over the edge. I can't take my eyes off her as I bring her leg up, allowing me drive into her that much deeper. She throws her head back as she continues to let her hands explore, driving me crazy in a way I don't think she realizes she's doing. It's mesmerizing.

"You're beautiful," I say as my speed picks up. "So fucking beautiful."

She opens her eyes, though I can tell she's fighting to keep them open as the pleasure rolls through her. I get it. I'm fighting to make this go as long as possible. I never want this night to end.

"Shane..."

"Yes, beautiful?"

"Make me yours."

That's the easiest request she'll ever ask of me.

I bring her other leg over my shoulder, allowing me to go even deeper. She lets out a surprised gasp as I ramp up my pace.

"You're mine," I mutter as I keep thrusting in and out. "I'm yours."

"Yes," she says as she grips onto each of my arms. "Yours."

That's all I need to hear to send me over the edge. Her body spikes up into me, and I know she's a goner too.

We're both gasping for air as we come down from the highs. I slowly pull out of her, take off the condom and dispose of it into the trash can next to my bed, and fall to her side. My arms immediately reach for her, bringing her into my body.

"That was…"

Amelia's words trail off but I don't say anything. What can I say? There aren't words in the English dictionary that could describe what we just shared.

So I do the only thing I know to do. I tilt her head up, kiss her with everything I have, and fall asleep with the woman of my dreams in my arms.

Chapter 19
Amelia

"Okay, you have to admit that was good."

"The only good part is when you let me kiss you."

I playfully smack Shane's arm. "We're thirty-five-year-old adults. I can't believe you wanted to make out in a movie theater."

He shrugs. "Let's just say I'm making up for lost time."

I smile as he gives me a kiss on the cheek before helping me out of the reclining movie chairs. I don't know who thought to install recliners as movie theater chairs, but I want to give them a medal. Best invention since wire-free bras and iced coffee.

When I said I wanted to keep this between us for a while, the biggest thing I wanted was to date. Be together. Do things together. Have outings and experiences, just the two of us. I know these won't vanish when we finally tell everyone, but they are going to be few and far between. Which is why I suggested an impromptu date night tonight. Luke is staying at a friend's house, and Mariah and Emerson went to a pool party. I might not get an overnight stay, but I'll still take the date while the kids are occupied. And I asked for the most mundane, boring, date ever—dinner and a movie.

And it's been perfect.

"Where to next?" Shane asks as we walk hand-in-hand back to his truck.

"Ice cream."

"Ice cream?"

"Yes," I say. "I want tonight to be the most basic date ever. Which means ice cream is next."

He laughs as he opens the truck door for me. "If basic is what you want, then basic is what you'll get."

We share a quick kiss before he helps me into the truck. I don't know if I'm supposed to be feeling butterflies at thirty-five years old because I'm on a date with my boyfriend, but I am. And even if I'm not, I don't care. This is the best I've felt in a long, long time.

"Ice cream, here we come."

Since we came up to Franklin for our date, Shane searches quickly for the nearest ice cream shop, which happens to only be a ten-minute drive from the movie theater.

"Thank you," I say as I lay my head on his shoulder.

"For what?"

"This. Tonight. I mean, everything really. But tonight specifically."

"Because I took you on a date?"

When he puts it like that, it does seem a little silly. "Yes, but it's more than that. I know you want everyone to know. And that you're keeping it quiet for me."

"Yes. Though I would like to point out that those who do know—Izzy and Betsy—heard it from you. And Porter knows because of you kissing me. So everyone who *does* know? That's all you my darling."

He's flashing me what is becoming my favorite Shane grin. A little teasing. A little naughty. A whole lot of hot.

"Yes, I realize that. And the irony isn't lost on me."

"As long we're on the same page that this is the worst-kept secret in Rolling Hills."

"It's not the worst."

"Name the worst then."

"Um..." How can I not think of one? There has to be at least one. "I can't think of any now. But there are worse."

"Sure..."

"What I was saying..." Shane laughs at my dramatic tone. "It's nights like this that made me want to keep it to ourselves. That we didn't have to feel obligated to include Wes or Betsy, or I guess Oliver and Izzy now. Or feeling guilty that I was excited when Luke told me he was hanging with friends. Just...I wanted nights with just the two of us. And this one is pretty perfect."

Shane doesn't say anything as he pulls into the parking lot of the small ice cream shop. I'm about to get out of the truck, when he puts his hand on my leg, stopping me from going anywhere.

"You never have to thank me," he says. "And I also want you to know—I promise that once people do know—we're going to make time for ourselves. Are we going to go out with the group? Yes. Is Betsy likely chomping at the bit for a double date? I'm sure. Will we go on said group date and take pictures to send to Simon because we can? Absolutely. And we're going to do stuff with the kids, and our families, and probably have to have standing Sunday dinners with our mothers. But never, and I mean never, will we forget about *our* time. I'll make sure of that."

I lean in and take Shane's face in my hands, kissing him with nothing short of love.

Love. Holy shit. Am I in love with Shane? I mean, in a sense, I always have been. But it's too early, right? We just started this. I can't be *in* love with Shane. I care for him. Yes, that's it. Because you don't fall in love with a person after a few weeks of dating and a few orgasms, right?

"Now," he says as he slowly pulls away. "I'm going to go stand in that long-ass line to get you peanut butter crunch ice cream with chocolate syrup on top. You go over there and snag that picnic table for us. That work?"

"You know my ice cream order?"

He kisses my nose, which somehow sends shivers through me. "I can't believe you thought I didn't."

Shane gets out of the truck, and because I forget, I get out as well. I see him shoot me a look once he realizes what I've done, but I just laugh and shrug it off as I go take a seat at an open picnic table. I use the time to check my text messages to make sure I haven't missed any from Luke or Mariah, and to check their locations. The dots are pointing to where they told me they were going to be, which makes me let out a breath. It always does. I trust my children. They are good kids who have never given me cause for worry. Okay, Mariah has, but she has a few more years before she'll get into the sneaking-out stage. Hopefully. But at least I know she's at the party then staying with Wes and Betsy until I come pick her up. That, and Emerson will call the cops herself if Mariah tries to act up.

Speaking of...

Betsy: How's date night *winky face*

Amelia: Great. We're getting ice cream now.

Betsy: Nice. Use it for later...

Amelia: Stop it. We're eating it like normal. Plus, Shane isn't spending the night. Not with Mariah home.

Betsy: Kids? What kids? Mariah is staying the night here.

Amelia: Since when?

Betsy: Since now.

Amelia: You don't have to do that...

Betsy: I know. But I am. Have fun and don't do anything I wouldn't. (For reference, that's not a lot.)

Amelia: I'm so glad you're in our lives.

Betsy: Yeah yeah, I'm great. Now, go get some. Talk to you tomorrow! Also, I know it may sound boring, but I recommend vanilla.

All I can do is laugh and shake my head as I put my phone away. I'm so glad Betsy came into Wes's life, and therefore ours. She's been the breath of fresh air he needed, and I must say, she's also the friend I didn't know I needed in my life.

I check out the line to see Shane's progress. It's busy tonight, which makes sense given it's a hot June Tennessee night, and I'm pleasantly surprised to see that he's only two people back. What also surprises me is that he's chatting with a woman.

Shane doesn't chat. Even if being polite, he'd give one-word answers. Yet, he seems to be actually having a conversation.

Do I know her? Is it someone from Rolling Hills? We're about a half hour outside of town, so it wouldn't be shocking to see someone we knew, but I also didn't expect to. Hence why we came out here for date night.

I tilt my head to try to get a better of a look at her, but I don't seem to recognize her. She's about my height at five-foot-five, with blonde hair that is currently piled up on top of her head in that way that's not supposed to look on purpose but is. She's wearing leggings that might as well be painted on and a tight tank top like she just came from the gym. Her body is lean and toned, and I can't help but put my arm around my not-flat stomach. I catch myself doing it, and try to put it down, but I can't help it. Old habits die hard when you're watching the man you are quickly falling for talking to a gorgeous woman.

But it's not just that she's beautiful; it's how she's looking at Shane. Smiling at him. It's genuine. Like they're old friends. Not over-the-top flirty like Emily. When I reacted the way I did at The Joint last week, I knew in the back of my mind Shane would never do anything with her. That reaction was a result of years of bullying, trauma, and being fed up with her and the shenanigans of her crew. This? Watching this is a hit straight to the gut. Because Shane knows her.

Like *knows* her.

And this feeling isn't one I was prepared to deal with tonight. Which I know isn't rational. Shane is a man. I know he's dated. He might not have brought them around, and he might not have called it dating, but I know he wasn't sitting at home every night alone. I guess I never thought I'd have to see it.

Which, again, is stupid. We're adults. We have pasts and baggage.

I see him walking toward me, waving goodbye to the woman as he brings over my sundae and his banana split.

"For my lady," he says. "And I got extra napkins because I don't want to get back up."

I smile, but don't look at him, doing my best to push down the feelings of unwanted jealousy. I dig into the ice cream for a few minutes, using it as the distraction I need to get my head right.

"Hey," he says as he takes my hand. "Everything okay?"

I quickly nod and give my head a little shake. "Yup."

He tilts his head, clearly not believing me. "Ask."

"What?"

"Ask," he says right before taking a bite of his ice cream.

"Ask what?"

"Is this how we're going to play this?"

I let out a breath. "I don't want to come across like a crazy girlfriend."

He shakes his head. "Not crazy. Believe me, if I saw you talking to a man I didn't know, I wouldn't have stayed sitting the whole time."

"Fair enough," I say as I picture Shane going caveman again. "What's her name?"

"Katie."

"And I take you know Katie?"

"I do."

"Biblically?"

"I do. Though I don't know anyone who uses that phrase anymore."

"Don't tease, Cunningham. I'm being serious."

He smiles as he slides his half-eaten banana split to the side. "I know you are. Do you remember when I once said that I have a story and you'd hear about it at some point?"

"Yeah."

"Ready for it?"

I look down at my melting ice cream sundae. I want to know. I need to know. Shane knows so much about me, from the little things to the huge things. I know a lot about Shane, but there are still parts of him that are a mystery. And if he's going to trust me to tell me these parts of him, then I'm going to push down every insecure feeling I have and let him.

"Lay it on me."

He smiles as he takes both of my hands in his. "Katie was a woman that I regularly saw, but we never officially dated. She lives around here, and there's a bar a few miles away I used to frequent."

"You were cheating on The Joint?"

"It wasn't like that," he says. "The Joint is good for when I want to have beers with you and the guys. Or if my brother stumbles into town. But I'd come out here when…"

"When you needed laid."

"For lack of better words," he says. "I wanted to always keep my private life private. I didn't need the drama of hooking up with someone in Rolling Hills. So I came out here. I always stayed at the woman's house. I never brought them to mine. I came out here when I felt like it."

"Was it always one-night stands?"

"Not always. Mostly, but in the case of Katie, we saw each other regularly."

"But you didn't date?"

He shakes his head. "It wasn't like that. Neither of us wanted commitment. She was fresh off a divorce, and I didn't want anything serious. It worked for us."

"Why weren't you? Looking to date, I mean."

That's the one thing I've never understood about Shane. From day one of us, he's been all in, headfirst, both feet in the water. But that energy didn't match how he's been in the past.

"Because they weren't you."

His words hit me so hard I think I'm about to fall back off this picnic bench. "Excuse me?"

He smiles and comes around to sit next to me. Good. He can catch me when I fall. "Since I can remember, the only person I've ever wanted to be with was you. Any of those other women? They weren't anything more than an itch to scratch. They weren't ever going to be more than that. You though? You're it. You're my forever."

Holy shit...

"Shane...I—I don't know what to say."

He shakes his head. "Don't say anything. You don't have to. And I'm not going to say anything more. I've had eighteen years to process my feelings for you."

"Wait..." I think about for a second what was eighteen years ago. "Prom?"

He nods. "When I first saw you walking toward me in that blue dress, it hit me that the feelings I had for you weren't friendly. Or like a sister. That was the first time I wanted to kiss you."

Wow. I mean, I had an idea, but nothing this specific. "Really? You wanted to kiss me? I thought that didn't happen until your party?"

He looks down, almost as if he's embarrassed. "Nope. It happened in your driveway."

Since we talked about it on our first date, I've thought about that night frequently. I remember the song. I remember the feel of the night on my skin. I remember feeling so comfortable in Shane's arms. At that time, I thought it was just because I was with Shane, who was my best friend. Of course, I was going to feel comfortable with him. What would have happened if he would have kissed me? Our lives would have literally changed...

"Why didn't you?"

He shrugs. "Rejection is scary."

"Shane...I never knew," I say, and I didn't. I never had even the slightest inkling he had those kinds of feelings.

"I know you didn't. And I didn't say anything. I thought maybe that night could have started something for us, but..."

His words trail off, but then it hits me.

Two days after prom, Paul—the guy I wanted more than anything in life to notice me—asked me out.

And the rest they say is history.

"I'm so sorry," I say. "I was a dumb teenager who couldn't see past the smile of the captain of the football team. And I swear, I had no idea that you—"

"Don't apologize," he says. "Everything happens for a reason. Without Paul, as much as I want to punch him every time I see him, there would be no Luke and Mariah. And those two—though I'm biased—are the best damn kids in the world. I probably wouldn't have gone off to the Army, which made me into the man I am today. I firmly believe what happened in the past is what was supposed to have happened. And we're here."

Shane pauses for a second, grabbing my hand and pulling me to his lap. "And here is pretty damn good."

I don't know if the words are even out of Shane's mouth before I move in to kiss him. I don't know what I did in this life to deserve this man, but I'm not about to look a gift horse in the mouth.

Because he's right. If he would have kissed me that night, everything would have changed. I don't know if I would have gone out with Paul. Which meant I wouldn't have had my kids. Who knows what else would have changed? I'd rather not think about that.

"Can I thank you for one more thing?" I say as I slowly pull back.

Shane's hold gets tighter on me. "Sure."

"Thank you for kissing me. Thank you for taking the risk."

He smiles as our foreheads touch. "Best risk I've ever taken."

Chapter 20
Amelia

What in the world is wrong with me?

I'm a grown-ass woman who has her house to herself. There are no kids within miles of me. Yet, why do I feel like right now I'm about to get caught with my hand in the candy jar?

The candy jar being Shane's pants.

Why am I nervous? This is silly. This isn't the first time Shane and I have been together. Or alone. But this is more than that.

This is the first time Shane has been in my house as my boyfriend. It's the first time he's been here with the intention of sex. In fact, it's the first time *any* man has been in this house for said capacity.

And it's freaking me out.

"You okay?"

I hurry and grab the remote to turn on the television. "Yup. Everything is fine."

"Are you sure?"

"Of course, I'm sure."

"I'm just saying, a lot was shared tonight. This wasn't the boring date you asked for. It's understandable if you want to talk more or want me to leave."

"No, I don't want you to leave," I say quickly. I see out of the corner of my eye Shane is staring at me, and clearly he doesn't buy one thing coming from my mouth. When I don't say anything else, he grabs the remote from me and turns off the television.

"I'm going to go out on a limb here and assume that when you say 'I'm fine' it doesn't mean you're fine."

"You're being ridiculous." He's not. Not at all. That's me. And I need to get my act together. "Want anything to drink?"

I don't wait for Shane's answer as I jump up from the couch and all but race to the kitchen.

"Get it together, Amelia," I whisper to myself, trying to take deep breaths to calm myself down. "It's just Shane. Don't be ridiculous."

Why am I acting like this now? I had no problem inviting Shane to come over as we drove back to Rolling Hills. I didn't have a problem when he double-checked with me once we pulled into my driveway.

Then I sat down on the couch. And it hit me like a freight train.

I close my eyes and tilt my head back, taking a few more deep breaths when I feel Shane's arms wrap around my stomach.

"Just admit you're not fine."

I chuckle as I lay my head back on his shoulder. "I want to be. It just hit me that you're here. At my house. In a way you've never been."

Shane kisses the slope of my neck before I turn around to

face him. Sometimes I forget we haven't been together that long. It's too easy. Too effortless. Then there are the times that it smacks me in the face that this is new, and a lot of things we do together are new. This is just one of those times.

"I get it," he says as he kisses my forehead. "How about something that will relax you?"

This man is a walking definition of the acts of service as a love language. "What do you have in—whoop!"

I don't think I've ever made that sound in my life. Then again, I've never been picked up under my arms and dropped onto my kitchen island without warning.

"Because of our talk, I didn't get to eat much of my ice cream earlier."

Shane comes in for an intense kiss that shocks me a bit. I'm just as surprised when he suddenly pulls away. "Since I didn't get to finish my ice cream, and I'm still hungry, I thought I'd have something just as sweet."

His mouth is back on me as he unbuttons my jeans. I lift up slightly as he starts tugging them down, even though I'm still not sure what is happening. I mean, I do. I'm just very confused. And shocked. I watch in awe as Shane throws my pants, along with my panties, to the side. When I look back at him, he's on his knees and taking each one of my legs and placing them on his shoulders.

"Shane! You can't do that here!"

"Who says?"

"Me! It's unsanitary. People eat here!"

He flashes me a devilish grin. "I know. And I'm about to feast."

That's the last thing he says as he licks me from back to front, the slow motion of his tongue making me throw my head back in ecstasy. I stay like that for I don't know how long—I just relax and let the feel of Shane's mouth, combined with the scratch of his beard, do their magic. I balance myself on one hand, letting the other comb through his hair. I gently scratch at his scalp, which judging by the reaction I get every time I do this, he quite enjoys. Like right now, just the lightest sensation of my nails against his skin speeds him up. He was taking his time before. Slowly building. But with just that little touch the man is now eating me like I'm his last meal.

"Holy shit," I let out in a breathy tone. "Shane, I can't..."

"Yes, you can." He takes his mouth off me for just a second, just long enough to insert two fingers, working them now in tandem with his skilled tongue. Damn, that tongue...one day it will be the death of me.

But what a way to go out.

I put my other hand back on the counter, needing it to hold myself up. That proves to be an effort in futility as Shane hits that perfect spot. My arms give out, the pleasure too much for me to handle as I fall back onto the hard surface of the island. I'm frantically searching for something to hold onto, but all I can find is the stack of today's mail.

My body is heating up, and suddenly the weight of this sleeveless blouse is just too much for me to handle. I rip it open, and I think I might have popped a button, but it's a small price to pay. All I know is that the second the cool air hits my skin, I feel a bit of relief. But not much, because at the same time Shane has made it his mission to give me an orgasm right here in the middle of my kitchen.

"Oh! Shane!" I scream as my hands find the top of his head, pulling his hair so hard I might leave a bald spot. It's a good thing I'm holding onto something, because before I know it I'm coming harder than I think I ever have in my entire life. My whole body is shaking. Why am I shaking? Am I supposed to shake?

"It's okay, beautiful. I got you."

And he does. Shane somehow brings my body down through gentle touches and kisses. I also feel a warmness between my legs as he takes care of me. The sensations, combined with the drop in adrenaline, is suddenly making me very tired.

"Are you falling asleep on me?"

I shake my head as I slowly open my eyes to see Shane standing next to me. "I think you killed me."

He smiles. "Nah, I think you have another one in you."

That wakes me up. "Another one?"

"I think so."

"Shane, I don't think I can walk, let alone do anything else."

"You don't need to worry about walking."

In one swift motion, Shane has me scooped in his arms, carrying me through my kitchen, living room, and then up the stairs toward my bedroom. I might be in an orgasmic coma, but it's not lost on me that Shane is carrying me like a bride over the threshold. Not that I know what that is like. Paul certainly didn't do it after our courthouse wedding.

What would that be like? To be in a white dress—would I wear white?—and have Shane carrying me to our bedroom after saying "I do." Shane in a three-piece suit, looking handsome as hell. Maybe his tie would be undone a bit. We'd be a little tipsy and tired from a night spent with our families and friends. But not too tired to come back to our space and spend the night in each other's arms.

I've never thought about getting married again. When I divorced Paul, I figured that was it. Sure, I might date again, but marriage? I wasn't rushing to do that again. Why would you want something a second time that sucked the first time? Plus, I figured that no man would want to take the package deal that is me and the kids.

Then again, I never thought about that man being Shane. Would he want to get married? We've never talked about it, even in casual conversation. Hell, before tonight I never knew he did anything in the realm of dating, let alone getting married.

"Amelia, please turn off your brain."

Wow, I must have been deep in thought, since I'm now sitting on my bed and a nearly naked Shane is standing in front of me. I wince. "Sorry."

"Anything I need to know about?"

I become lost in trance again, only it's because this time Shane is sliding down his boxer briefs. "Nope."

He chuckles as he comes down to bed, but not before slipping off my shirt that's been dangling open and my bra. "Come here."

Shane brings me into him, and we fall into a deep kiss, wrapping ourselves around each other like vines on a tree. I love the feel of our bare skin against each other. I don't know what it is. Shane is so warm, like he could heat me through the night if he just held me close enough. And yes, feeling every dip and valley of his defined chest and arms helps, but it's not that.

It's the intimacy. It's the comfortable feeling of being like this with him. I've always hated my body. I never had curves. I only got boobs when I was pregnant. My body went from underdeveloped teenager to mom body with a stomach that was never tight in the blink of an eye. Doesn't help when you have an ex who not only told you that he doesn't find you attractive, but also goes out and seeks other women because you don't do it for him.

Then there's Shane. As I sit straddled on him, his hands gently sliding up and down my thighs, I can't help but feel beautiful. He makes me feel that way. Looking at him now, I see nothing but love and adoration in his eyes.

Love. I know he was going to say it earlier. I could tell it was on the tip of his tongue. But I'm glad he didn't. Even though I do love him, I don't know if I'm ready to say it out loud.

But I can show him.

I reach back behind me and take his hard cock in my hand. I give it a few slow strokes, which makes him tense for just a second until he relaxes into my touch. His eyes are closed, so he doesn't see me as I lift up to center myself to him.

"Amelia. Wait." His eyes open in an almost panic. "Hold on. I have a condom in my wallet."

I shake my head. "Only unless you want it. I have an IUD. I'm clean and...I want to feel you, Shane."

He sits straight up and grabs my face, crashing our lips together.

"Is that a yes?" I say though a smile.

Shane nods against me. "I want nothing more."

He stays sitting up, lifting me up slightly so I can slide slowly onto him. I slowly sink onto him, and with every inch I feel more and more complete.

"Fuck, Amelia," he moans, wrapping his big arms around me. "You feel so damn good."

"So good," I echo, loving the closeness we're sharing right now. Neither of us are moving much, but it's just enough for this moment. I never understood that phrase of "I don't know where he ends and I begin." But now I do. I now understand it.

And I don't ever want it to end.

Shane slowly pulls me back and rolls me over, putting him back on top. Which is fine. My legs are still weak from the kitchen. Plus, I love it when he takes charge. The man knows me better than I know myself, inside the bedroom and out. Why wouldn't I? Especially when he's driving into me with such force, yet such tenderness, that I don't know whether to scream or cry.

"Shane..."

His name from my lips only makes him go in deeper, which I didn't know he could, but that's what this has to be. That's the only explanation for the fact that I swear I can feel him in my stomach. My back arches and my hips lift, giving it a whole new sensation that makes me immediately claw at his back. The poor man has to have scratches there, but he doesn't seem to mind. If anything, it spurs him on more.

I feel my orgasm slowly start to build, but before I can settle into the feeling, Shane takes my leg and picks it up, only to cross it over my body, almost twisting me in half. This is new.

But I like it. I like it a lot.

Shane holds me in place as his pace picks up, bringing that orgasm back front and center as his new position has me panting and begging for more.

"Please, Shane," I moan. "

"Give it to me," he growls. "Give it to me now."

Like his finger has some sort of magical powers, just a few circles over my clit, combined with his powerful thrusts, send me over the edge. My eyes were open, watching every second of this, but now they are officially rolled into the back of my head. Hell, I don't think I was over the first one from earlier. Now with this? I've officially seen stars.

"Amelia!"

That's the last word out of Shane's mouth as he spills into me. As soon as he comes back to Earth, he slips my leg back down before he collapses on me, though somehow he keeps his weight off. I wish he wouldn't. I want to feel him on top of me. Every inch of him covering every inch of me.

Our heavy breaths are all that's in the room as Shane pulls

out of me. I feel him crawl up the bed next to me, but I can't open my eyes. I can barely move.

I think the man killed me tonight with orgasms. And love. We might not have said it, but I know that's what this is. So I fall asleep to visions of Shane and I, me in that dress and him in that suit, and I have the best night's sleep I've had in years.

Chapter 21
Shane

THE MORNING LIGHT HITS MY FACE, AND I BASK IN THE warmth. Normally I'd be upset I allowed myself to sleep in. But not today. I just spent the night with the woman I love. Her body is pressed behind me, doing all she can to be the big spoon despite the fact I'm much taller and bigger than she is. Her bed is warm, her skin is smooth, and I don't see how anything can ruin today.

Then I hear a door open and slam shut.

Amelia...Morning light...Fuck...fuck, fuck, fuck....

I nearly jump out of her bed in a panic, which also wakes her up.

"What's going on?"

I start looking around her floor for my pants. "I spent the night."

My words don't register right away, which is making me panic even more. I know she was asleep five seconds ago, but I need her to catch up. "Amelia. We fell asleep. It's morning. By the look of how bright it is, I'm guessing it's not early, and I'm also going out on a limb to say the door I just heard shut is because Luke and Mariah are home."

Her eyes slowly get bigger and bigger as my words sink in.

"Shit!" She throws off the covers and leaps toward her drawers to put on a T-shirt and shorts. "Oh God, Oh God, Oh God...What time is it?"

I pat my jeans pocket before I remember that I left my phone downstairs last night before the...activities started. "My phone is downstairs."

"Mine too." She starts pacing around her bedroom as I finish getting dressed. "Shane! My pants and underwear are downstairs. In my kitchen!"

"Maybe they didn't notice?"

The death glare Amelia shoots me is downright scary. Actually, I take that back. Scary isn't a good enough word. Terrifying is a little better, yet still not quite doing justice. "Shane. My clothes are on the kitchen floor. Our phones are laying out. Your truck is in my driveway. It's safe to say they noticed."

She sits on the bed and covers her hands with her face. "Oh, this is bad. This is so bad."

"Hey," I say, doing my best to calm her down as I sit next to her. "They were going to find out sometime."

"But not like this. I wanted to sit down with them. Explain everything. And I know they are teenagers, and I know you're not a stranger. But still. This is big, and I didn't want it to be like this."

"I know," I say. "But that plan is out the window. So we need a new plan."

This perks her up. "Yes! Window! You climb out the window. I did it for you. Time to pay up, bucko."

I look over to her window, then back to her. "Amelia, you're on the second floor. There isn't anything to break my fall. I love you, and I'll do a lot of things for you, but I will not jump out a window."

"We're going to forget that you just said 'I love you' for the first time *during a crisis* and we're going to focus." She stands back up and starts pacing again. "Okay. If you refuse to sneak out the window, which I think you should reconsider, then I guess we only have one solution..."

"Yup," I say, standing up and putting my hands on her shoulders. This stops her from pacing and coincidentally makes her take a few deep breaths. "We have to go face the firing squad."

She nods and starts shaking her limbs out like we used to do before football games. "You ready, Cunningham?"

I bring our foreheads together. "Let's do it, Evans."

I put on my T-shirt, and with one more big breath—and a double-check to make sure there wasn't anything out of place or lingering—we walk out of her bedroom door and head downstairs to the living room. I don't hear Luke or Mariah, but as soon as we are the bottom of the staircase there they are—sitting on the couch, neither of them saying a word. Their arms are crossed, their looks are stern, and all of a sudden I feel like I just got busted by my girlfriend's parents for sneaking over.

"Come in and have a seat," Luke says, his tone even.

"Kids, let us explain," Amelia says.

"Oh, there will be explaining," Mariah says. "Because we have some questions."

Amelia and I look at each other and do as we're asked, because clearly any thoughts of us controlling this conversation are long gone. We sit next to each other, but with a few inches between us. I don't dare hold her hand, because I have no idea which way this conversation is about to go. I'd hope because they know me, and I've been around so long, that they'd be okay with this. But on the other hand, maybe they like their life the way it was. They might be scared that Uncle Shane is now more than that.

No matter what their feelings are, I know I'm about to be put through the wringer. These two love their mom. They will protect her just as much as she does them. Especially Luke. He was old enough to know, at least somewhat, how bad things were before the divorce. He knows what she's sacrificed to raise them basically alone. So, the fact that they're sitting us down like this doesn't surprise me. These are two cubs looking out for their mama bear. And I must say, I'm damn proud of them for this.

"First, we need to start by saying we're not mad, just disappointed." I glance over to Amelia, and both of us are trying to keep our laughs in. Luke sounds so serious, and I want him to have this moment, but he had to know that was going to make us crack.

"I understand," Amelia says, pushing down her laughter. "And we're sorry. We didn't want you both finding out like this."

"What are we finding out?" Luke continues. "Because this morning has been a little odd for us. It started with Mariah texting me to come pick her up from Uncle Wes's house."

"And I had to do that because Betsy was being weird about me asking to leave. She was almost begging me to stay longer. I told her thanks but that I had other plans today and I needed to get home. And since you weren't responding to my calls or texts, I got a hold of Luke to come get me."

"So consider us confused that when I pull into the driveway to see Uncle Shane's truck here. Which isn't abnormal, but it was strange since it's ten in the morning."

"But again, we didn't think anything of it. That is, until we walked into the kitchen..."

"Oh God," Amelia says, hiding her head out of embarrassment.

"We're not going to talk about it," Luke says. "Mariah and I have decided that it's best that we just don't ever bring it up again."

"Thank you."

"I'm not done."

Amelia sighs. "Carry on."

"In exchange for us never speaking about seeing what we saw on the kitchen floor, we each get one get-out-of-jail-free card to be used at any point in the future. And we get to pick the offense."

"And we're talking a *big* get-out-of-jail-free card," Mariah adds. "I'm not wasting this on something small like not cleaning my room. We're talking a makeup haul like you've never seen."

"Deal," Amelia says quickly. Hell, I was about to say deal too just to be safe. "I'm so sorry. You should have never seen that."

"Agree," Luke says. "But that still doesn't explain the elephant in the room. What did you two not want us to find out?"

I look over to Amelia, whose face is still red. She reaches out for my hand, which I gladly give her. I don't know if it's more for the moral support, or a symbolic gesture to the kids. Maybe both. I know it makes me feel better, and I can only hope it's the same for her.

"We're together. Dating. Whatever you kids call it these days," Amelia says.

I stare at Luke and Mariah, waiting to see some type of reaction from them. But these two are made of stone right now.

"How long has this been going on?" Luke asks.

"We've been seeing each other for about a month," I say. I

don't bother telling them about the wedding or my nearly-twenty-year unrequited love. They don't need to know that yet.

"Wow," Mariah says. "But it does make sense. Mom's been in a much better mood recently."

I look over to Amelia, whose face is turning red. "I can relate."

Amelia looks over to me, and we share a smile. "Kids, again I'm sorry. We were going to tell you soon, and I'm not just saying that because we got busted today. We just wanted some time for ourselves as we are figuring this out."

"Wait, does Betsy know? Is that why I spent the night last night and she was weird today?"

"Yeah," Amelia says. "But, we didn't tell her. She figured it out on her own."

"Who else knows?"

"Just Whitley, Betsy, and Izzy," Amelia says. "Oh, and Porter. Don't ask about that one. None of the uncles know. Grandma doesn't know. Before it got out to anyone else, we wanted to tell you two. I promise."

Luke and Mariah look to each other and have a silent conversation. This goes on for about a minute, which is kind of scaring me. Luke is always a hard one to read. He has a hell of a poker face. But Mariah? The girl can't act for anything. And right now, I see a slight smile sneak onto her face before she pushes it back.

I instantly relax, knowing this is all going to be okay.

Amelia cracks. "Say something. Ask questions. Be mad at me. Be mad at Shane. Be happy for us. Something, because I've freaked out a lot this morning without coffee, and I can't sustain this calm facade much longer."

The two of them nod at each other before turning back to me.

"I do have one question," Luke says as he turns his attention to me. "Shane, what are your intentions with our mother?"

I chuckle at his wording, but I'm glad he asked this. These two need to know I'm in it for the long haul. And I want them to know that from the jump. "I love your mom. I always have. My intentions are to make her happy. I want the only tears she ever cries again are to be happy ones. I want to be her partner. I want to share my life with her. And not just her, but you two as well. I want to be a family. Maybe not the traditional one, but one that we know is right for us. That is, if y'all want me?"

I look over to Amelia, who at some point started crying. I turn back to Luke and Mariah, and there's no more hiding—the smiles on their faces say it all.

"Good answer," Luke says.

Mariah gets up from the couch and wedges herself between me and Amelia. "Great answer."

I reposition my arm to hug her while silently saying a thank you that this is all going to be okay.

"Wait!" Mariah pops back up off the couch. "Is this why you had me get you a new lipstick?"

I look over to Amelia and grin. "Was the new lipstick for me?"

"I'm already not liking you two ganging up on me," Amelia says.

"Mom! Now I'm actually mad you didn't tell me. I was just pretending before. I could've done your makeup! And your hair. Oh God, who is dressing you?"

"Don't worry. Aunt Whitley has me covered."

"Phew, that's good," Mariah says. "I love you, but I don't want Uncle Shane having to see you after a failed makeup attempt. Wait! Do I not call you Uncle Shane anymore? Or do I? Is that weird? What if you two get married? Then what?"

We all laugh at Mariah's dramatics. "Let's slow down. This

is new still. Remember, you're now persons five and six who know this. And we need to tell everyone in our own way, on our own time."

"That makes sense," Luke says. "Grandma is going to flip."

"So will Uncle Oliver."

"Oh my God! I need to be there when Dad finds out," Mariah says. "He's going to lose his mind."

"Exactly. To all of that," I say. "So, we need to keep this quiet as we tell everyone on our own time. I know there's a lot to figure out. And we will. But at least now I don't have to keep coming over under the ruse of mowing the lawn."

"Aw, man," Luke groans. "Now I have to go back to doing that, don't I?"

I laugh. "How about we split it?"

Luke stands up and extends his hand for me. "Deal."

We shake on it, and I think we both know that this is more than just shaking about the lawn. This is about him trusting me to be part of his mother's life. This is him welcoming me as more than a surrogate uncle, but as now a member of this family.

"Okay," Amelia says. "I need coffee, and I'm guessing you guys haven't eaten. What do want to do for breakfast."

"Mona's." The three of us answer in unison.

Amelia smiles. "Fine. Everyone go get cleaned up and we'll go."

Luke heads upstairs, and Mariah gives me a hug before she makes her way as well. I look back to Amelia, whose is all smiles, a rare event pre-caffeinated.

"So that happened," she says.

"Yes, it did," I bring her into my arms. "I think it went pretty well."

"Easy for you to say. You're not the one whose panties are still in the kitchen."

"True," I say as I drop my forehead to hers. "But now they know. Two down. A bunch to go."

"Two down."

Amelia flashes me a smile before tilting her head up to find my lips. I reflexively pull her in tighter when I hear a groan from the top of the stairs.

"Gross," Luke says while also making a gagging sound. "I take back everything I said. I'm not a fan."

We look up to him, and he might have said that, but the smile on his face says otherwise.

Yup. Everything is going to be just fine.

Chapter 22
Amelia

"Betsy, I know we just met, and I know you have a man and don't swing my way, but I think I love you."

Betsy laughs at Kendra as she hands her a glass of sangria. "As a woman who thought for two seconds in college she might be bisexual, I appreciate that."

"You did?" Whitley asks. "When?"

"I took a women's studies class. Things got confusing."

We all laugh as the four of us lie back on our loungers around the pool at Betsy and Wes's. When Betsy called, asking if I wanted to come over and lay by the pool with her and Whitley, I hated saying no, but I had made plans with Kendra. Since we hadn't been on the same shift in weeks, I would have felt bad canceling. Betsy fixed that problem by telling me that the more the merrier and once Kendra heard the words "drinks" and "pool," our once-urgent errands didn't seem so time sensitive.

"Well, thanks again for inviting me," Kendra says as she holds up her drink. "To good drinks, good people, and hopefully a good suntan."

"I'll drink to that," Whitley says as she and the rest of us hold up our drinks. "It really is the perfect day for this."

"It is. Just sucks Izzy isn't here," Betsy says.

If things weren't weird enough for Oliver and Izzy with that whole wedding thing, Izzy got a call that her dad had suddenly passed away. From what Oliver told us, she and her family don't really get along, so he had no idea what to expect.

"I love how casually you say his name now in conversation. Like we don't all know that he was telling you this lying naked next to you in bed."

"He was not!" I say to Betsy, who is smiling from ear to ear.

"Where was he when he told you this bit of information, then?"

"Um…" Well, I walked right into that one, didn't I? "In bed. He just wasn't naked."

"Ha!" This gets a laugh from Betsy and a round of applause from Kendra and Whitley.

"Wait! Is this a safe Shane space?" Whitley asks. "Betsy! How did you not tell me you knew?"

"Because I didn't know you knew! It was supposedly a secret." She shoots me a glance and I look away.

"And I've known from the beginning, because I don't know any of you so it was safe for me to know."

"So we all know?" Betsy says, double-checking with everyone. "Good. Now we can dish."

"No, we can't," I say, looking toward her house. "Wes doesn't know."

Betsy waves me off. "Let's be honest, if any of the guys were to find out first, wouldn't you rather it be Wes?"

That's true. "Yes, but I want to tell all the guys together. It just feels right."

"I get that," Betsy says. "I just want to point out that for the woman who didn't want anyone to know, I find it odd we all know."

"I know," I groan. "I'm really the worst with this."

"It's okay. You're happy. And it shows."

"Thank you, Betsy. We're going to start telling people soon. The kids found out."

"What!" Whitley screams. "How?"

Kendra sits up and rubs her hands together. "Oh, this is about to be good."

I tell them every embarrassing part, including the panties on the floor and the blush on my cheeks when my kids called me out on it. I of course tell the sweet parts too, and the parts where I had to hold in laughter as my kids tried to play the parts of scolding adults.

"That's fucking amazing," Kendra says.

"It really is," Whitley adds. "So are you going to tell everyone now?"

I knew one of them was going to ask the million-dollar question. "Yes and no."

Kendra gives me a look that screams "you've got to be kidding me."

"It's not that easy," I say as she shakes her head. "Once we let this cat out of the bag, our relationship is going to change."

"Didn't you already let your cat out of the bag and that's how your kids know?"

"Kendra!" I scream, though I must admit, that's pretty funny. Betsy is laughing so hard I think she's about to fall out of her chair. Whitley might be hyperventilating.

"What I was going to say...we have to do this delicately. The kids, while I knew they'd have some feelings about it, were the easy ones."

And they were. After the initial shock, and a day to process, we all sat down and they asked more questions and we laid down some ground rules. They requested minimal PDA as they get used to us. But they also said that they didn't care if Shane spent the night. When I asked if they were sure about that, they reminded me they already know what's happening. No sense in making everyone pretend.

For now they are going to continue calling him Uncle Shane, but that's more for keeping up the secret than anything. When I said they could continue calling him that even after everyone is in the know, Luke described a scenario where we're all out, Shane and I are holding hands, and he or Mariah ask Uncle Shane for something.

After a good laugh, we acknowledged Shane's days as an "uncle" are officially limited.

"So who's next?" Whitley asks. "I haven't told your brother yet, which is killing me."

"You can tell him," I say. "It's not his reaction I'm worried about."

"The guys?" Betsy asks.

I nod. "Yeah. I don't think they're going to be mad. It's just...it's going to shift the dynamic. I've always been the sister. Sometimes the mother. Shane has always been the single guy who people think is a monk. It's just going to hit like a lightning bolt. When we do tell them, it has to be in a controlled space."

"Makes sense," Betsy says. "You can come over here. Neighbors far enough away that everyone can yell or fight and no one will call the cops."

"You mean call Shane? Or my husband?" Whitley says, snorting.

"True. I still forget I'm living in a small town where I know half the police force."

"Thanks, but it's not them I'm most worried about." I look over to Whitley, who immediately picks up what I'm thinking.

"Oh goodness gracious, your mother might die from a happiness-induced heart attack."

"Bingo."

"Really?" Kendra asks. "I've only met her a few times, but she seems pretty relaxed."

"She is. Mostly. Except when it comes to me dating. And especially when it could involve Shane and me."

"Why?" Betsy asks.

"She's been best friends with Shane's mom since they were kids. When they had us within months of each other they started planning the wedding. And Shane's mom is just as bad. She tried to ask Whitley and Jake to add him to their bridal party just so we could be partners."

"Are you serious?" Kendra looks to Whitley. "Are Shane and Jake friends?"

"Yeah, but not bridal party friends," she says. "They work together and know each other because of Amelia. That's pretty much the extent."

"Wow," Kendra says. "Okay, crazy moms. That would be definitely a reason to wait for a minute."

"Exactly," I say. "Once they know we're together, be ready for the wedding, because it will happen within a week."

"It won't be a week," Betsy says.

"Oh, it will," I say. "I've already had my mother pressure me to get married quickly once in my life. I know exactly how fast that woman works. I don't need for it to happen again."

"Really?" Whitley asks. "Is that what happened with your ex?"

At this point, we are all sitting in our loungers, and unfortunately, my sangria is long gone. I should ask for another if I'm about to talk about my lackluster wedding to a lackluster groom.

"I got pregnant spring of my senior year. Of course, I was

scared, mortified, and all-around confused. I was so panicked that I told Shane before anyone else. Even my mom or Paul."

I remember that day like it was yesterday. How I cried. How he held me and told me everything was going to be all right. How he walked with me to my parent's house and stayed with me when I told them. Not Paul. Shane.

I should have known then what I know now...

"I told my mom a few weeks before graduation. My dad was long gone by then, so I didn't need to worry about him. I was afraid she was going to kick me out of the house. Which, I mean, I was eighteen, she could have. She didn't. However, she very strongly kept asking if Paul and I were going to get married. The asking became nudging, which ended in her and Paul's mom sitting us down and all but forcing us to get married. I mean, we *were* in love. At least we said that to each other at the time. So one Wednesday night we went to the courthouse and got married in our jeans and T-shirts. Six months later, Luke was born. The rest is history."

"Damn," Whitley says. "What I'm confused about is your dad left when you and Jake were young. She was a single mom most of y'all's lives. Why was she so gung-ho on you getting married?"

"I wondered that too," I say. "Years later, right after my divorce, I asked her that. She said she knew how hard it was for her as a single mom. She thought if we were married, it wouldn't be so hard for me."

"Was she right?"

"In some ways," I admit. "At the beginning, things were good. We were young and dumb and in love. Then Luke came. For the first few months, Paul was always there. Slowly he started going out more and more on the weekends. Sometimes he'd be gone all weekend, saying he was going with buddies to different college parties in Nashville or Knoxville. And I let him. I mean, he didn't give me a choice, but I didn't fight it. That's what we *should* have been doing, partying and having fun, not budgeting for the week to make sure we could afford diapers and groceries."

"You raised Luke by yourself, didn't you?"

I shrug my shoulders to Betsy. "Basically. I made excuses for Paul. And don't get me wrong, we had some good times. There would be weeks he'd be home. We'd do things together as a family. Then as soon as I'd get used to that, he'd be back out and I'd never know when he was going to come home."

"That had to be horrible."

"It was," I say. "Then we had Mariah. Before it was just the partying and drinking. Then it became so much more than that. At that point, I was a stay-at-home mom. I was completely reliant on him, and he knew it."

"Oh, I do not like where this is going," Betsy says.

I nod. "It started with just little mind games. He was gaslighting me before I knew what that word even meant. He'd tell me if I took care of myself that we'd have sex more. That if I was a better wife, he wouldn't leave all the time. Things like that. It then became more and more evident he was sneaking around. But even with all that, and part of me knowing he had to be having an affair, I was still in denial about it."

"How did you find out?" Kendra asks.

"The guys," I say. "They told me that they saw him at The Joint kissing another woman. At first I didn't believe them. They always hated Paul, so of course I wasn't going to believe them."

"What was the tipping point?"

I push down the tears and the anger that threaten to build up every time I talk about this. Which granted, isn't often. But I don't think that matters. I think this will always make me emotional.

"I was out with the guys. Mom had taken Luke and Mariah. We went out for Simon's birthday. I had texted Paul what I was doing, but either he never got the text or didn't care, because when we showed up at The Joint, there he was, his tongue down the throat of Jessica Mozzaro."

"This is why I hate men," Kendra says.

"For a while I did too," I say. "I don't even remember reacting. I just know I turned and ran away. I still don't know what happened after that. All I know is that the next time I saw Paul he had a black eye and was full of apologies and excuses."

"No fucking way!" Kendra says as Whitley and Betsy's eyes almost pop out of their heads. "That brazen fuckhead! Also, my money is on Shane for decking him."

"Probably," I say. "That was the beginning of the end."

Maybe it wasn't the true beginning, but that was the first night I realized everything that had been bad in our marriage. The late nights. The lying. I couldn't excuse it anymore. Two days later I confronted him. And he lied. He told me I was seeing things. I asked him about the black eye, and he said he ran into something at work.

The man sold cars.

A week later I told him I was leaving.

And I did, just not the way I thought it would go down. I'm not going into that story. What I've said is enough for one day.

"Well, I'm just glad you got out," Kendra says.

"Same. I can't imagine still being with him. Then again, I got Luke and Mariah out of it, and I wouldn't trade them for the world."

"I get that," Betsy says. "Especially now when you see what it's like to be with a man who puts a permanent smile on your face."

I feel my smile growing, because she's right. "Yes, that does help. But no matter what, I'm better for being away from him.

It took me a while to get here. But all that matters is that I'm here."

"I'll drink to that."

I hold up my empty glass. "I would if I could."

"Oh! What kind of hostess am I!" Betsy gets up and grabs the pitcher of sangria, filling me right up.

"Thank you," I say. "And thank you for this. I've never really had a lot of girlfriends."

"Hey!" Kendra yells. "I'm right here!"

"I said friends. As in plural." Kendra harrumphs. "All I'm saying is, I never felt comfortable talking to people about this. But now? With the three of you…"

Shit, why am I crying?

"All I'm saying is that I'm grateful that you women are in my life."

"Oh, girl!" Kendra hugs me so tight I might burst. "I'm so glad I'm in your life now. And that you're happy. And getting good dick."

"Amen!" Betsy yells.

I laugh. "Y'all are ridiculous."

"Yeah, we are. But you love us."

I tip my glass to Betsy. "That I do."

Chapter 23
Shane

"Porter! Get me a whiskey neat, a basket of wings, and make sure to put everything on this motherfucker's tab."

Porter nods. "You got it, Simon."

"I already said I was buying," Wes said. "It's the least I can do for the *hard* manual labor I made you do today."

I can't keep in my laugh at Wes's sarcasm.

"What are you laughing at?" Simon asks. "We worked hard."

"We did," I say, pointing to Wes and I. "You, though...I don't know if supervising the bounce house crew really constitutes working."

"Those men were putting in place an apparatus that will entertain my goddaughter and her friends," Simon says. "I needed to make sure it was up to snuff. And, did you forget that I helped put out the tables? That was hard."

Wes shakes his head. "I'm sorry I made you sweat."

Simon waves him off. "Anything for Magnolia."

We laugh as Simon looks at the dirt under his nails—there isn't any—as Porter brings us over our drinks. I'm a big believer that there are tiers of beers. Not necessarily quality, but based on when you drink them. The number one is a shower beer. A close second is a cold beer at the end of a day of hard work, like today. Because while Simon got away with doing the bare minimum to help set up Magnolia's birthday party Saturday, Wes and I took care of the lawn and landscaping, strung lights around his patio and did any other thing Betsy, and Magnolia, told us to. I swear that girl is the most outspoken seven-year-old on the planet.

"I do have a question," Simon asks. "You aren't poor. I know you're not playing professional football anymore, and you paid your ex-wife a likely stupid amount of money to leave you alone, but why were you doing your landscaping today? You know you can pay people for that."

"Because why would I pay people to do something that I, along with my friends, can do ourselves?"

Simon shakes his head. "That, my friend, is the difference between you and me."

"It ain't the only one."

Some people would take that as insult. Not Simon. He just tips his glass to Wes. Because you can't argue with the truth. Those two are as different as night and day, but they just work. That's actually the crux of our friend group. We're polar opposites on many things, but at the end of the day, we're brothers. Amelia says our differences keep us balanced. I think we've just been friends for so long we don't know how to not be, differences or not. Either way, it works.

"Anyone heard from Oliver?"

"Yeah, he texted me yesterday," I say. "They're traveling back today and were probably going to lay low for a bit. Apparently some shit went down. But he'll be at Magnolia's party."

Before we can talk about Oliver, or anything else, my attention is drawn to the front door. That's what happens when it's a dark bar and the bright light of the afternoon hits your eyes. When I get them refocused, I have to shake my head to make sure I'm seeing what I think I am.

Because walking into the bar, for who knows what reason, is Paul fucking Sanders.

Wes and Simon notice the anger growing on my face and turn to see what I'm looking at.

"What the fuck is he doing here?" Wes asks.

"Apparently wanting an ass beating," Simon growls.

The three of us stare at him as he saunters into the bar. Even if he wasn't Amelia's ex-husband, I'd hate this guy. He was a pompous asshole in high school because he could throw a football and his dad owned the car dealership in town. He and Wes went rounds in the locker room, mostly because Paul was jealous that Wes was going to play college ball and he was going to be staying in Rolling Hills and selling people used sedans. Simon hated him because Simon hates everyone. And, well, I think it's self-explanatory of why we didn't get along. He always accused me of having feelings for Amelia, which I always denied. But feelings or not, he's still an asshole.

"Well, well, well...shocking to see you three together. Where's your fourth musketeer? Off getting turned down by a woman, I'm guessing?"

"What brings you into town, Paul? Is it already time for the yearly meeting of the 'I Peaked in High School' club?"

"Always a pleasure, Simon," Paul says, ignoring his question. Seriously, what the fuck is he doing here? "Porter, how about a drink? And get one for my friends."

"We'll pass," Wes says.

"Apologies. I figured you could use a round. You know, now that you don't have that big football money coming in. Speaking of, how is your ex-wife? I heard that alimony you paid her had a good number of zeros in it."

"Worth every penny," he says. "You know, I should introduce you two. I feel like you'd be a great pair."

Porter comes over and hands Paul his drink, but he doesn't make his way back to the bar. There's no one here, so he doesn't have anyone to serve. But even if he did, I have a feeling he'd be here monitoring the situation.

"I appreciate that, Wes, but I'm off the market."

"That so?" Simon says. "Let me guess, barely legal so she doesn't know better?"

"Jessica finally snag her hook into you?" Wes guesses.

"Oh! You met someone on a dating app that you catfished, but she stayed with you after you paid her off."

Wes and Simon laugh as I stare Paul down. They're the ones better to go verbal rounds with him. I'm going to do what I do best: sit back and picture all the ways I could pummel him.

"You guys are always such a riot." Paul laughs off everything just thrown at him. "If you must know, her name is Staci. She works for me at the dealership."

Wes looks to Simon. "Secretary. We didn't guess secretary."

"Damnit!" Simon says, holding his fists in the air in mock anger. "It was right there, and we missed it. We're better than that."

Paul doesn't respond, instead finally turning his sights to me. "Hello, Shane. I see you are still holding up your role in the group."

"Paul."

The two of us stare each other down. Years of hatred are passing through our eyes, yet every time I see this fucker I only think of one day—the day Amelia left him.

It had been a week since Amelia saw with her own eyes Paul cheating. We all knew it had been happening for years, but she didn't. And she wouldn't believe it when we told her.

But when we saw him at this very bar that night, we knew it was the straw to break the camel's back.

She wanted to leave him that night, but she also needed answers. And she had to get her things to be able to leave with the kids. This wasn't something she could do on a whim, even though all of us offered her places to stay and money to help her get on her feet.

Amelia was too proud for that and refused our help. We ended on the compromise that me, Oliver, and Simon were going to make routine, random check-ins on her. Wes was in season, so he couldn't come down. But he made sure his mom and brother helped make up for it. We just wanted to make sure she and the kids were okay. And, if and when she was ready to go, we'd be there with the getaway car.

During one of my check-ins, I knew something was off as soon as I pulled into the driveway. Maybe because Paul was home in the middle of the day when he should have been at work. Maybe because I could hear them screaming at each other the second I stepped out of my truck. Maybe because I've known for years this day was going to come.

I THROW *open Amelia's door and the first thing I see are suitcases at the doorway. The second thing I see is a lamp flying into the wall.*

"Amelia!"

I race down the hall and turn into their living room, where the lamp came flying out of. I see Paul breathing heavy as he stands over Amelia, who looks afraid for her life.

"What the fuck did you do to her?" I storm toward him and grab him by his shirt, dragging him away from her.

"Why are you in my fucking house?"

"What. Did. You. Do. To. Her?"

My grip is getting tighter on his shirt. He has three seconds to answer me before my fist goes into his face. He still has the remnants of the bruise Simon gave him the night we caught him cheating. I'm about to give him one that matches.

"It's none of your fucking business, Cunningham."

"That's where you're wrong. Amelia is my business. She always has been. And she always will be. And after this day, she's no longer your concern."

"Ha." His face goes from scared to calm. Like he suddenly grew a set. "This must make you happy. You're finally going to get your chance. Just remember that you're getting my leftovers."

I punch him so quickly I don't even realize I did it. Square across the face so he drops to the ground. I stare down at him before I stomp on his chest hard enough I might have cracked a rib.

Ask me if I fucking care. He's lucky I'm not breaking every bone in his body.

"If you ever, and I mean ever, come for her again, I will end you. That's not a threat. It's a promise, do you understand me?"

Paul doesn't say anything as he rolls on the ground, holding his midsection. My breathing is only getting heavier as I stare at him, wondering if I could actually get away with murder.

"Shane?"

Amelia's trembling voice pulls me away from all thoughts of ending Paul. I run over to her and pull her off the ground into my arms.

"Shhhh. It's okay. I'm here." I pick her up and her arms immediately go around my neck, holding on for dear life. "He's not going to hurt you anymore. I've got you."

I took her back to my house after that, where she cried in my arms for hours. In between the tears she told me that he never hit her, and the lamp flying was the closest it ever came. But she was also convinced that if I was two seconds later, he probably would have. They had a fight about her leaving. He couldn't believe she was actually going through with it.

Well, she did. And she's better for it.

"What the fuck are you doing here Paul?" I ask.

"Not that it's any of your business, but I'm in town to take my kids for a few weeks. I thought a summer vacation would be fun. Figured I could introduce them to the woman who hopefully one day is their stepmom."

I rack my brain trying to think if Amelia told me this, but she hasn't said anything. No. This has to be a surprise, because even if somehow Amelia forgot to tell me, I know I would have heard it from Mariah. She would have had *something* to say about a vacation with her dad and his new girlfriend.

"Is that so? Does Amelia know this?"

Paul shakes his head. "She doesn't. I don't need permission to take my kids. Mel can deal with it."

I stand up and walk a few steps, so I'm now toe-to-toe with him. "You don't. But I find it comical that you're deciding to evoke visitation that you've never taken before. And as a surprise? I'm sure that's going to go over well."

"Why the fuck do you care? Oh, that's right. You don't have a relationship or a family, so you like to pretend my family is yours. Well, guess what, asshole? They aren't. They're mine, and as much as you want them, they will never be yours."

"That's where you're wrong." I lean in a little closer, making sure he hears every word I'm about to say. "Where were you when Mariah fell off her bike and needed stitches? Where were you when Luke was learning to drive? Where have you been for every Christmas and birthday over the past ten years? You've never *once* seen Luke play a down of football. Your daughter won a track meet this year, and you know who she ran to? Me. Not you. She didn't even care that you weren't there. You're not a fucking father. You for sure weren't a fucking husband. You're barely a man. You make me sick."

"You fucking watch it," Paul says as he pushes me, but I see it coming and plant my feet. I don't move an inch, which makes his eyes go wide.

"I will fucking watch it," I say, taking a step back toward him. In my periphery, I see Wes and Simon stand up. Porter moves so now they're circling us. I know they're prepping for backup, but lucky for them I won't need it. This is my fight. "I'll fucking watch your kids fade out of your life. No vacation is going to fix that. I'll watch as the woman you threw away falls even more in love with me."

"What the fuck is that supposed to mean?"

Shit. I don't know what I was thinking when I just said that. Correction. I wasn't thinking. But I'm in it now. And like hell I'm going to take those words back. Especially in front of him.

"You heard what I said. She loves me. And I love her. One day I'll watch her walk down the aisle toward me. I'll continue being the father to your kids that you've never been. The best part? We won't even think of you. Because you mean nothing to us. Nothing."

You can hear a pin drop right now. I don't look over at Wes or Simon, but I can only imagine their faces. If I had to guess, it's either shock or confusion. Probably both. I don't look to see. Like hell if I'm going to be the one to break the stare down I'm having with Paul.

"You love Mel? I mean, I've known that for years. But she loves you back? Oh, Shane, when are you going to get it through that thick skull of yours that she's never going to feel that way about you?"

"It's true."

All eyes turn to Porter. Shit, I almost forgot he knew.

"Oh, Porter," Paul says. "You don't need to cover for them."

"They were making out in the back hallway a few weeks ago. I'm pretty sure you know the spot, since you frequented it while you were married to Amelia."

He narrows his eyes at Porter. "Stay the fuck out of this."

"Why? He's not lying." This is coming from Wes. "They've been together for months. Happier than I've ever seen them. The wedding is going to be epic."

I look over to him, wondering if he's just going along with what he thinks is an act or if he actually knows. Who cares? I could kiss him right now.

"Wedding?" Paul asks. "Mel isn't getting married. I'd know."

"Would you?" Simon jumps in. Okay, now I know these guys are just playing along. But I'm grateful they are. "I mean, we'd know because we're all best friends. You're a gnat that we can't ever seem to get rid of. I'm so excited for it. I got ordained to officiate. I'll make sure to emphasize that this is Amelia's first real wedding."

"Fuck off, Simon. This is all bullshit."

"Is it?" Porter asks. "They've been friends for years. Makes sense for them to take this jump. You should have been here when the town found out. It was all the buzz. If you were around more, you probably would've heard about it. But hey, you have your new girlfriend, so what should you care?"

Paul's eyes go wide and looks to each of us, all now with smug looks on our faces.

"What?" I ask. "Cat got your tongue?"

"Fuck all of you," Paul says as he turns and storms out of the bar.

"Holy shit!" Wes yells as he pats me on the back. "I didn't know you could lie like that."

Porter laughs. "Oh, he wasn't lying. Let me go get us a round of shots."

Wes looks to Porter then back to me. "What does he mean that you weren't lying?"

Simon and Wes just stare at me. Like with the kids, this isn't how I planned on doing it, but here we are.

"How about we sit down?"

"No," Wes says. "Tell us. Right now."

I take a deep breath. "Amelia and I are together. We've been for a few months now. That wasn't a lie. It's the truth. I love her."

Porter comes back with four shots, which we all down in one gulp.

"Thanks," I say to Porter. "You didn't need to do that."

"Yes, I did," he says. "That fucker used my bar for too many years for his side pieces. It was about damn time karma came and bit him in the ass."

"Wait!" Simon shouts, turning all our eyes to him. "Is Amelia Mary?"

I nod. "Yes. Amelia is Mary."

Simon jumps out of his seat and starts pacing. "Holy shit! How could you not fucking tell me?"

"Mary is Amelia?" Wes joins in.

"Holy shit, this is huge," Simon says, now pacing back and forth. "I have so much to say. There's so much to unpack."

Wes pulls out his phone. "I have to tell Betsy. She's never going to believe this."

I hope Betsy's ready for some Academy Award acting, or she's never going to hear the end of it. My phone dings.

> Amelia: Why is my ex-husband wondering
> why I didn't tell him we're getting married?

"Fuck!" I yell as I jump up from our table.

"What?" Wes asks.

"We need to go. Amelia just got a text from Paul."

"Holy shit! This day just keeps getting better!" Simon says as we sprint out of the bar. "The manual labor was totally worth this day."

Chapter 24
Amelia

"Who's going to tell me what the hell happened?"

Shane, Simon, and Wes continue to look at the floor from their seats on my living room couch. None of them are making eye contact with me. They know they're in trouble.

They're right.

"Okay, so if no one is talking, I'm going to say what I think happened and please, someone correct me if I get anything wrong." I start pacing in my living room, feeling like a mom scolding her teenage sons who just got caught drinking. "You were at the bar. Paul walks in. You guys start having a pissing match."

"It wasn't a pissing match. He was being his normal douchebag self."

I shoot a glare at Simon for interrupting. "I wasn't done."

"Sorry," he says, bowing his head back down to look back at the floor.

"As I was saying. You guys were going back and forth because someone said something, and I'm going to go on a limb that Paul started going after me, which caused Shane to Hulk out. Before we know it, our relationship is outed, and I'm suddenly engaged. That sound about right?"

Not a word from Larry, Curly, or Moe. They just continue to hang their heads.

"Hello? Anyone want to say anything?"

I know I'm not saying names, but I really need Shane to speak up. Apparently my telepathy skills are working today as he looks up at me, his face covered in remorse. "We fucked up."

"You think?" I know he feels bad, but I'm sorry, I don't know how to react right now. I continue marching around my living room, trying to wrap my brain around how in the matter of hours my relationship with Shane became not a secret, and on top of that, I'm now somehow engaged.

"In our defense," Wes begins, "he was being horrible."

I clutch my nonexistent pearls. "Oh! Shocking! My ex is a dickhead! That is brand-new information!" I try to calm down, but it's not going well. "Guys. I know you hate him. So do I. And I appreciate the solidarity, but do you know what you've done? The can of worms you opened?"

I fall down on a chair, because I can't think and maybe this will help. "Please, someone tell me what happened before I fucking lose it."

The three of them look up and share a nod, and I see Shane take a breath. "You're right. Mostly."

"It started with him existing," Wes says.

"Then he walked into the bar and started running his mouth," Simon interrupts. "Though I must say, Wes and I were doing a stellar job at knocking him down a few pegs. Wes even suggested setting him up with the Wicked Witch, which I think is a fantastic idea."

"That's when he brought up that he has a girlfriend—we can only guess she's half his age—then he turned his sights to Shane," Wes says. "During all of this, Shane was just sitting there stewing, which at the time we thought was just Shane being Shane and wanting to pummel him because it's another day that ends in Y."

"Who knew that our boy here was trying to keep his cool because he was talking shit about his woman? We sure as hell didn't."

I can't help but laugh at Simon's rendition of this encounter. I might be mad at them, but they will never not make me laugh. "Yeah, sorry about that. I promise we had a good reason for keeping it quiet."

"Oh we'll get to you...*Mary*," Simon says. "Anyway. Paul is being Paul, and then he tells us about the vacation he's going to take with the kids."

"What vacation!" I yell. "Shane? What vacation?"

I see him balling his fists. "For the first time in years, Paul wants his two weeks. That was another trigger for what happened."

I take a few deep breaths. Legally, he's allowed. But fuck him. He's never wanted the kids for his extended summer visit. Now I'm hoping this story ends with one of them punching him in the face.

"Okay," I say, trying to stay calm. "Shane? What happened next?"

"He was talking about how he didn't have to ask you permission to take the kids, and that he could do whatever he wanted. How he could be a dad whenever he chose to. I snapped."

My heart immediately sinks, knowing this all started because Shane wasn't just defending me, but Luke and Mariah as well. Now I'm not as mad.

And I still hope there's a punch in this story.

"I just lost it," he continues, his voice pleading. "Amelia, I didn't mean to. But years of hatred and things I've wanted to say to him just poured out. So many times I wanted to tell him what a shitty husband he was. Or a shitty father. It all just came barreling out. Before I know it, I was professing my love for you and the kids to him, which then somehow led to talk of a future hypothetical wedding."

"That was our fault," Wes admits. "Well, mine. In my defense, I didn't think any of this was real, and I was just playing along to piss off Paul. Which is always fun."

"You should have seen the look when I told him I was offici-ating," Simon says. "Oh, by the way, when you guys get married, I'm performing the ceremony. I will not be taking any objections at this time."

I think Shane is legitimately about to cry, and I can't take it anymore. I walk across the room to him and sit on his lap, wrap-ping him in my arms.

"Ah! Wes! Look at our two friends in love!" Simon says. "I can't wait to tell Oliver that I got to see this before him. He's going to flip."

Shane and I laugh. "And there's one of the reasons we kept this to ourselves."

"What do you mean?" Wes asks as he moves off the couch to another seat, making room for me. As I do, Shane grabs my hand and links our fingers. We share a look, and I know exactly what he's trying to tell me: This is it. This is the official start. And he's right.

"When we figured out this was for real—"

"Correction, when she came around to the realization she couldn't live without me."

I look over to Shane, who has apparently channeled his inner Simon. "Watch it, buddy."

He laughs. "I'm sorry. Go on."

"When we knew this was for real, we knew it would affect

a lot of people in our lives. The kids. Our families. And you guys."

"Aw, Wes, they thought of us."

"Of course we did. But when we did, we also realized that there might be a potential for freakouts and overreactions."

"A.K.A. Oliver."

"Yes. And our mothers," I say to Wes. "We just wanted some time to ourselves. To not rock the boat for a bit."

"And so we didn't have to hear shit from Simon."

Simon nods. "You guys are smart. I would've been relentless. I'm still going to be, Mary. That's your name now."

"Exactly. So we snuck around."

"Wait!" Wes yells. "The night at The Joint when we met Izzy. And Emily was trying to flirt with him, and you guys came over like a gang."

"Oh yeah," I say with a chuckle. "Betsy and Izzy knew. They figured us out that night. That was a coordinated attack."

"Betsy knew and didn't tell me? I texted her an hour ago with the news and she played dumb. Oh, I'm going to get her..."

"Yes. But don't be mad at her. She was just doing what I asked."

"Fine," he groans. "So now who knows?"

"You two. Porter. Betsy, Whitley, Izzy and my friend Kendra. Oh, and the kids."

"Excuse me!" Simon shouts. "You told me I'd be the first to know!"

"I'm sorry!" Shane says. "In my defense, she was the one who made me promise to keep the secret and then told people."

I look over to Simon with puppy dog eyes. "Forgive me?"

He narrows his eyes at me in a way that I know he's pretending to be mad. "Fine. Earlier I was joking. Now I'm serious. I'm going to get ordained and will officiate."

"Deal," I say. I see Shane shoot a look at me. "What? It's either that or he's your best man."

"True," he says. He looks hard at Simon. "Just don't pull any bullshit."

Simon shakes his head. "I promise nothing."

"Speaking of weddings," Wes says. "While I'm happy for you two and am going to be anxiously awaiting the rest of the story of how you two got together under our noses, that doesn't change the fact that your ex-husband thinks you're engaged."

"And because we are stubborn as hell, we're not about to admit to him we made this shit up. So, when's the wedding? I'll go online right now and fill out the form."

Simon's right. We are stubborn as hell. And I'd rather have Edward Scissorhands give me my yearly exam than admit to my ex-husband that Shane and the rest of them lied about the engagement.

"Who else was at the bar that would know this?"

"No one," Shane says. "Just the three of us and Porter."

"Good," I say. "That means no one will actually go up to Paul and talk about the wedding."

"True. But could he blab?" Wes asks.

I shake my head. "No. He knows everyone in town picked me in the divorce. Especially after his dad closed the car dealership. It's why he rarely comes back. People don't kiss his ass like they used to."

"So what's the plan?" Shane asks.

"Unfortunately, I'm going to have to see him soon, because I'm required by law to grant him two weeks of summer visitation. So it looks like the kids are going on vacation," I say. "All we have to do is pretend to be engaged when we drop the kids off and pick them up. Obviously, we'll fill them in. I'll go get a cheap ring, and we'll play the part. As long as no one else finds out, we can just let this fade away."

"Won't he start asking questions if you're engaged too long?" Wes asks.

"I see him twice a year, when he remembers he's a father. Let's cross that bridge when we get there."

"Easy enough," Shane says as he puts his arm around me. "Do you want me to propose?"

I shake my head. "Save it for the real thing, okay?"

"Gladly."

Shane comes in for a kiss, which is met with immediate boos and Simon telling us to get a room.

"Get used to it, guys," Shane says. "I'm not about to stop kissing her."

I smile as I lean into his hold.

"While this is all sweet and everything, there's one more thing," Wes says.

"What?"

"We forgot the biggest problem."

"What's that? We figured out the engagement. What else is there?"

Wes looks at all of us with a distressed look. "When, and more importantly how, are we telling Oliver?"

Chapter 25
Shane

"Okay, let's go over the plan one more time."

Luke, Mariah, and I all nod our heads at Amelia, who is doing her best impression of a coach getting her team ready for a game.

"I'm lurking around and making sure no one is talking about the engagement," Luke says.

"Good. And if anyone asks either of you if it's true, you say—?"

"It's Rolling Hills. Do you really think you'd be hearing about my mom and Shane getting married like this?"

"Perfect." Amelia turns to Mariah. "And you?"

"I'm finding out if Magnolia knows. If she does, I'm shutting it down. And quick."

"Good. That girl is a loose cannon we need to control."

I can't help but laugh, but it's true. Magnolia will say what's on her mind on any given day, let alone on a day and a party all about her.

"What about you?"

"To make sure our friends don't do stupid shit. Or give

anything away. Which again, I don't know how I'm supposed to stop that."

Amelia shakes her head. "I don't care. Bribe them. Pay them off. I don't want Oliver feeling bad that he doesn't know, so we need to be the ones to tell him. And we need to do this somewhat discreetly since it looks like half of Rolling Hills is at this party."

We all break our huddle and damn, Amelia's right. Sometime in the last ten minutes I think every kid going into first grade at Rolling Hills Elementary has arrived at Wes's house. Then again, this is the birthday party of the year—or so Magnolia said when we got here today to help Wes and Betsy finish setting up. There's a bounce house, a face painting station, the swimming pool, and in a little bit, Disney princesses are going to be here.

If this is Magnolia's party when she turns seven, I can't imagine what it will be like when she's sixteen.

"There they are," Simon says as he saunters in, drink already in hand. "Rolling Hills' newest couple."

"Really?" Shane says as he signals to the red Solo cup.

Simon shrugs as he takes a sip. "Listen, after the events of the last day, I've officially cemented myself as the fun, drunk uncle of the group. Might as well live up to it."

"Hey, I'm fun," I say.

Amelia hugs my arm. "Of course you are."

"What's that supposed to mean?"

"You're fun in other ways." She sends me a wink before she walks to where Betsy is getting kids in line for the face painting.

"I'm fun," I grumble.

Simon pats me on the back. "Sure you are, buddy. Sure you are."

We take a seat and I observe the mass chaos that is at least fifty kids running through Wes's yard.

"Do you want this?"

I look at him, a bit confused. "Want what?"

"This," he nods out to the party. "Kids. The whole family thing."

"I don't know," I say honestly. "At this point in my life, I kind of figured that ship sailed. Plus, I haven't talked to Amelia, but I don't know if she's eager to have any more considering Luke is about to start his senior year."

"You never know," Simon says as he lounges back in the chair. Which is true. We haven't had any of these talks yet. We've been too focused on navigating the now to really think about the future.

"What about you? Are you going to be the forever single man standing? Or are you ready to finally settle down?"

"Ha!" He laughs. "You're hilarious."

"Never say never, my friend."

"Oh, I will. Never. Never getting married. Never having kids. I'm the fun uncle for these kids. I'm the fun uncle for my sister's kids. It's a role I play well. Plus, I have yet to meet a woman who holds my interest more than ten minutes, let alone for the rest of my life."

"Oh man," I say. "When you fall, it's going to be so fucking hard."

He gives me a challenging look. "Wanna bet?"

"Absolutely," I say, holding out my hand. "Hundred bucks?"

"Deal."

We shake hands as Amelia starts walking back toward us.

"Shane?"

"Yeah?"

"In all seriousness, I'm happy for you two. I didn't see it coming, but I can see clear as day now that it's in front of me. You two are good together. And I might give you two shit, but I want you to know it's out of love. No one deserves this more than you."

"Thanks, man," I say as I slap him on the back.

"One warning though," he says.

"What's that?"

"If you make her cry, I'll hit you harder than I hit that asshole ten years ago."

"Wait, what?" Amelia says. "You hit Paul? I always thought it was Shane who hit him."

Simon gets a smug look on his face. "Oh Amelia. When are you going to learn that this guy isn't the knight in shining armor? It's been me all along."

Simon gives me a pat on the shoulder, then kisses Amelia on the cheek before he walks away.

"He's really the one who hit Paul?"

I nod. "He was. I didn't even know he did it when it happened. Apparently after we got you out of the bar, Simon went back. The story goes that he walked in, tapped him on the shoulder, then laid him out."

"Wow," Amelia says. "Maybe Simon's right. Maybe he has been my Prince Charming?"

I pull her in, choosing at this moment to not care who sees us. "Don't you dare."

She smiles up at me, a smile that I know has a promise attached to it for later. "I wouldn't dare."

"Break it up, kiddos, the eagle has landed."

Simon's words break us apart as we watch as Oliver and Izzy walking into the party. They only get a few steps inside before Magnolia runs over and seemingly steals Izzy.

"Are we ready?" Amelia asks.

"As we'll ever be."

"He's alive!" Simon exclaims, handing Oliver a beer as he makes his way to us. "We thought you went dark again on us."

"Sorry. Just been a little hectic after we got back."

"How'd it go?" I ask.

"Good," Oliver says. "Well, not good. But good."

"You're going to have to use more words than that," Amelia says.

It's at that moment I see Oliver look at us a little funny. I'm not touching her, and she's not touching me. Are we standing too close? I don't feel like we are, but maybe?

I slightly take a step away from Amelia as Oliver recounts their time in Nebraska for Izzy's father's funeral. The main takeaway: Izzy's family is horrible.

Soon, Wes and Betsy come and join us, both of them looking worse for the wear.

"Are you two okay?" Amelia asks.

"No," Wes says. "Kids are exhausting."

Betsy falls into one of the chairs. By the looks of it, she might not get back up. "Be a nanny, they said...it will be fun, they said...They didn't tell you that you might fall in love with your boss and then have to be a bonus mom and plan extravagant birthday parties."

"Hey, you're the one who said we needed face painting. This was after you already convinced me to hire princesses."

Betsy snaps her head to Wes and shoots daggers at him. "Wes. I love you. I love the kids. But right now I'm going to need you to stop using my own actions against me and just support me when I'm ignoring the problem that I created."

We all laugh as we take seats on the patio, away from the chaos. Amelia and I sit next to each other, but since I can see Oliver trying to catch glances at us, I do my best to keep a little distance. As we all find seats, Emerson comes over and plops into the seat I'm assuming Oliver left for Izzy.

"You okay, Em?" Betsy asks.

"I just need five minutes," she says through her heavy breaths. "Five minutes away from the kids. I just...I need this."

"Who says you can sit at the big kids table?" Simon teases. Except I'm not laughing at Simon. I'm laughing at the look of death he's now receiving from Emerson.

"I'm a teenager now. I've earned my place in this circle. Plus I don't see you taking a turn as event coordinator."

Simon holds his hands up in defeat. "I stand corrected. Sit with us."

"Room for another?"

We all greet Izzy as she takes a seat on the arm of Oliver's chair. The two of them whisper hellos as I feel a pat on my hand. I turn to Amelia, who's giving me the nod. I nod back, knowing that this is just as good of a time as any. Except before Amelia can say anything, Betsy lets out a scream that stops the whole party.

"OH MY GODDDD!!!!!!!"

We all turn to Betsy, who's pointing at Izzy.

"What?" Wes asks.

Emerson stands up and pats Wes on the back. "Dad, I love you. And you're smart. I know this. But for a smart man, sometimes you are very dense. Izzy's wearing her wedding ring."

Everyone's attention turns to them. Everyone except Amelia.

"I tried," she mouths.

I nod and give her hand a quick squeeze. "Soon."

We both nod and return to the conversation, not wanting to steal the thunder from Oliver and Izzy. Especially Oliver. The man has waited for this moment his entire life. I'm not about to ruin it.

Later. We can do this later.

～

"WHEN DID THEY LEAVE?" I ask.

Wes laughs. "About the same time Mariah and Luke left to go pack for their trip with daddy dearest."

Amelia's eyes go wide. "Izzy and Oliver left an hour ago, and we're just noticing?"

"They pulled an Irish goodbye," Simon says. "Respect to them. They did it well."

"Can you blame them?" Betsy says. "They're in their honeymoon phase. I'd have left too."

The five of us settle around the fire pit on Wes's back patio as we take in the warm summer night. Amelia tries to take her own seat, but I grab her and sit her on my lap. Everyone here knows. I'm not taking that situation for granted.

"Is this what I'm going to have to put up with now?" Simon asks as he nods toward Wes. "Him I could deal with."

"What's that supposed to mean?" Wes asks.

"It means you've always been the relationship guy. You and Oliver. So I was used to you guys. But Shane? Shane was my man. My brother in single arms, even though he'd never be my wingman. Now look at him. All in love and shit."

Amelia laughs as she leans into me a little more. I take her hand and kiss her for longer than necessary, making sure I stare at Simon the whole time.

"I fucking hate you," he says.

"No, you don't."

"So what now?" Wes asks, changing the subject. "When are we going to tell him?"

"I don't know," Amelia says. "I want to tell him soon so he doesn't feel like we're purposefully not telling him. But on the other hand, I don't want to steal his thunder."

"Makes sense," Betsy says. "You don't have to worry about us slipping. We leave for vacation at the end of the week. I doubt we'll see Oliver before then."

"Same," Amelia says, turning and smiling at me.

"What do you mean, 'same?'" Simon demands.

"We decided since the kids are going to be with Paul, and because we both have PTO we haven't used, that we'd take a little vacation ourselves."

"When were you going to tell me this?"

"Sorry, Simon," Amelia says. "I didn't realize that you were so interested in my itinerary."

"I don't care about your itinerary. I would have just liked a heads-up that I'm going to be all by myself for the better part of the next month."

"You have other friends," Wes says. "What about your old college buddy, Emmett? You used to hang out with him all the time."

"How in the hell do you remember Emmett?"

Wes shrugs. "That one weekend you two came and hung out with me. He seemed like an all-right guy. And to be frank, that's the only other friend of yours I think I know, and I needed to prove a point."

"You're right. Emmett is a good guy." Simon pulls out his phone. "Maybe I will give him a call. He's still in Nashville as far as I know."

"There you go," Amelia says. "We have a sitter for Simon, so we can all go on vacation." Simon narrows his eyes at Amelia, but she just smiles at him. "We'll make sure to bring you back a souvenir."

"Please," he says. "Just make sure it's not a real engagement. Or a wedding. There's been too many of those for my tastes. That goes for both of you."

Simon points back and forth as Wes and I both hold up our hands in agreement.

"You have my word," I say.

And he does. Amelia and I aren't coming back engaged. No, I have a different plan for the day that happens.

Hell, I already have the ring.

No, this vacation is about no one but us. No friends. No jobs. No kids. No exes. Just me, Amelia, a beach, and a few days where we hopefully don't leave our beds.

And it's going to be perfect.

Chapter 26
Shane

"I come bearing food!"

I'm not even two steps into the kitchen before Mariah grabs the boxes of pizza and breadsticks out of my hands. "Thanks, Uncle Shane!"

I laugh as the tornado known as dinnertime unfolds in front of me. When it comes to this crew and pizza, you don't get in their way. It's a once-a-week meal, and they are very particular about their order. I should know. Once I forgot that pepperoni only went on half of one of the pizzas, and I heard about it for a month.

"Did you get the snacks?" Amelia asks as she grabs drinks from the refrigerator.

I hold up the plastic bag with every treat each of them requested—and a few I know they like but didn't ask for. "Of course."

Amelia walks past me, giving me a drive-by kiss. "You're the best."

I smile and take off my shoes as Amelia and Mariah grab their food and drinks and head into the living room for family movie night. That's when I see Luke, who is moving like molasses. He slowly picks a slice up and just lets it fall onto the paper plate.

"Everything okay?"

He nods but doesn't make eye contact.

"I know what it's like not wanting to talk about things. Believe me, I try to do it as little as possible. But if you want to talk, I'm here."

Luke looks out to the living room—I'm guessing to make sure Amelia and Mariah are out of earshot—before looking back at me.

"There's this girl..."

I pat him on the shoulder as we take a seat at the kitchen table. "There always is."

"She's...funny. And pretty. So pretty. And she likes baseball. Uncle Shane, she can name the starting lineup of the Tennessee Arrows for the past five seasons. I like her. I like her a lot. We danced together at prom—neither of us had dates and went with friends—and, I don't know. There's just something about her."

I know that time evolves, and things change over the course of generations. I know my high school experience is nothing like Luke's. But it's good to know that the feeling is still the same when you meet the first girl to turn your world upside down. Because I swear to God, this was how I felt about Amelia when I was Luke's age. Also, the prom coincidence is just spooky.

"I'm guessing there's some sort of problem?"

He nods. "I think I'm in the friend zone."

"I know that all too well," I say. "But why do you say 'think?'"

Luke shrugs as he aimlessly plays with his pizza. "Sometimes I think she might like me too. I've never had a serious girlfriend, but I think I know when a girl is flirting with me. She'll touch my arm when she laughs. She'll send me funny memes. We text all the time. Except, last night she went out with another guy and…"

Luke trails off, but having been in his shoes, I know what he was going to say. And while I do think that everything happens for a reason—and who's to say Amelia and I would have worked if I had gotten up the courage all those years ago—I don't want Luke to have to go through what I did.

"Have you told her how you feel?"

He shakes his head. "No. I've wanted to ask her out a few times, but it never felt right. Also, what if she turns me down? I don't want it to be weird if she does."

"I get it. Rejection is a paralyzing fear," I say. "It was the reason I didn't ask your mom out in high school."

"Really? You liked her back then?"

"I did. She was always my friend, but one day, I realized she was more. Except I came up with every reason why I shouldn't ask her out. I thought things needed to be perfect."

"I do that too," he says. "And now look where it got me."

"I get that," I say. "I had to watch your mom with your dad."

This makes him laugh. "That had to suck."

"It did. Big time. But it doesn't have to be the same for you."

Luke looks up at me, a little bit of hope in his eyes. "Really?"

"Do you know if this girl is now dating the guy she went out with?"

He shakes his head. "They aren't. I asked her how it went today. She said it was fine."

I smile and pat him on the arm. "You've still got a chance."

"What?"

"Luke, I've had the honor of teaching you a lot of things

over your life. But this might be the biggest one I've ever taught you." I lean in closer to him, which he does as well. "When women say fine, they aren't. And nine times out of ten it means not good."

He sits up, a sudden look of hopefulness on his face. "Really?"

"Really. But now you have to do the scariest thing you've ever done."

He nods. "I have to ask her out, don't I?"

I nod. "Yeah. And yes, she might say no. You might, in fact, be friend zoned. But Luke, don't be like me. Don't be scared. Take the risk. Ask her out. Tell her how you feel. Don't have the regret."

He lets out a breath and pulls his phone out of his pocket. "What do I say? 'Hey, can we go out in two weeks after I get back from a vacation I don't want to go on?'"

I look at the time and see that it's only seven. "Ask her out tonight. See if she wants to get ice cream or something."

"You know I can't do that." Luke looks toward the living room then back to me. "Mom was all about having family night before we left. I can't tell her I'm ditching to go get ice cream with a girl. And who knows if she'll even say yes. I'll just wait until I get back."

He starts to put his phone in his pocket before I grab his wrist. "Don't wait. I'll take care of your mom. Believe me, she'll understand."

With a worried look and shaky hands, Luke takes his phone back out and starts typing. I get it. My hands would have been trembling if I had done this with Amelia in high school. Hell, they still do sometimes.

"Okay. Done," he says as he lets out the biggest breath of maybe his life. "Now let's go turn on the movie so I have something to think about other than if she's going to text me back."

"Sounds good."

We both stand, grabbing our sodas and pizza, but Luke doesn't move.

"Shane?"

"Yeah?"

"Thanks," he says. "For...well, everything."

"You never need to thank me," I say. "But I appreciate it."

We each grab another slice and head out to the living room. Mariah has already set up shop on her oversized bean bag. I take a seat next to Amelia on the couch as Luke heads to the recliner, remote in hand.

"Which one are we on?"

"Last week we watched the one with the hot blond guy."

"*Thor*," Luke says with a dry look. "The movie was *Thor*."

"Whatever," Mariah says. "My description wasn't wrong."

Amelia and I laugh as the two of them bicker. This. This is what I've always wanted. A normal night with just me, Amelia, and the kids. I've been over to Amelia's house dozens of times for dinner. But being here now, Amelia snuggling into me, the kids carrying on like they always do, it just feels right. Like I'm home. Like this is where I was always meant to be.

"Oh! Does this one have Captain America in it?"

I can see Luke rolling his eyes. He's probably silently begging for that girl to text him back just to get away from Mariah. "Yes, Mariah. This is *The Avengers*. They are all in it."

"Good," she says as she finishes off her pizza.

"How about Tony Stark?" Amelia asks. "Which one is he?"

"Iron Man? Really?" I ask.

Amelia wags her eyebrows. "Heck, yeah, Iron Man. Money and looks? Sign me up."

I let out a groan. "He's my least favorite."

"That makes sense. He's the Simon of *The Avengers*."

This makes everyone crack up. "Oh my God, he is!"

Mariah says. "Can I call Uncle Simon that? I feel like he'd really like that."

"No," I say to Mariah. "He doesn't need to think he's a superhero."

Everyone laughs as Amelia gives me a kiss on the cheek. "Don't worry. I'll pick you over Tony Stark, or Simon, every day of the week."

"You better."

She smiles and cuddles back into my side as the movie begins. It plays for about twenty minutes when I see Luke nearly jump out of his chair.

"She said yes!"

If it were just the two of us, I'd get up and celebrate with him. But I have to play it cool. I just smile and nod. "We'll see you later."

"Thanks Shane," Luke gets up and gives his mom a kiss on the cheek. "I won't be late. And don't worry, I'm all packed."

Amelia looks to Luke, then to me, then back to Luke as he grabs his keys and heads out the door. "What did I miss? Where's he going?"

"He's going to see his Amelia."

I don't say anything for a second, as I hope she's not going to be mad I overstepped my boundaries. But that worry quickly fades as I see the realization on her face. And it comes with a smile.

"Really? He's going on a date?"

"He's taking her for ice cream. I heard ice cream is a very important part of the dating experience."

"It is. Wait. Do we know who she is? Do we like her? What did he tell you about her?"

All of a sudden I don't hear the noise of the movie anymore. Amelia and I look down to see a clearly annoyed Mariah. "Her name is Kylie. She plays softball, and they started talking on the bus during away games. She's like the best softball player at the school. She also plays volleyball, and she's probably going to get a scholarship. She was in the big group that went to prom together. Purple dress, if you look at the group photos. They danced that night, and Luke has been a mess since. She went out with another football player last night, and Luke was a wreck all day. But, I heard that it bombed, so good for Luke to move in now. There. You're all caught up. Can we go back to watching the movie?"

For being four years younger than her brother, Mariah sure has all the information. I bet she'd be a hell of a detective.

"Oh my God, she really is me," Amelia says.

I laugh and bring her back into my arms. "My man has good taste."

Chapter 27
Amelia

I know Shane and I haven't talked about the future in detail, but I need to inform him that yearly trips to the beach need to be in the mix.

The Florida sun is warming my body and soul. The sand between my toes is soft and I love the feel of it on my body. I read a book for the first time in years. I never thought I'd be into romance books, but this one Betsy recommended was quite...enlightening.

Then of course there's the other reason I'm relaxed and possibly the happiest I've been in years. I open my eyes to look over at Shane, who's laying back in the beach chairs we rented for the day. The man is so gorgeous sometimes it hurts to look at him. His tanned skin is shimmering in the sunlight. His red swim trunks are hugging his thick thighs. His defined chest is making me, and every other woman on this beach, drool. That's not an exaggeration. I've noticed at least ten women staring at him.

Sorry, ladies, he's taken.

"Are you staring at me?"

"No..."

He moves the baseball cap he was using to cover his face and turns to look at me. "It's okay. I like it."

I laugh as I reach over for his hand. "This is perfect."

He starts rubbing his thumb over my hand, and I can't help but notice that where he's rubbing is where a ring would sit. I also know we've avoided the conversation long enough. It's probably time I ask him what's been on the tip of my tongue for days now.

"Are we going to talk about it?"

I'm not just talking about how when we get back to Rolling Hills we have to pretend we're engaged. Luckily, we avoided anyone who might know before we left—including Paul. To prevent any dustups or cause any further scenes, Whitley and Jake took Mariah and Luke to meet him at the neutral location of Mona's.

But no, that's not what I want to talk about. I mean, yes, we'll eventually have to game plan—we have to pick them up from Paul, because Whitley and Jake will be on their own vacation—but what I want to talk about is something deeper than that. Something that's been weighing on me over the past few weeks since this happened.

"Which part?"

I mean, that's a fair question. "Which part do you want to talk about?"

He turns a little in his chair to face me. "First, I know I need to apologize."

I shake my head. "You don't. I know I was angry at the time, so I appreciate this, but I also know how things can get out of hand with Paul."

"Want to know the funny thing? I didn't even hesitate telling him that I loved you. Or that we'd get married one day. I wanted to see his face. I wanted to watch the color drain from it. I've punched him before, and it felt good. But seeing that reaction? That was fucking great."

"I know," I say. And I do. Everything Shane is saying makes sense. "But do you?"

Shane tilts his head in confusion. "Do I what?"

"Want to get married?"

Shane quicky gets out of his chair and sits down on the blanket, gesturing me to sit across from him. "Of course, I do. I'd love nothing more. The question is, do you?"

"Can I be honest?"

"Always."

I take a breath, wanting to make sure that I choose every word correctly. "Four months ago? I'd have said no. I had no desire to get married ever again. Then my best friend kissed me."

Shane grins. "Your best friend stands by that decision."

I softly laugh. "And I'm glad he did. And yes, I have thought about it. And every time I have, I've thought, yes, this is something I'd one day want."

"That's good, right?"

"Yes..."

"I now know to wait for the 'but.'"

"You know me so well. But...I don't want to rush. I rushed last time. Yes, most of that was because of Luke. But I was pressured, and it was rushed, and I remember feeling completely out of control of a situation that was literally about me and my life."

"I hate that for you," he says. "I remember when you told me about it. I wanted to tell you not to do it, but I knew it wasn't my place."

I nod. "It wouldn't have mattered. It was happening, whether I liked it or not."

And it was. Our mothers made sure of that. Looking back, I

don't think either of us wanted to. But we felt like our hands were tied. "All I'm saying is that I've done rushed before. I've done the 'we're just doing this because we feel like we have to.' And while I want to marry you, I really do, I don't want us feeling like we're doing it for anyone but us. I want it to be because we both think the time is right. We know this is what we want forever. We're ready for the next chapter of us."

Shane smiles while taking both of my hands in his. "I promise. We're going to get through this ruse of a fake engagement. We'll piss off Paul, which is really fun, and the second he's done being a dad, it will be back to normal. Because, beautiful? When I ask you to marry me, I want you to remember it for the rest of your life."

I smile. "Good. I must say, it was rather disappointing getting engaged and not even being there for it."

This makes him laugh. "God, I'm so sorry. What can I do to make it up to you?"

I lift my eyebrows, which immediately puts a confused look on Shane's face. "I have an idea."

"You KNOW we could have done this at home?"

I laugh as I take my helmet off. "Not like this. Here we got to ride up the coastline. See beaches and beautiful homes. In Rolling Hills we'd be driving past old gas stations, through our two stop lights, and on dirt roads that lead to the hunting trails."

"Fair," Shane says. "Now, get up here so I can hold you."

I smile as I dismount the motorcycle, only to get back on in front of Shane. I lean back into him, my back to his front, as we sit and watch the sun set over the Gulf of Mexico.

I don't know what Shane thought when he said he wanted to make it up to me, but I'm pretty sure he didn't think I'd suggest a coastal motorcycle ride. I thought it was a perfect way to spend the day. Shane loves riding his bike, and I found a place that rents any kind of motorcycle you could want—including a limited-edition Harley Davidson that made Shane's eyes sparkle when he saw it. The air was warm, the scenery was beautiful, and I got to spend it by holding on to the man I love.

Because I do. I love him. I love him so much it hurts sometimes. I love him in a way I've never known before.

"Shane?"

"Yeah, beautiful?"

"This is where I want to get married."

"Really?"

I nod. "Yeah. I just keep staring at the shoreline. The sun setting in this perfect orange and pink backdrop, and all I can think about is that when the time comes, this is where I want it."

"I like the sound of that," he says, kissing me on the top of my head. "Tell me what else you see."

I smile, and suddenly the whole picture is unfolding in front of me. "You're wearing khakis and a white shirt with the sleeves rolled up."

"I'm liking this already. I'd put on a tuxedo for you, but I wouldn't like it."

"I figured," I say through a laugh. "I'm wearing a silky white dress. Both of us are in bare feet. Because...sand."

"Obviously," he says. "Can I make a request?"

"Of course. It's your hypothetical wedding too."

He laughs. "I know our friends will want to be part of it—and we probably have to let Simon officiate if we ever want a moment of peace again—but I think I'd like only one person standing next to me."

I tilt my head back to look up at him. Only one? Between

Oliver, Wes, and his brother Noah, I'm curious who he'd want. "Who?"

"Luke."

I don't even have a chance to try and fight the tears. "Really?"

"Of course," he says. "This wedding wouldn't just be about us. It would be about becoming a family. So, it's fitting if Luke is next to me. Mariah next to you, if that's what you want. The four of us becoming a unit. A family."

Oh, this man... Every time I think he can't do, say, or show any more how he loves me, he goes and says things like that.

I stand so I can turn and straddle myself across his lap. I take his face in my hands and bring him in for a kiss that I hope communicates everything I feel for this man.

"I love you, Shane," I say as I still have his cheeks in my hands. "I love you so much."

"Oh Amelia," he says as he brings our lips back together. I'm mad when it doesn't last longer, but that's only until I hear him say four words I'll never forget. "I love you too."

We fall back into a kiss that's not appropriate for public consumption. Luckily, we found a secluded part of the beach, and even if there were people here right now, I don't care. I love Shane, he loves me, and for the first time in my life, I feel at peace. I feel truly loved. I feel whole.

And it's all because of him.

Our mouths move together in perfect harmony as his hands travel under my T-shirt. It's nothing indecent, but the feel of his gentle touch and callused fingers against my skin is always a welcome sensation.

The kiss deepens, and I can feel Shane getting harder under me. My hips start moving because I'm desperate to find relief in my aching center. Shane's lips move down to my neck, kissing, making me arch back so far that I think I might touch the handlebars of the bike. He starts sucking on my breasts through my shirt, and somehow it's pleasure and pain, because I want to feel him on me. It's actually hurting that I'm only getting fractions of what I could be if his mouth was on me, sucking and nipping in ways only he can do.

"Shane...please..."

He brings me back up so we're looking eye-to-eye. "Here?"

I nod while simultaneously looking around to make sure we haven't been joined by anyone. The sun has set, and there's barely any light on the beach. The only sound is the waves crashing against the sand.

"Yes. Here. Now."

Shane's lips plunge back into mine before he starts inching back. "Stand up."

I do as he says, carefully backing myself up so I can swing my leg over the seat. As soon as I'm standing, Shane appears next to me, turning me around so I'm facing the bike.

"You are so beautiful."

He reaches around me, somehow undoing my jeans from behind.

"So sexy."

He pushes them down my legs, just low enough so I can spread them apart for him.

"And mine."

"Yours," I whisper as I hear Shane undoing his belt. I close my eyes, brace my hands on the bike and lean over from the side, waiting for Shane to take me like only he can. The second I feel his tip lining up to me, I relax, allowing him to slide right in.

I let out a low moan as he dives into me. I know I need to be quiet, but I can't keep this in. Between the thrill of being seen and the sensation of Shane thrusting into me, I'm absolutely lust drunk.

Freeing.

That's what this is. Over the past few months, being with Shane, I've started feeling like a new me. I worked for years to shed the skin I grew when I was married. I fought and clawed to become the me I almost forgot I was.

But with Shane? He's helped me find me. The parts that were missing. The parts I thought disappeared. The parts I never knew I had.

He's made me whole.

I don't know if I can ever thank him enough for that. But I know I'll try.

I'll try for the rest of my life.

"Amelia." My name is a whisper from his lips.

"Yes," I say, needing the release.

Shane starts pumping harder into me. I try to hold onto the bike, but there's nothing for me to grip onto. I feel Shane's hand wrapping around my stomach, his fingers traveling down to rub the spot that sends me every time.

And he does.

I yell so loud I know anyone could hear me, even if they are miles away. Shane follows me, his lower and guttural. He falls over on me, both of us using the motorcycle underneath us to hold on. It's the only thing stopping us from falling to the ground.

But it would be okay. We'd be doing it together. And I think that if we're together, everything is going to be okay.

Chapter 28
Amelia

"This feels weird."

For the hundredth time in the past ten minutes, I play with the fake engagement ring that's now sitting on my finger. It's been a while since I've worn anything there—even when I was married, it was just a wedding band. This ring is a thirty-dollar cubic zirconium that we picked up from a store on our way back from Florida. But unless Paul's new girlfriend has schooled him in fine jewelry, I doubt he'll notice. But he *would* notice if I wasn't wearing one. And we need to keep the ruse going for today. So fake engagement ring it is.

"I'm not going to lie; it looks good on you."

I laugh and bite my lip, my eyes wandering around to see if anyone is looking at us as Shane takes both of my hands in his. We're in the back corner booth, but still, this is Rolling Hills. Spreading gossip and rumors is the town's pastime.

"We need to be careful. Remember, people still don't know. Oliver doesn't know. And if he finds out through the town's gossip page, it will break his heart."

I might have said those words, but my actions don't match. I haven't pulled my hands away. The shit-eating grin is still on my face. And I'm pretty sure the look I'm giving Shane screams, "We had sex this morning and that's why I'm walking a little funny."

"I know," Shane says as he slowly pulls his hands away. "After we get the kids today, I'll head to his place. He'll know today, and then we can tell our moms. After that, we've covered everyone who should hear it firsthand that we're together."

"Good plan," I say as Mona approaches our table with coffee and water. I quickly hide my left hand under the table. Last thing I need is for Mona to catch me with the ring on. That's a recipe for disaster.

"So how long has this been going on?"

My eyes nearly pop out of my head. Shane's face is slowly losing color. "What do you mean?"

Mona shakes her head. "Quit your damn lying. I saw you two holding hands. You think you're slick? You're not. Amelia here looks like a whole new woman, and this one over here is smiling. I haven't seen him smile since the Fury won the championship. So we can do one of two things: You can either tell me now so I know what to tell everyone. Or you can let my imagination run wild."

I look over to Shane, hoping we can silently agree on the first option, when the sight of Paul's Hummer pulls in. I mean, you can't miss it. The thing is huge.

"I see your ex is here in the car he's using to compensate for what I'm guessing he's lacking in other departments."

I can't even laugh at Mona's joke. My stomach is in a sudden knot, and my hands are sweating. I've never been a liar, let alone a good one. Yes, I was able to sneak out a few times back in high school. Yes. I've expanded on the truth. But keeping up a completely untrue story like this? I don't know if I have it in me. Hell, I cracked the first time my kids asked me about Santa.

"Hey," Shane says, taking my hands back in his, despite Mona as our audience. "You and me. We got this."

I nod and squeeze his hands. "We got this."

We stand up from the booth, and that's when I hear the loud gasp from Mona. I turn back to look at her and she's pointing to my ring.

Fuck.

"What's that!"

I turn to look outside, then back to Mona. "Listen, we have to get the kids and put their bags in the car. And I don't want Paul coming in here. Let us go take care of that and when we come back in here, we'll explain everything."

"You can explain over waffles. We're about to have another Rolling Hills wedding!"

I ignore Mona, knowing I need to get outside. Yes, the kids could come in here by themselves, but it's Sunday at Mona's. There's barely room for people, let alone suitcases, backpacks, and whatever souvenirs Mariah bought. But if they come in, I have a feeling Paul will as well. And the last thing I need him doing is starting shit at my favorite breakfast place in front of the town and people I consider friends and family.

Shane takes my hand in his as we walk toward Paul's monstrosity of a car. He's staring at us as the kids unload their bags.

What a guy...

I do notice that there's no sign of his new girlfriend. Interesting...

"Mom! Shane!"

Mariah drops the bag she was holding and sprints over to us, jumping into my arms. I didn't realize until now I how much I truly missed them. This is the longest we've ever been apart. "Did you have fun?"

"The good parts were good. The bad parts were both bad and entertaining." I look down at her, and her smile that is both sweet and terrifying, before she moves to give Shane a hug.

Oh hell, what did my daughter do...

"Hey, Mom," Luke says, walking over with an armful of the bags.

"Hey, sweetheart," I say, giving him a hug and a kiss on the cheek. "Did everything go okay?"

He shrugs. "We'll talk later."

Luke and Shane give each other a quick "bro hug" as I like to call it, when I feel Paul's hateful glare directed our way.

"Enough with the family reunion," Paul mumbles. "Nice ring."

I smile, loving that the plan is working. "Thank you."

He rolls his eyes. "Can we talk, Mel?"

Shane whispers something to Luke, who leads Mariah toward Mona's, before taking my hand. "You can talk to us."

Paul rolls his eyes. "I didn't say I wanted to talk to you. I want to talk to my wife."

In the emergency room, there's a slight moment of calm before you hear the blaring sounds of the ambulance's coming in.

This is that silence. Shane's grip becomes tighter on my hand. I see his face turning red out of the corner of my eye. This man is about to Hulk out more than he ever has in his entire life.

"That's not your wife. She's going to be mine. Don't you fucking ever call her that again."

This only makes Paul laugh.

Wrong move, my man. Wrong move.

"Last I checked you weren't married. Hell, I don't even think you're really engaged."

"You think what you want. But last I checked, you're the one who fucked every woman in this town when you had the best one right in front of you."

The two are toe-to-toe right now, and if I don't stop this, there's going to be a freaking fight in Mona's parking lot.

"Just wait," Paul says. "After a while she'll stop giving it to you, too. You'll understand where I was coming from."

I see Shane pull back his arm, but I'm quick enough to grab it.

"Don't."

I don't know how I stop him. His arm is bigger than my thigh. But somehow I do. Shane slowly backs away, lowering his arm as I step in front of him. Paul's smile is downright bone chilling. It's a smile that used to haunt me in my dreams. The one where he thought he was getting away with things. Back then I just ignored it.

I'm not anymore. I'm not that woman anymore. I'm stronger. Tougher. Smarter. I'm the Amelia I was always meant to be.

"You wanted to talk. Let's talk. But Shane stays. He's my partner and my fiancé. Get used to it."

Paul looks at Shane, who I think is actually shaking from rage right now, before looking back to me. "Fine. I guess congratulations are in order then?"

"Thank you," I say, even though I know he's not being sincere. "But I doubt you wanted to talk to me about my engagement."

"No. I wanted to talk to you about the kids."

"What about them?"

"Mariah and Luke were very rude to Staci during the trip.

And me. So much so that she left early and isn't returning my calls."

Okay, if he just said that about Mariah, I could see it. But Luke? My child, who still scoops up spiders so he can release them into the wild? If he did do this, my boy was pushed to the limit.

"What happened?"

"Mariah was making rude comments all trip. About what Staci was wearing. Or asking her how old she was. She even asked her if they were going to be in the same class next year."

How I push down my laugh I don't know. Also, my girl is about to get the spending spree of a lifetime at Ulta. "Did something happen to instigate it? I'm sure Mariah didn't just start saying something without reason. And you said Luke was in on this?"

"Are you accusing Staci of starting this?"

I shake my head. "I'm not accusing anyone. I'm just trying to get your side of the story before I talk to the kids."

"Oh, I talked to the kids," he says. "I told Mariah she needed to apologize."

"Did she?"

"I told her not to."

The words are from Luke, and I barely recognize his tone. It's deep. Firm. His stance is protective.

It reminds me of Shane.

"You wouldn't stop asking us about Mom and Shane," Luke begins. "It was all he would talk about for the first few days. Grilling us to see if you two were together, or if this was fake. Or if you were doing it just to make him mad. That's all we heard."

"That's not true," Paul says, though judging by how his voice pitches upward, I'm going to guess that's a lie.

"Staci was pissed. I mean, she seemed bored anyway. I

doubt her dream vacation with her new boyfriend was him and his two kids at Myrtle Beach. We heard her on the phone one night complaining about you, about us, and then started talking crap about Mom. She was saying horrible things, Dad. Mariah and I both heard them."

"Quit lying, Luke," Paul says.

"I'm not lying. We weren't trying to eavesdrop, but when we heard what she was talking about, we stayed and listened. She caught us but didn't acknowledge us. Just got up and walked away. Next day comes, and she's horrible to us. Told Mariah she needed to cover up because she didn't look good in her bathing suit. Made me basically be her cabana boy. I sucked it up and kept my mouth shut, and I tried to tell Mariah to do the same thing, but we all know how that was going to go. You're lucky I reined her in as much as I did."

Paul looks at Luke, then to me. "Well, he admitted it. Aren't you going to say something to him? Punish him? They should, at the bare minimum, apologize to Staci."

I can't keep the laughter in anymore. Because that's fucking funny. "Oh, you're serious?"

Now it's Paul's turn for the beet-red face. "Yes! Is that how you're going to raise our children? To be able to talk to elders like that?"

"She's twenty-one, Dad. I don't think you can call her an elder."

My son doesn't throw out burns often, but when he does, they are scorching.

"You stay out of it."

Okay, that's enough. "Paul. From what I heard, Luke and Mariah did nothing wrong. Yes, they shouldn't have eavesdropped, but I can't say I blame them for that. You started this with your inability to process that I'm happy, and mad as hell that I've found that happiness with Shane. Then you take it out on the kids and try to put them in the middle. Hell, you didn't even do that when we got divorced. Then, you're going to blame them because your *very young* girlfriend talked shit about me and treated your kids like crap? I've never understood how your brain works, and today is just another day of that. Because if you think Luke and Mariah are at fault, you're more delusional than I thought."

I stand up a little straighter, proud of myself for standing up to him and the kids. I didn't use to do that. Even within the last few years if we had an argument, I would back down if I didn't think I could hold my own.

But not anymore. Especially now that I see Shane standing on one side of me and Luke on the other.

"I'm done," Paul says, typically not taking any accountability. "It's clear you've poisoned my kids against me."

"You did that all by yourself," I say. "You didn't need any help from me."

Paul turns and looks at Luke. "See? She's blaming you. Not taking any accountability."

"Don't talk about accountability, Dad. You don't know the definition of the fucking word. Now leave. We don't want you here."

Out of all the things said in this exchange, Luke dropping an F-bomb might be the most shocking. Because that might be the meanest thing my son has ever said.

I'm so proud.

"Luke. Don't talk to—"

"He said to leave, Paul. I'd suggest you do that."

I've held the Hulk back long enough. I'm not stopping him this time.

Shane steps in front of us, slowly backing Paul up to his Hummer. He goes to grab the rest of the bags, his eyes never leaving Paul.

"I'll take good care of them, Paul. Don't worry."

And with a huff and a slam of the car door, Paul peels out of the parking lot.

"Mom, I'm so sorry," Luke says. "I know I swore, but I was mad and—"

I pull Luke into the biggest hug I've ever given him. "Don't you apologize for a thing. You said what you needed to say, and frankly, there is no one more fitting to get your first F-bomb than your father."

He laughs. "Thanks."

Shane comes over and pats him on the back. "Proud of you. What you said here? What you probably had to navigate on the trip? That was a lot."

Luke nods as we hurry to drop the bags into my car before heading back into Mona's. "It was. Being on Mariah duty was a full-time job."

"Don't I know it."

We start walking back toward the diner when I catch a glimpse of something through the window I can't quite make out.

Are those balloons? And streamers? And is that my mom? When did she get here?

"Shit..."

The three of us are silent when we get to the door and see Mariah barging out, her eyes as wide as saucers.

"I'm sorry, guys. I couldn't stop them."

As soon as we walk in, I realize what she's talking about.

This is about to get bad. Really bad.

Chapter 29
Shane

"Happy engagement!"

The screams and the cheers are so loud I am nearly knocked over from the volume. I take Amelia's hand to brace myself, because...what in the actual fuck is going on?

The diner isn't the same place we walked out of twenty minutes ago. Earlier it was just the normal, busy Sunday breakfast crowd. Now there are balloons and streamers all over. Everyone is standing and cheering. And is someone pouring champagne?

"When did this all happen?" Amelia asks. "How long were we outside?"

"Long enough for this to get out of fucking control."

All of a sudden Simon appears, looking gassed.

"When did you get here?" I ask.

He bends at the waist as he tries to catch his breath. "I was driving past when I saw you and douchebag about to square up, and I haven't been in a fight in a while so I thought it might be fun. But when I pulled in, Mariah grabbed me and told me that she needed me inside. When I came in, I was informed that everyone just found out you two were engaged, and since no one knew you were even dating, that a celebration was in order. And don't ask me where Mona got the champagne. I'm too scared to ask. She then made me go get the balloons and streamers I had in my car."

"How? Why? What do you mean you have balloons and streamers in your car?"

"I keep them on me just in case," Simon says. "Mona asked me if I had any leftover from when we surprised Oliver. And she's scary right now, so I followed directions."

I take a deep breath as I try to grasp my bearings. But when I look around, I'm even more off kilter.

"Oh my God."

Amelia said it, but I was thinking it. This place is insane. I'm pretty sure I'm barely blinking as we start walking through the crowd that is sending us congratulations. Then I see the booth we were sitting at with a cake now on top of it.

And it's being occupied by Barb Cunningham and Tammy Evans.

And they look pissed.

"Shit," I say under my breath. I'm guessing Amelia heard me because her hand tightens against mine. "Mom alert."

"When did they get here?" she whispers back. "Also, what the hell are we going to do?"

"Go with it," I whisper back, doing my best not to move my mouth. Instead, I plaster on a smile I know must look fake as hell. Maybe since I rarely smile, people will think this is what I look like?

"Everyone! Can I have your attention please?"

I look up at Simon, who has taken it upon himself to stand on a chair in the middle of the diner and play master of ceremonies. I pull him down so I can whisper, because if I didn't, everyone right now would hear me cuss him out. "What the fuck are you doing?"

"Getting control of the situation."

"By putting all eyes on us?"

"Would you rather have me do this or Mona? Or better yet, do nothing so you are forced to go talk to your mothers, who look like they're about to internally combust?"

"Good plan." I pat him on the back. He may be my most frustrating friend, but he's damn good under pressure.

"Everyone, I know today is coming as a surprise to many of you. Me as well. I had *no* idea two of my best friends were sneaking around on us this whole time. You two are sneaky, I tell ya."

This gets a laugh out of the crowd, and a fake one from Amelia and me. She steps in closer, and I put my arm around her so she's flush against my side. I hate that the first time we're in public together that everyone is staring at us. And I hate that I'm holding her because we're nervous, not because of happiness.

"I kid. I was one of the few who knew they were together, but I should have seen it long before that. The two of them have never been happier. Did anyone know Officer Shane Cunningham could smile? Well, he can! And boy does he do it anytime he hears Amelia's name."

As if on cue, I feel myself smiling as I look down to Amelia. A few tears have escaped as she looks up at me. I know Simon's doing this to take the pressure off us—and to continue our story because none of us know what the plan is—but that doesn't make his words any less true.

"Amelia...I'm going to save the speech about how I defended your honor, multiple times, for the wedding. But know this. I love you like a sister. And there is no one, I mean no one, better matched for this man than you."

"Thank you," I hear her whisper. Simon nods in return and grabs a coffee mug from the table beneath him.

"With that, raise your cups of coffee—or champagne. To Shane and Amelia!"

"To Shane and Amelia!"

Everyone in the diner starts applauding, including Luke and Mariah, who somehow found noisemakers.

"Thanks," I say as Simon steps down from the chair. "You didn't need to do that."

"Oh, but I did, my friend. That's a glimpse of my best man speech."

"I thought you were officiating?" Amelia asks.

"Who says I can't do both?"

"You're not doing both," I say. "Speaking of best men, do we know where Oliver is? I don't want him finding out like this, or walking in and seeing everything."

"First off, rude," Simon says. "Second, he's been in his dark place."

"Why?" Amelia asks. "Is he okay? Did something happen with Izzy? We need to go see him."

Simon shakes his head. "Don't. He told me he'd come up for air when he was ready, but not now."

Before we can ask any more about Oliver, I hear the very loud, and very distinct, noise of my mother clearing her throat. It's her tried and true way to get anyone's attention.

"Good luck with that," Simon whispers before he ducks and weaves back into the crowd.

"Here we go," I say, taking Amelia's hand as we walk over and sit in the booth. Our mothers are sitting across from us, their faces blank. I'd rather have angry right now. Anger I know how to deal with. Not knowing what's about to hit us? That's the worst.

"Mom, I'm—"

Tammy cuts me off. "No. We're going to start."

"Mrs. Evans, let me—"

"She *said* we're going to start, Shane."

I hang my head. "Yes, ma'am."

"Tammy, did you know our children were dating?"

"I didn't, Barb."

"Don't you think that's odd, that we're the last to find out?"

"I do, Barb."

"Actually, you're not the last," Amelia speaks up. "We haven't told Oliver."

"Oh!" Tammy says, dramatically throwing her arms in the air. "Well, since *Oliver* doesn't know, that makes everything so much better."

"First of all, why are you keeping that boy in the dark?" Mom says. "And second, why are we in the dark? We should have been the first people you told. How long has this been going on?"

Amelia and I look at each other and nod. This part is easy. This we can tell the truth on.

"I told her how I felt in the spring," I say.

My mom narrows her eyes. "*When* in the spring?"

I brace myself for the impact from what I'm about to say. "At Jake and Whitley's wedding."

I see the moment of recognition on my mom's face. "Shane Thomas Cunningham, are you meaning to tell me that I asked you if anything happened at the wedding and you lied to my face?"

I nod, and internally wince from the use of my middle name. "I'm sorry, Mom. I promise though, at that conversation, nothing was happening. We were figuring things out."

"How could you not tell me? And even after that, once this started? How could you keep this a secret?"

"Don't be mad at Shane, Mrs. Cunningham. It was my idea to hide it," Amelia says.

"Why?" Tammy asks. "You had to know we'd be excited. Even though we're mad now, we're happier than pigs in slop."

"I know...it's just...." Amelia looks at me. Her eyes are a little sad, and I get why. Our bubble has just burst wide open. I take her hand in mine, holding it on top of the table."At first, we wanted to make sure this was the real thing. That we both felt the same way for each other. We didn't want to tell people, and then quickly realize that we weren't compatible."

"But clearly you are." Tammy makes a gesture to our joined hands. And the fake engagement ring. "So why the secrecy after? And how do you not tell us you're engaged?"

"Because we wanted some time to ourselves," Amelia says. "I know that was probably selfish, but we knew what the reaction was going to be."

"Reaction? Do you think we'd have a reaction?"

Amelia looks at me, and if she's wondering if this is a trick question, we're on the same page. "Mom, in second grade you made sure that I had a special card for Shane for Valentine's Day because the 'cheap ones weren't good enough for my future husband.'"

"You two dressed us up in couples Halloween costumes until we were five, and you only stopped because Amelia refused to wear another princess dress," I add. "Can you blame us for wanting to delay the freakout?"

Mom and Tammy look at each other, their faces still blank. I'm holding my breath, and I'm pretty sure Amelia is too. We don't have to do it for long though, because our mother's faces turn from angry to the happiest I've ever seen in a blink of an eye.

"This has been my dream, our dream, for so long," Mom says as she reaches over to grab my hand.

"When you had to marry Paul, I knew it was the right thing at the time," Tammy says to Amelia. "But in my heart I always wanted it to be Shane for you."

"Thanks?" Amelia says. "We're very happy, but you need to know something about the engagement."

"Yes, the engagement. We want to hear all about that later," Tammy says as she stands up out of the booth. "But not now. We have so much to do."

"What is there to do?" I ask. "Because we'd really like to talk to you both more about it. Now."

"Oh, Shane, you just sit back and be the groom. Which means show up when we, or Amelia, tell you."

"Um, but we need to tell you something."

Amelia and I quickly jump out of the booth. We need to stop them.

"It can wait," Mom says. "We have to start making calls."

"I'll get a hold of Whitley," Tammy says. "So nice now to have an event planner as a daughter-in-law."

"Good. And I'll go find that binder we started making a few years ago. It has all the samples of things we liked."

"Binder?" Amelia asks with a touch of panic in her voice. "Mom, Mrs. Cunningham—"

"Oh Amelia. Cut that Mrs. Cunningham crap. You're about to be my daughter. You call me Barb. Or Mom. Whatever you like. Hopefully soon it will be Gigi."

Amelia looks over to me for help, which I don't know how to give her right now. This is like being able to see the car accident in progress but not being able to do a damn thing to stop it.

"Mom. Tammy. How about we take a breath? Maybe go back to Amelia's house and sit down and talk. Away from all of the craziness."

"We will, but we need to get this all rolling," Barb says. "Mona!"

Mona turns toward my mom, six plates somehow balanced on her arms. "Yeah?"

"Hold a spot for me for the groom's cake. I know Shane loves your red velvet. I'll call you later and let you know the date."

"You got it!"

"Mom, I don't think we'll—"

"You shush," Mom says to me after she gives me a kiss on the check. "We'll be over early next week so we can start going over everything. But you two just sit back and relax. Tammy and I have this all under control."

I stand, slack-jawed, as our mothers walk out of Mona's hugging everyone who congratulates them. Amelia and I don't move. How can we? I'm trying to process everything that's just happened, and, oh yeah, we're still in the diner, where everyone thinks we're engaged.

I see Simon, Luke, and Mariah walk toward us, concerned looks on their faces.

"What just happened?" Mariah asks.

"I have no idea, Pipsqueak. I have no idea."

Amelia

I PACE WHEN I'M NERVOUS. OR STRESSED. OR FEEL LIKE I'm not in control of a situation. Needless to say, I've made so many laps around my living room in the past hour that I'm pretty sure I've walked a marathon.

"What in the hell just happened?"

I'm asking the question out loud, but I don't expect Shane to have an answer. He looks just as lost and confused as I do. Only he doesn't pace. He sits and stares at the floor with his hands clasped.

"Mom? Shane? We have another problem."

I roll my eyes in frustration as Mariah comes down the stairs. "What now?"

"Grandma and Shane's mom created a Facebook event for your official engagement party. They've invited the whole town. And they're asking for people to submit pictures of both of you over the years for their slideshow."

"Oh, for fuck's sake!"

I plop down on the couch next to Shane. I can't pace

anymore. I feel like this is a freaking tornado, and we're caught in the twister.

"Thanks, sweetie," I say. "Can you give Shane and I a minute? Also see if Oliver has RSVP'd? He still doesn't know because this keeps spinning out of damn control."

"On it. I'll hack into their Facebooks. I'm pretty sure Grandma's password is her birthday or something. I can also change the settings to cancel it, but for Grandma to still think it's there. Anything else?"

"See if anyone posted pictures of today and get rid of them. Any means necessary." I realize that yes, I'm telling my child to violate someone's privacy. But at least she's using her powers for good.

Mariah gives me a nod as she heads back upstairs. When I look over to Shane, he seems even more defeated than just a minute ago.

"An engagement party? Shane, what in the world is going on?"

He slowly sits up and looks at me, and my heart immediately hurts from the sadness in his eyes. "I'm so sorry. This is all my fault."

I shake my head. "No, it's not. I'm in this as well," I say as I hold open my arms. He comes into them, and for a minute we just sit like this, comforting each other. For the first time in what feels like hours, I feel some sort of peace.

Then I see the ring still on my finger. In the chaos I must have forgotten to take it off.

"This is just as much my fault as any," I say. "I was so desperate to control the situation, and now it's completely out of control. If I would have just allowed us to come out with the truth at first, maybe it wouldn't have blown up like this."

"No one could have seen this coming," he says as he sits

back up, but makes sure to take hold of my hand. "I guess all we can do now is regroup. Figure out what to do next."

I nod. "You're right."

Except neither of us say anything. We sit on my couch in total silence. I'm begging my brain to come up with something, anything, to figure out how to control this situation, but I can't think of anything.

"Option one," I begin. "We sit our mothers down. Tie them to a chair if we need to. And tell them that we are together. We are dating. But the engagement was a lie that spiraled out of control."

Shane shrugs. "Would they believe us? At this point they probably would just think that we're trying to get them to quit planning the wedding."

"True, or if they do believe us, they won't let up. Remember how hard they pushed for us in high school to date? This would be that times a thousand."

"So what I'm hearing is letting them believe this is actually the best option?"

"I don't know if it's the best, but it's not worst."

"Okay." Shane pauses before his eyes light up with an idea. "You said everyone in town chose your side in the divorce, right?"

"Yes. Well, everyone except Paul's mother, Jessica, her crew, and a few of his old high school buddies."

"So enough people that if we came out and said that we aren't getting married..."

"It will get back to him and he'll gloat for months. That is, without a doubt, the last option."

I know this is insane right now, but I need my pride. And I need Paul *not* to say I told you so.

"You're right." Shane goes quiet for a second, and I figure he's trying to come up with a solution. That's what I'm doing.

More specifically, trying to figure out how to gently tell our mothers, and the town, what happened with the least amount of collateral damage.

"Can I ask you a question?"

I look over to Shane, whose head is now resting on the back of the couch. "Sure."

"What if this wasn't fake?"

Now that makes me sit straight up. "What do you mean?"

"I mean what if we just did it?"

"Get married?"

"Yeah. Get married."

I blink a few times to make sure this is real. I even bite the inside of my cheek to make sure I didn't fall asleep on the couch out of mental exhaustion. Because no way is Shane asking me this. Not like this. Not on my couch out of desperation.

"Because we can't."

Judging by the confusion on his face, I don't think that was the answer he expected. "Why not?"

"Because!" I say, standing back up. I need to pace again. "We just started dating. Despite that yes, this feels easy and I love you, we've barely been together three months. And you want to get married because we started a secret, that turned into a lie, that is now completely out of our control? How is that going to help anything?"

"Yes, it does fix things, but that's not why I want to marry you." Shane stands up from the couch and puts his hands on my shoulders as I pass by, stopping me from my pacing. "I want to marry you because I love you. I want to marry you because I want to start our life together. This might not be how I envisioned it, but what if this is just the way it was supposed to happen?"

I shake my head and walk away from his hold. "No, Shane. I love you. I do. But we aren't ready for that kind of step."

"What do you mean we're not ready?"

"We're not!" How can I make him see this? How does he not see this? "I wanted time for us to date. To get to know each other as a couple. Which we did, and we still are. Just because I know what side of the bed you like now doesn't mean we're ready to get married."

"We can figure that out!" Shane says, his voice rising. Shit, I don't want the kids to hear this.

"Yes, we can," I say at a lower volume, hoping that he follows my lead. "And I'm not saying that we have to wait forever. But I *am* saying that doing it now isn't the answer. Getting married because you feel like your hands are tied isn't the answer."

Believe me. I know.

That's how I want to end that statement to Shane, but something inside stops me from saying that. Because Shane knows that's how I felt before. I don't want to have to say it out loud. The last thing I want to do right now is reiterate to Shane that I've already been pressured into getting married once, and I'm not about to do it again. But I need him to see that. Because comparing his proposal just now to what happened with me and Paul will likely end in a fight I don't want to get into right now. Or ever.

"I guess," he says. In no way is he seeing what I'm saying, but, like me, he doesn't want to turn this into a fight. "Then what do we do now?"

"We go along with it," I say reluctantly. "But every time we're with our mothers, we try and softly bring up that we don't want to rush, and we want to take this slow. Maybe if we get them to take their feet off the gas pedals, we can eventually talk to them in a rational tone they'll understand."

"Okay," he says. "Whatever you want."

"Shane..."

He starts walking out of the room before stopping to turn around. His face is sad, and it breaks my heart. I want to go to him. I want to take that look off his face. But I know the only thing that will make that happen is for me agreeing to marry him, and I can't do that. At least not right now.

"I'm sorry."

He shakes his head. "Just forget I said anything."

Easier said than done.

Chapter 31
Shane

"Th at chicken piccata was th e best thing I've ever tasted, and if you don't have it at your wedding I will boycott."

"Don't threaten me with a good time."

Simon slams his foot on the brake of his BMW. Luckily, we just pulled into the parking lot of the last caterer appointment of the day, so we aren't in danger of causing an accident.

"Do you see any other friends here helping you pick out food for a wedding you don't intend to have? No. That's just me. So joke all you want, but if I boycott, you might be without a bridal party for this pretend bash."

I roll my eyes as I get out of his car. He's technically right, he has been the only one able to help me through all of this. Wes got back from his extended vacation but then had to jump right into his new job as the Rolling Hills High School football coach. Oliver is out of commission, which is a saga in its own right.

That leaves me with Simon.

Yay.

"You know there's going to be a bridal party, asshole," I say.

"For your pretend wedding? Or is there a real one you've failed to inform me about?"

I give him a glare as we approach the front desk of the catering company's public entrance, which gives all the vibes of a small restaurant. I do my best to put away my sour mood, but I don't think it works.

"We have an appointment. Name's Cunningham."

"Yes, right this way," the receptionist says as she takes us into another room, where there are a handful of tables. "Just give us a minute and one of our staff members will be out to go over everything with you."

"We're in no rush. Thanks, darlin'."

Simon's smile and deployment of his exaggerated Southern drawl makes the receptionist giggle as she leaves the room. I just shake my head, because I can't believe that shit works for him. I've seen him use it many times over the years, and it has an impressive success rate. Impressive in the fact that I don't know how he gets women to go home with him.

"What's on the menu for this place?" Simon asks as he looks at the menu that's waiting in front of us. "Because if it's another piccata, this place has already lost."

"I don't know. Don't fucking care, either."

And I don't. Because I'm over it. I'm over tasting different kinds of chicken. I'm over Simon's smartass comments. And I'm over pretending to plan a wedding Amelia doesn't want but I do.

"Okay, I need to ask, what the fuck is up with you?"

I look at Simon to see if he's asking this in a genuine way or a smartass way. It's usually smartass, which means I can give my normal minimum word answer and we can sit here in silence and wait for the food.

But when I do, the cocky look isn't there. Gone is the playboy of a minute ago who was trying to pick up a woman he just met. This is the Simon only a few know. And this Simon is the reason why he's one of my best friends.

"Last week, after the insanity at Mona's, Amelia and I tried to sit down and figure out what we were going to do about the engagement. I suggested we go through with it."

Simon's eyes double in size. "You asked her to marry you?"

"Doesn't matter," I say. "She says we're not ready."

"One, it does matter. Two, if that's what she says, then that's what goes."

"Apparently this is how it works." My comment comes out sarcastic and bitter. I know it does. And I don't care that it did.

"Whoa!" Simon says. "That was a fucking dick thing to say."

"Why?" I ask. I know my anger is bubbling up right now, but I can't help it.

"Why did you say it like that? If she doesn't want to marry you, then she doesn't. Hard line, my friend. Hard line."

I feel my blood starting to heat. I do my best to push it down, but I don't think it's doing much good. "I'm just a little tired of giving her everything, and the one time I ask her for something she turns me down. And she wouldn't even consider it. It would solve everything, and she dismissed it."

Simon gives me a look like I'm an idiot. And I probably am. But I'm mad. And the more this goes on, the angrier I get.

"Listen, I know you love her. I know she's been your dream girl for apparently our entire lives. And you want to make her happy. Which is great. Everyone wants Amelia to be happy. We also want you to be happy. But this isn't bringing her coffee or conceding on where you're going for dinner. This is marriage. That's a big fucking ask. Something, might I remind you, she's done before—and it didn't end well."

"Are you comparing me to that asshat?"

"No, I'm not, Hulk. Calm down. I'm just saying you might

think marriage is an easy solution, but for Amelia, it probably isn't. She probably doesn't associate that word with anything happy. So maybe cut her some slack."

He's right. I hate it when he's right.

I should know this. And her happiness means everything to me.

But I thought mine did too.

"I just want her to consider it," I say. "She wouldn't even do that."

"Maybe because you guys just got together. Or maybe because it's been a whirlwind since you have. Or maybe because she doesn't want to marry your grumpy ass."

"It's not that," I say. At least, I hope it's not that. No. It's not. I remember back to our night on the bike in Florida. Picturing our wedding. The beach. Our family. Our friends. She wants it. I know she does, so why not now? Why would she say all of that if she didn't want it?

And on top of that, why am I here? Why is she at the florist? Why are we still entertaining and placating our mothers? Because it's one thing to let them believe we're engaged, it's another to actively plan a wedding.

"I bet it is." Simon stands up and flashes his phone to me. "It's Emmett. I have to take this. If the food comes out, don't you dare start without me. And if there's piccata, just send it back."

I wave him away, which is returned with a middle finger of his own. Just as he walks out of the tasting room, I see a woman carrying a tray of food over my way.

"You must be Shane. Hi. I'm Charlie. I'm one of the sous chefs here, and if you pick us, I'd be the one cooking the food for your wedding."

"Nice to meet you." I plaster on a smile. I don't know what she knows, but I'm guessing she thinks this is a regular tasting, just like the last two. Granted, the first was with Mona, because she insisted she could cater the wedding with breakfast foods.

"Just you today?" Charlie asks. "Whitley wasn't sure if it was going to be you or your fiancée as well."

"My fiancée is meeting with the florist today. You know Whitley?"

She nods as she sets out the plates. "I've worked with Whitley on a bunch of weddings, including her own. Honestly? That's how you guys got in here today with such short notice. Whitley called in a favor."

"Interesting."

Whitley knows this is fake. At least I think she does? At this point, I don't know who fucking knows what. If she does, why would she use a favor for something that she knows isn't real? But what if she doesn't? If that's the case, and she thought this was on the up-and-up, at some point I'd have to believe that Amelia would have told her not to bother.

Is Amelia changing her mind? Or at the least maybe reconsidering? Is that why I'm here? For the first time all day, I feel a little more at ease. Not as angry. Like there's hope. I know I'm grasping at straws, but I'll take anything right now.

"Okay, let's get started with the appetizers." Before Charlie can go on, I watch her cheerful demeanor turn to straight rage as she looks over my head toward the direction of the entrance. When I turn around, I see Simon standing there, leaning in the doorway, a smug look on his face.

"Hey, Bug."

"What the hell are you doing here?"

My head is turning between Simon and Charlie like I'm watching a tennis match. How the hell do they know each other? At least I'm assuming they do. I'd assume that Simon hooked up with her—and then didn't call her back. That's the easy guess. But he used a nickname for her. That is way too intimate for one of Simon's one-night conquests.

"Out of all the catering companies in all of Nashville, I have to be at yours?"

He starts walking back to our table as Charlie continues to glare at him. Ten minutes ago, I'd have described her as having a very pleasant demeanor. Perky, even. But now I'm terrified.

"What are you doing here?"

He pats me on the back as he comes back to our table, but doesn't sit down. "I'm the best man at this guy's wedding. I'm here to taste the food. Make sure it doesn't have poison in it."

"He's not my best man."

"Don't listen to him," Simon says. "So what do we have here today?"

He makes a show of pulling out his chair and sitting back down. He even snaps the napkin in the air before setting it across his lap. With everything he does, Charlie's face gets more and more red. I know they call me the Hulk, but she's three seconds away from smashing Simon into this table.

"I don't think it's a good idea for you to be here."

"Why not, Bug? Can't concentrate with me around? It's a problem for many."

"Why are you the way you are?"

"We've been asking that question for years," I offer in solidarity.

"Oh, stop. You love me," he says to me. "Now, what are we eating? I just had a mean chicken piccata that it's your job to beat."

Charlie narrows her eyes at Simon before visibly taking a few deep breaths to calm herself. I sneak a glance to Simon, who's sitting back in his chair, foot resting across his leg, like he doesn't have a care in the world.

I don't know how, but I'm going to bet my pension that he fucked this woman over. And bad.

"Shane, I think it would be best if we rescheduled. Maybe when you can come with your fiancée. Or I can have one of our servers bring you out the courses for you to choose from."

I look over to Simon, who looks quite pleased with himself. "Can you just fucking stop it?"

"What? I'm not doing anything."

"You're existing."

"Fine," he says, standing up. "I'll leave. Because I'm a gentleman. You remember that, Bug, don't you?"

I know I'm a police officer, and if I witness a crime I should do something about it. But if Charlie were to kill Simon right here in front of me, I'd testify that I didn't see a thing.

"Please leave, Simon."

Simon doesn't say anything, and for just a second, I feel like I see a hint of apology on his face. But as quickly as it appeared, it vanishes, and he walks out of the tasting room.

"I'm sorry," I say. "Whatever he did, I want you to know, you're right and he's wrong. No questions asked."

She laughs, and I can tell she's pushing back tears. "Thanks. I'll go ahead and bring out the rest of your food."

Charlie turns and hurriedly walks back toward her kitchen. She doesn't come back out, instead sending out a server to present me the dinner options.

Oh, Simon, what the hell did you do to this poor woman?

Chapter 32
Amelia

"Oh, Amelia! You look absolutely stunning!"

"My baby girl is finally in a wedding dress. I think I might cry."

I might cry too. But not for the same reason my mother is going to be.

Horror. Straight horror. This wedding dress might be the worst thing I've ever put on my body. I didn't know that much tulle could exist in a dress. And then there are the beads. And the random additions of lace and sequins.

If I didn't want to get married before, I definitely don't now. I hate to judge people, but who in their right mind would wear this?

I turn around from the mirrors to look at Mom and Barb, who are both sitting on the couch at the bridal store, and I swear I see hearts, angels and song birds coming out of their eyes. And tears. So many happy tears.

I sneak a look over to Kendra, Whitley, and Betsy, who are shaking their heads so fast you can barely tell that they are moving. They also haven't blinked.

"What do you think?"

"I think I want to keep trying things on," I say to the woman waiting on me at the bridal store.

"Oh, of course," Mom says. "You have to try them all on. We need to make the most of this day!"

I force myself into a fake smile as I walk back to the dressing area. The second I get into my room I strip off the dress, hand it to my consultant, and throw on a robe. "I'm not telling you what to do with your inventory, but you should burn that dress."

She laughs as she puts it back on the hanger. "Believe me, if I could, I would. Which one would you like to try on next?"

I look at the wall where my options of dresses are hanging. Since I didn't really know what I wanted—on top of the fact that I don't want to be here—I told everyone that they could each pick one dress for me to try on today. The one I just had on, which was my mom's pick, was the worst. I didn't think it could get worse than Barb's dress that made me look like I was going to prom in the eighties, but I was wrong.

I was so wrong.

"Actually, can you give me a minute?"

My consultant, whose name I think is Jessica, nods. "Of course. If they ask where you are, I'll make something up. I'm really good at being dramatic."

"Thanks," I say with a small smile.

I wrap the robe around tighter and sit down in my dressing room. The second I hear the door close the first tear comes out.

And I just cry.

How did this get so out of hand? I fooled myself into thinking that things were calming down. That maybe my plan about taking things slow, and eventually they'd get to a point where we could tell them rationally, had worked. It had been two weeks since

Shane went to the caterers—which was organized by Mom and Barb with the help of Whitley. She didn't want to do it, but I had tied her hands with the secret. She had to play along. And when she said she didn't think she could get appointments, you know, to help me out of this, Barb and Tammy sat and watched her make phone calls, on speaker phone, to see if they could sneak us in.

But since then, things had been silent on the wedding front. I should have known it was just the eye of the storm.

In the past week alone we've gone cake testing, talked to a DJ, visited three different florists from the one we originally went to—because their roses weren't bloomed enough. Oh, and I had an appointment with a travel agent to talk about a honeymoon. You know, so we can have some time to ourselves to make grandchildren.

Barb's words, not mine.

The more places we went, the more I knew I needed to say something. The only thing I took solace in was that we didn't put down a deposit for anything. Then I was told yesterday that I was going to get picked up in the morning for a girls' day to try on wedding dresses.

So here I am, in a bridal suite, crying in a robe, because this is supposed to be a happy and joyous day, and all I want to do is sneak out of the back door and go hide where no one can find me.

"Amelia?"

I try to quickly wipe my tears away as I hear a knock on the door.

"Can we come in?"

"Yeah."

Whitley and Betsy ease into the room and take seats on either side of me.

"You okay? We came to check on you but I don't know how

long Kendra can distract the Monsters of the Bride and Groom."

I look over to Whitley, and as much as I want to keep it together, I can't. "No."

I fall into her arms, the tears no match for me. She wraps me up and lets me cry as Betsy softly rubs my back.

"You need to tell them."

I nod and lift my head, but the tears are still coming. "I know. I just thought...I don't know what I thought. Every idea I've had has gone to shit. I don't know why I keep trying."

"Hey," Betsy says as she hands me a tissue. "Cut yourself some slack. No one could have seen this insanity coming."

I shake my head. "I did. Yet somehow I convinced myself I could cut it off. Control it like I want to control everything. Not only did I not stop it, it's morphed into a beast I don't think anyone can contain."

"That's why you need to tell them now," Whitley says. "Will they be upset? Probably. But at least this stops and you two can go back to normal."

I laugh. "I wish it was that simple."

"What's that supposed to mean?"

I didn't want to tell Betsy and Whitley this, but I need to get it off my chest. "Shane wants to go through with it."

Neither of them say anything. I look to each of them, and they both have stunned looks on their faces.

"Shane wants to go through with what?" Betsy asks. "Because the only right answer in this situation is telling your mothers that you aren't engaged."

"No. He thinks we should get married."

A mixture of "oh my" and "What the actual fuck" are the reactions. Which tracks. Because I've said all of that since he suggested it.

It's all I've been able to think about since those words came out of this mouth. He said to forget it, but I know it's been weighing on him as well. Things have been...tense...since that day. I know we're both trying to ignore the elephant in the room, but it's starting to get to us. He still comes over. He eats dinner with us and has stayed the night a few times. But I can feel the tension. I think we've had sex twice, and both times he felt distant. I probably did too. Even the kids have noticed he hasn't been around as much. Luke asked at dinner last night if everything was okay, and of course I said things were fine.

They are anything but fine.

"What did you say?"

"I said no."

"Good," Whitley says. "What would make him ask you that?"

I shrug. "I mean, we talked about it before all hell broke loose. But it was more hypothetical. At least, I thought it was."

"Do you want to marry him?"

I nod. "Yes. Someday. Not now. Not like this."

"Not forced."

I look to Betsy and nod my head. "Exactly. I've already been forced into one marriage, and we see how that turned out."

"Did you say that to Shane?"

I shake my head. "I wanted him to realize that. I know now that wasn't the best move. I should have just spoken it. But I have before. He knows how I felt about my first marriage, and what led to it. And things were heated when Shane suggested it. I didn't want him to think I was comparing him to Paul. That would have led to a whole different fight. But he doesn't see it. Oh, and he didn't even ask me! He just said 'maybe we should.'"

"Clearly he didn't go to Oliver for proposal advice," Betsy says with pursed lips.

This makes me laugh through the tears. "Apparently not. But yeah, he basically said 'why not, since we already are?' Those are the words I always dreamed of hearing when asking for my hand in marriage."

I get up and start pacing around the dressing room. "Am I asking for too much?"

"Too much for what?" Whitley says.

I shrug. "I don't know, to have the proposal. To have the big moment. I didn't have it with Paul, which I understand why. I guess I just thought with Shane I'd get that. He...he's so thoughtful. And present. Remember that whole 'if he wanted to he would' conversation we had? That's Shane to a tee. The man is the walking definition of loving by acts of service. So when he just threw it out there... I don't know, it just felt so impersonal. I guess I thought when he asked me to marry him I'd finally have the moment. And that I'd feel like this man would move heaven and earth to spend the rest of his life with me."

"The moment?"

I nod as I feel the tears starting to return. "The moment. The one where I'm taken by surprise when I see him on one knee. The one where I can barely hear him through my racing thoughts and tears when he asks. Watching him slip the ring on my finger. I've just...I know I'm not the girliest girl, but I've always wanted that moment. I thought I was never going to have it. I honestly gave up on it. But...I don't know, I thought maybe Shane would be the one to make that memory with me."

"Oh, Amelia." Whitley stands up and brings me in for a hug. "You deserve that. Every person does."

"I don't know, maybe I'm selfish," I say, now feeling ridiculous actually saying all of that out loud. "I'm thirty-five years old, for Pete's sake. I'm too old for butterflies. Maybe I should be practical."

Betsy pops up and grabs me out of Whitley's embrace. "Oh no, ma'am, we're not talking like that. You're not going back to the woman who would apologize for wanting things. Or pushing her feelings down. You aren't ready, and you don't want to get married under these circumstances. Therefore, you're not. And if he wants to piss and moan about that, then that's a him problem."

She's right. I know she is. It's just with every day this continues, I feel myself wanting to give in, just to put an end to this. It's my natural reaction. It's how I kept the peace for so many years. In my mind, saying yes, and putting aside my feelings, solves all the problems. It makes Shane happy. Our mothers. Probably our friends, even though they're not pushing us. At the end of the day, me saying yes and turning this fake engagement into a real one makes everyone happy.

Except me.

"You're right," I say. "I need to talk to him. We need to get on the same page. And then tell everyone the truth. Hurt feelings be damned."

Just saying that out loud was hard. I can't imagine what this conversation will feel like with Shane.

"Exactly." Whitley says. "Except we have one problem. Well, two."

As if on cue, we hear a knock on the door, and Kendra popping her head in. "Ladies, I can't keep this up. Amelia, I love you, and I hope you're okay, but if you don't come out in a wedding dress soon there is going to be a search party sent. Those two are relentless."

I nod. "Okay. I think I can finish."

"You got this," Betsy says. "Get through it, then we'll sneak you out before they can suddenly get the idea to start looking at bridesmaids' dresses."

I nod. "Let's do it."

I take the dress off the hanger—I think it's the one that Whitley picked for me—and slip it on. I don't mean to look at myself in the mirror, but I do, and I'm stopped in my tracks.

It's the dress. *My* dress. The one I envisioned myself wearing during my beach wedding to Shane. The silk hugs me in all the right places. It's plain—there isn't a drop of lace or beading—yet somehow it doesn't look boring. It has a shimmer to it, and I can imagine the sun hitting it as the sun sets over the Gulf.

"Oh my God, Amelia..."

Whitley comes behind me and puts her hands on my shoulders. "You look beautiful."

"It's my dress," I say through another round of tears. "This is my dress."

"Do you need a minute?" Betsy asks.

I nod my head yes as the two women who have become such special friends leave the room. And all I do is stare at my reflection in the mirror and wonder why I don't want this.

Because I have the dress. I have the man.

I just don't want the wedding.

Chapter 33
Amelia

The second I hear Shane's truck door slam shut my stomach immediately tightens. I grab one of the pillows I bought for his couch and hold it against me, like somehow it's going to either soothe my nerves or shield me from what's about to come.

I wish it could do both.

I went straight to Shane's after dress shopping today. I knew if I didn't, I'd chicken out. I've been here for over an hour, just sitting and waiting. Stewing. Practicing over and over again what I'm going to say. Because I don't want this to be a fight, even though it probably will become one. I love him. I really do. With my whole soul. One day I want to be Mrs. Shane Cunningham.

Emphasis on one day.

I tense as I hear him come through the garage door. I close my eyes and remind myself of things I want to say.

Don't give in. Tell him you love him. Take ownership of what you need to. Make sure he knows you're in this together. But marriage, right now, isn't the solution.

"Hey," he says as he walks into the living room.

"How was work?"

"Fine," he says as he takes a seat next to me.

"That's good."

"How was dress shopping?" His tone is interested. Enthusiastic even.

"Fine. I tried on a few hideous ones our mothers picked."

"Sounds about right. Did you find one you liked?"

The image of me standing in my perfect dress takes over my mind, and I do all I can to not start crying.

"I did," I admit.

"That's great."

The smile on his face breaks my heart. He looks so hopeful. It reminds me of just a few short months ago when he had all the faith in the world that we were right for each other, and I had nothing but doubts.

"When it comes to the possibility of us? I'm eternal."

I just hope he feels that way once I say what I need to say.

"Shane...I can't keep doing this. We need to come clean. I know we thought it would taper, but it isn't."

He falls back against the couch and he looks up at the ceiling. "You want to call it off?"

"Yes."

"The idea that *you* had about keeping it a lie?"

I swallow a frustrated groan. "Yes. I was wrong. It's not working. It's out of hand."

I keep in the comment I have about us only being here because of him and his loose lips originally. That's a fight for another day. And I don't want to rehash that.

"So me going to the caterer's? And you wedding dress shopping? The florists. What was that? Just part of the lie? Playing the part?"

I tilt my head out of confusion. I thought he knew that was

what we were doing? "Yes. I didn't know how to tell them no, so I went along with it. And in turn made you. And that was a mistake. I'm sorry. I take ownership of that."

I look closer at Shane, and he doesn't seem mad. It's more sad. Defeated. I wasn't expecting that. Unless...

"Shane? Did you think going to those things *wasn't* part of the lie? Why did you think we were doing it?"

"I don't know." He falls into his classic Shane pose—hands clasped, elbows on his knees, staring at the floor. "Whitley arranged it. You could have stopped her. And dresses are a big deal. At least that's what I always assumed. I didn't think you'd go unless maybe..."

Is he thinking and about to say what I think he's thinking and about to say? "Shane? Did you think I was changing my mind?"

He doesn't say anything. He just nods his head.

"Shane...why would you think that?"

"Because!" He shouts so loud I physically jump back. "Why wouldn't I? I love you. You love me. I don't see why we're not doing this!"

"Because we said that we weren't doing that!"

"No, Amelia. *You* said you weren't doing that. I never agreed. That was all you. Just like everything in this relationship, it's all you."

Excuse me? Did he just...

"Wow," I say, letting his words process. "How long have you been waiting to get that off your chest?"

"Never mind," he says as he stands up. He slowly turns his back on me, not saying a coherent word. All I hear are deep breaths and a few muttered words under his breath.

"Shane. Don't you never mind me. You're going to turn around and say what you need to say."

I don't know why, but it's at this moment I know I'm not

the Amelia of ten years ago. She would have cowered from this fight. But not today.

"Everything I've done for the past four months has been for you," he begins, but he doesn't turn back around. His voice is lower. More sad than mad, but it still has a bite. "I waited for you. I let you dictate our timeline. Being a secret. When we were going to tell our friends. Our families. That was all you."

"But did I twist your arm?"

"What?" He turns back around to face me.

"Yes. I'll take blame for all of that. Because you're right, all of those were my ideas, but did I force you? I didn't think I did. I thought you understood. But if you had such a problem with it, why didn't you say anything?"

"Now you sound like Simon."

"I never thought I'd say this, but good!" You know this is a jacked-up situation when Simon is the voice of reason. "But why not, Shane? If you had a problem, why didn't you say anything?"

I sit back down because I need to wait him out. He needs to answer this question, not just sit in silence until I crack.

"I waited for you," he says. "I waited so long. I didn't think I had a problem with those things because I wanted you. I wanted us. And if it meant being in secret, then I was good with it. If it meant not telling people, fine, I could live with it."

"What changed?" I ask. "Why all of a sudden is it marriage or bust?"

He doesn't say anything. I feel him shutting back down. He turns back to face the wall and doesn't move.

"Don't do that," I say. This is reminding me of that very first night. The fight we had before he kissed me. Where he'd yell, then retreat. I'd yell then he'd shut down. Somehow though, I don't think this fight is ending in a kiss. "Do you have something to say to me? I might not like it, but clearly there's something eating at you. So say it. Say whatever is on your mind because I can't take the Shane shut down right now."

I should have been more careful what I wished for. Because when Shane turns around, I don't know if I've ever seen a more tortured look.

"Eighteen years, Amelia! I waited eighteen fucking years. Then I had you. We had us. It was perfect. And I thought we were there. We talked about it. *You* talked about it. So when you said no—when you wouldn't even consider it—it felt like... fuck...I don't know. It fucking hurt. It hurt, and I felt like you weren't as in this as I was. And then all these appointments kept popping up I thought maybe you were changing your mind. But apparently not. Now it's not even a discussion. It's once again what you want goes and I'm just sitting here hoping for a scrap like I did for nearly two decades."

"Why are you yelling at me like this?" I stand up, squaring up in front of him. "What do you want me to say? I'm sorry, okay? I'm sorry I thought we could fix it. I'm sorry we didn't tell everyone from the start. I'm sorry I came up with this stupid idea. I'm sorry! I apparently forced you into so many things. I'm fucking sorry. There? Happy?"

He doesn't respond. He just stands there and slow bobs his head in agreement.

"Really? Back to stoic Shane? Anything else? Maybe an apology?"

"What am I apologizing for? You're the one who wants to tell everyone this is fake. That's your decision. I'm just going along for the ride."

Yup. Should have been careful about what I wished for.

"You're the reason we're here in the first place!"

There. I said it. And I'll probably regret it at some point, but not now.

"So now it's my fault?" he asks.

"Well, I'm not the one who told Paul we were engaged. No, that was you and your merry band of brothers."

"Fine. I'll take that," he says, his face now fire red. "But that doesn't change the reason for this entire argument."

"And what would that be?"

"That you don't want to marry me."

I shake my head. "I never said I didn't want to marry you. I just said that I didn't want to marry you *now*. There's a difference."

I think a vein is about to pop out of his head. "Quit fucking mincing words, Amelia. Why won't you marry me?"

"Because you never asked me!"

There. That's it. The root of the problem. He never said the words. He never asked me the question. He suggested we do something that was an idea born out of a lie.

But he never asked me.

"Are you kidding me?"

I shake my head as the tears come hot and heavy. "You didn't. You didn't ask, Shane. You told my ex-husband we were engaged, I said let's go along with it, then you suggested we just do it. There was never a question in there. And you want to know where my mind went? Back to me at eighteen, pregnant, and being forced into a marriage. And I'm not doing that again. I refuse."

He looks away and doesn't say anything. Which I could have guessed was going to be his reaction. Another flashback in the history of Shane and Amelia.

I take a few breaths to calm myself. Because I want him to hear this. I *need* him to hear this. "I've wanted you to come to this conclusion for yourself for weeks. But you haven't. So here it is. I want to marry you. I want to spend the rest of my life with you. I want to build our family together. But not like this, okay?"

He doesn't say anything, which again, no surprise.

"Do you remember all those years ago when we were sitting on Simon's porch, the night before you left for the Army, and you asked me whether or not I wanted to marry Paul?"

"Yeah." His word is so soft I could barely hear him.

"Do you remember what I said?" I don't wait for him to respond. "You asked me what I wanted. And when I told you it didn't matter, I believe your exact response was, 'the fuck it doesn't.' So yes, it was my decision for this to be a secret. It was my idea to do this stupid fake engagement. It's also my idea to make sure we do something because we both want to. Not because one of us does. Or we think it's the easy fix. But because both of us, mutually, want to be together for the rest of our lives."

I walk and grab my keys off his end table and sit back down next to him, placing a soft kiss on his cheek. "I love you. But I'm going to leave, because we both need time to think. And to cool off. We need to make sure this is what we want. And not because of whose feelings we're sparing, or pride, or what we think everyone else wants. Because of what we want. Both of us. No one else."

I start to get up but Shane grabs my hand, stopping me from taking a step.

"I love you," he says. I see his eyes watering, and I know I need to go. If I see this man break down I'll lose it.

"I love you too," I say. "Call me when you know what you want. What you *really* want. When you've thought everything through. You waited for me. Now it's my turn to wait for you."

Chapter 34
Shane

In all the years I've had the photos on my mantel, I don't think I've ever just stared at them. Since Amelia walked out yesterday, I haven't been able to take my eyes off the photo of us. It's been staring at me. Taunting me. Making me face the woman whom I've let down so badly.

Because that photo happened to be taken the day that everything changed, I can't stop thinking about if I did the right thing that night. In some ways, I did. I might not have done it the best way, but finally showing her how I feel led me to a happiness I've never known.

It also led me here: alone, angry, and wondering if my best friend, who is also the woman I love, just walked out of my life forever.

I fucked up. Badly. She's right. I was pushing her. I wasn't listening. I was coming up with ways in my head to justify what I wanted to happen instead of talking to her about what *we* wanted to happen.

I didn't give her a choice the night I kissed her, and I have been basically doing the same thing since this whole fake engagement thing started.

I know I was wrong. I know I need to apologize. The problem is I don't think just an apology is going to be good enough. And for the life of me, I can't figure out what else to do.

A knock on the front door startles me, and also makes me wonder who's coming by this early in the morning. If it were my mom, she would have just let herself in. Oliver is still away. Wes is likely at football. Who knows what Simon is up to. And Amelia...I know that's not happening.

So when I open the door to see Luke and Mariah standing in front of me, I immediately get choked up.

"What the hell, Shane!"

I don't know if I'm more startled at Mariah's choice of words or her pushing past me as she stomps into my house. Then there's Luke. Unlike Mariah, who chose to use her words to tell me how she's feeling, he's going the opposite way. Silent. Staring. It's a look I know well.

"Come in." Luke barely makes eye contact with me as he follows Mariah into the living room. The silence is deafening as they make their way to my couch and take a seat. I pull up the ottoman so I can sit across from them with only the coffee table between us.

"What are you two—"

"What happened?" Mariah asks with an edge. Okay, then. No small talk.

"I don't know."

"You don't know?" Mariah asks. "How can you not know?"

"It's complicated."

"Complicated?" she yells. I've never been on the receiving end of a Mariah verbal whipping. I've always been proud of the way she can speak her mind. I'm still proud of her now, even if it hurts that her words, and her anger, are directed at me. "It doesn't seem complicated to me. You're here looking sad and mad. Mom's at home crying in her bedroom, which she's been doing since yesterday, with the door locked. Doesn't take a genius to figure out you two had a fight."

I nod and do my best not to avert my eyes to the floor. I don't want her to think I'm not acknowledging her. But seeing the fire in her eyes right now physically hurts. It's a look I saw yesterday. Because now more than ever, Mariah is the spitting image of Amelia.

"Why is she crying?" Mariah continues. Her face is getting redder, and I can tell there are about fifteen emotions ready to explode. "We could *hear her*. She hasn't come out of her room. Do you know when the last time she did that was? Right before she left Dad."

The gut punch I feel is immediate. I was injured in war. I've taken punches that I've felt for weeks. But nothing has ever hurt me like those words just did. And it's not just the words. It's knowing that now, for the second time in two days, I'm being compared—and rightfully so—to the man I've spent years trying to be the exact opposite of.

"What happened?" Luke asks the same question Mariah did, but his tone is drastically different from hers.

"We got in a fight."

"Obviously," Mariah says sarcastically.

"Mariah, chill," Luke says, which makes her cross her arms and sit back against the couch in a huff. "Shane, what happened? I know couples fight. But this seems...you and Mom have never fought, at least I didn't think you did, and this seems bad."

"It is," I say. No bother in pretending or lying to them. "I messed up."

"About the engagement?"

I nod. "We...didn't see eye-to-eye on some things."

"Then fix it!" Mariah yells. "Why do adults make everything so complicated?"

From the mouths of babes...

"It's not that easy." I can tell Mariah isn't believing a word coming out of my mouth, even though it's the truth. "I said some things that, while they weren't lies, were delivered in a very cruel way. I didn't listen to her. I was assuming things without talking to her about them. We had a fight and, well, it's going to take a lot more than for me to say I'm sorry."

That's the one thing that I've realized since Amelia walked out yesterday. It's what kept me up all night. I said things—hurtful things—that had truth in them. They were what I was feeling. Whether I was in the right or wrong, they were, at the time, my truth. And instead of talking to her about them in a rational way, I exploded like a bomb and left it to burn.

"So what are you going to do?"

I don't say anything to Luke's question, because I don't have an answer.

"Nothing?" Mariah says, clearly exasperated. "You're not going to say anything? Do anything? Uncle Shane, you're better than this."

"What do you want me to say, Pipsqueak? I messed up. I don't know how to fix it."

"Don't Pipsqueak me," she snaps, and just at that moment, she can't contain her tears. They are coming out hard and heavy, and it's breaking my heart with every second. "My whole life you've been the man who could do anything. The man who would always come through. You were my own personal superhero. The one I could always count on. *We* could always count on. And now you're just going to, what, give up? That's not my Uncle Shane. I don't know this guy."

Mariah pushes herself off the couch and sprints out the door. I stand up to go after her, but Luke stops me.

"Don't," he says. "You got off easy compared to what she told me she wanted to say to you on the way over here."

I do as he says and sit back down. I hate the fact that in a matter of twenty-four hours I made two of the most important people in my life cry. But that's what I get. It's my punishment. And it's still not enough.

"Luke, I am sorry," I say. "I know I need to apologize. And more. I just...I don't know what that is yet. And I don't want to do the wrong thing. Or say the wrong thing. Or worse, make her think it's not genuine, or that I've rushed this, and she rejects me."

"I get that," he says. "But don't you love her? Don't you want to make it right?"

"I do. I love your mom more than anything. I love you and Mariah. I hate this. I just...it has to be perfect. It has to be right. I don't want to mess this up. I have one shot."

"Isn't that why you didn't tell her how you felt for so many years?"

This stops all trains of thought. "Excuse me?"

"You told me that you didn't ask Mom out in high school because you were scared of rejection. Or that you'd lose your best friend. Maybe both."

Well shit...

Luke stands up, and I follow. "And weren't you the one telling me about doing the scary thing? About taking the risk? Because you didn't want to live with regret?"

Well, well, well...if it isn't my own words coming back to bite me in the ass.

"Yes."

"Then don't. Don't have the regret of not trying everything. Who cares if you fail? Just try. Because won't you regret it if you don't do anything? If you just assume you can't fix it? Or think it needs to be perfect?"

I nod, getting exactly what he's saying.

Luke returns my gesture as he starts walking back toward my door. I open it for him and he takes a step out, but turns to look back at me.

"When I heard her crying, I thought she had a fight with Dad," he says. "I never even thought it was you. Not until we walked in and saw your face did I think it was you. Do you want to know why?"

I'm scared of what he's about to say. "Why?"

"Because you promised."

I tilt my head, confused about what he means. "Promised?"

"You said you'd never make her cry."

I take back my earlier statement. This. This is the worst I've ever been hurt. That was the ultimate knife in the chest.

"I'm sorry," I say, fighting back the tears about to spring.

Luke doesn't say anything as he walks back to his car, a crying Mariah in the front seat, and I just sink to the ground.

Oh God, I've hurt them. So much.

I need to fix this. Somehow. And Luke's right. I need to try everything.

Except I have no clue where to begin.

Chapter 35
Shane

Oliver: I'm back! Oh my God, I have so much to tell you guys. Drinks. Tonight. On me. Who's in?

Wes: Thank fucking God. And I swear your story better have a happily ever after. I can't believe you fucking left me with two weeks to go before the season starts.

Oliver: I promise it did.

Simon: I'm in. Been a minute since I've graced The Joint with my presence. Not since the incident.

Oliver: What incident? What's he talking about? What has happened? I know you've been leaving me out of things but that ends tonight. I demand to know what's been going on.

Wes: That, my friend, we need booze for. And Shane needs to tell it.

Oliver: Shane? Shane, why aren't you responding? What's going on? I know you're keeping something from me, and I have a feeling it's about Amelia. I know you wanted to tell me something before I left. What the hell is going on? TELL ME. I NEED TO KNOW THINGS.

I read the text message but I don't respond. I don't have the strength for Oliver and his golden retriever energy tonight.

Shane: Nothing. You guys have fun.

Oliver: Unacceptable. I'm back. I got my girl because of you. Now, you're meeting us out or I'm coming over and dragging you to The Joint myself. I also have a lot of questions that I won't shut up about until they're answered.

Shane: I said I'm not coming.

Oliver: Fine, then we're coming to your house.

Shane: The door is locked. I'm not opening.

Simon: I made keys after I couldn't get in that one morning. Make sure you're dressed, asshole. We'll be over in twenty.

I put my phone down, but I don't leave my recliner. It's where I've pretty much lived for the past week.

After the kids left from verbally whipping me, the rest of the day was a blur. I remember sitting down to think about what they said, and to try and come up with a plan, but I never did. The next day I barely moved. I ignored calls and texts. None of them were from Amelia, anyway. I knew she wouldn't be contacting me, but I had to check. I had to hope.

The One I Love

The day after that, I was supposed to have a shift, but I called off. It was the first time in my six years on the force that I've done so. I told them I needed a few days, that I needed to sort some things out.

I'm in no better shape now than when she left. I'm a mess. I'm confused. I'm angry. My heart is breaking, and I can't seem to pull myself out of the dark.

It's all my fault.

And I don't know how to fix it.

My phone vibrates again, and I hesitate to pick it up, figuring it's one of my three asshole friends again. But I sit straight up when I see Mariah's name on my screen.

Mariah: Shane?

Shane: Hey, Pipsqueak.

Mariah: First I want to say that I'm sorry. Well, I'm not sorry because I meant what I said. But I'm sorry I yelled.

Shane: You don't need to apologize. I'm the one who should be apologizing.

Mariah: Are you going to? I mean to Mom. She's still sad. At least she stopped crying. She told me not to text you, but I'll use my get-out-of-jail-free card if I have to. I just need to know you're not giving up.

Shane: I'm not giving up. I promise.

Mariah: Just freaking fix it. Please.

Shane: I'll do my best.

Mariah: I'm holding you to that.

"Fuck!" I yell while trying to pull my hair out. I throw my phone across the room for good measure.

"Whoa!" Simon says as he, Wes, and Oliver, walk in just in time to see my phone hit the wall. "What the hell was that?"

"It—" I stop myself before I say too much. "It was nothing."

"Well, I'm going to call bullshit on that," Simon says as he makes himself comfortable on my couch. "Wes, hand me a beer."

"Shane, are you okay?"

The concerned question comes from Oliver. Fuck, I've missed this guy. I don't blame him for not being here during all of this—he's had just as much of a whirlwind over the past four months as I have. Yet I know while he might be shocked at all that's happened with me, he's not going to be angry. Or hurt. He's going to try to fix it. Because that's what he does.

That's what best friends do.

I shake my head. "No, I'm not okay."

Saying it out loud isn't as cathartic as I hoped it would be. Then again, I still feel like I'm bleeding from that text from Mariah.

"Okay," Oliver says, pulling up the ottoman so he can sit down in front of me. "Talk to me. Start from the beginning."

Everyone laughs except me. "Oliver, I don't have the energy to start from the beginning."

He looks over to Wes and Simon. "Can you guys fill me in?"

"We got it," Simon says, cracking his knuckles. "It started when Shane kissed Amelia at Whitley and Jake's wedding."

"The wedding! That's when Izzy and I—"

"Yes, we know," Wes says. "Now quiet and let him talk."

"Fine, but I already have a thousand questions."

"Shush," Simon says. "Anyway, she didn't want to ruin the friendship, but he didn't give up, so they started dating but she insisted they keep it a secret. They didn't tell anyone. Well, they told some. But not us, which is rude since I'm his new best friend. Anyway, one day we saw Paul and accidentally told him they were engaged. And then it got out of hand and now we're here, and judging by the state of Shane's beard, I'm guessing they had a fight and he hasn't showered in at least a week."

The room is silent as Oliver processes. Then, because this man is who he is, he says the most Oliver thing I've ever heard.

"You proposed without me?"

I shake my head. "I didn't propose. That's actually the whole problem."

"What?" Wes asks. "What happened that we don't know about?"

"Wait! Am I caught up?"

"Seems as if you are," Wes says.

"Good. I mean, I'm still very confused, but I'm appeased for now. Also, I'm super happy for you, and you owe me a lunch to answer every question I have. After that story, the question count is at roughly ten thousand."

I laugh, and honestly, it's my first real laugh in I don't know how long. "I really could have used you."

"Hey!" Simon says in protest. "I did pretty good."

I shoot him a look. "You got kicked out of the caterers."

He waves me off. "Bug didn't know what she was saying."

"Who's Bug?" Wes asks. "What the fucking hell has been happening this summer?"

"Enough!" I yell. "We will catch everyone up over everything. But first you assholes need to help me get Amelia back, because I'm pretty sure if I don't figure something out, this is over, and it can't be over. It can't."

Oliver pats me on the knee. "We will. Now, what happened, and how are we going to fix this?"

I fill him, and Wes and Simon, in on the events of the past

few weeks. Everything since the day of the catering appointment. Wes and Simon knew about some of it, but no one knew about the fight.

And I must say, as I retell it, I'm even more of an asshole than I thought I was.

"Ouch," Wes says.

"Yeah, man," Simon adds. "Even I know you're supposed to *ask* a woman to marry you."

"I don't need your smartass remarks," I say.

"Well, he's right. Rule number one of proposing is to actually ask her," Oliver says. "And to make sure she wants to. That's rule number two."

"How could I be so stupid?" I yell, grabbing my hair in frustration. "Here I was, thinking that I was helping her, when I was trying to push her into something she didn't want. Just like our mothers were doing. Just like before. I'm no better than fucking Paul."

"Hey!" Oliver says. "Don't talk about my best friend like that."

"Um—" Simon raises his hand. "You've been MIA. I'm the new best friend. But I agree. Don't talk about Shane that way. I don't want to punch you. I always want to punch Paul."

"Enough with the best friend shit," Wes says. "Shane. What are you going to do?"

I stand up and start making laps around my living room. "I don't know. That's why I've been going around in circles for the past however many days."

"What if you proposed? For real?" Wes asks.

I shake my head. "She's not ready. She has said that multiple times. And she's right. We're not. I just got the idea in my head and I ran with it."

"Been there," Oliver says.

"Plus, she'll think I'm doing it just because she said that I didn't *actually* ask her. I don't want her to think that I'm doing that just to correct the blunder."

"That's fair," Wes says. "Do your moms know yet that it's fake? The kids?"

I shake my head. "My mom doesn't. Which I'm guessing means Tammy doesn't either. The kids know it's fake, and they know we're fighting. Other than that, I think everyone still believes we're engaged."

No one says anything for a second. I know I'm racking my brain. I'm sure they are too. I'm in deep thought of what I could do when Oliver literally jumps from his seated position.

"I got it!"

We all look at each other then back to him. "Are you going to tell us?"

I swear to God, Oliver perks up so high I think I see the actual light bulb turn on above his head. "We're going to do something I never thought I'd do, or help someone do, in my entire life."

"What's that?"

"We're going to *un*propose."

Chapter 36
Amelia

I've never been a fan of confrontation.

It's why I put off leaving Paul. It's why I kept delaying my talk with Shane. And it's why I'm just now sitting down with my mom and Barb to tell them that there is no wedding. At least for now.

Hopefully that's true.

When I told Shane the ball was in his court, I knew he'd need a few days. I didn't expect a week. Now with every day that goes by, I'm getting more and more scared that he's taking my words as an ultimatum. And I never meant that. I just wanted him to think about things, to take a step back to see the bigger picture.

But what if that bigger picture is him and I not together?

"Don't freak out," I tell myself as I see my mom's car pull into the driveway, Barb sitting in the front seat next to her. I called them over today because no matter what Shane decides, I have to tell them there's not going to be a wedding, and there never was an engagement.

And there might not be an us.

I didn't want to tell them without Shane, but my hands are tied. They had Whitley make appointments to look at venues today. Dresses, flowers, and DJs were one thing, but venues? I know if there is a date available, money would be put down. They wouldn't even blink twice. And we can't have that.

"Hello? Amelia? Are you ready?"

"In the kitchen, Mom."

I sit at my table, clasping my third cup of coffee of the morning like my life depends on it.

"Amelia? Why aren't you dressed? We have to be at the banquet hall in a half hour."

I look up to Mom and Barb, who each look concerned as I sit at my kitchen table, still in my pajamas. "Have a seat. I need to talk to you both."

"Is everything okay?"

I shake my head as they each take a seat. "No. Yes. I don't know."

Mom reaches for my hand. "Amelia, you're scaring me. What's the matter?"

"Mom. Barb. There's something I need to tell you."

"What is it, dear?" Barb takes my other hand. "No matter what you say, we're here for you. And for Shane. Where is that son of mine, anyway?"

I don't answer the last part of her question. "It's about the engagement."

"Is it about the party?" Mom asks. "I know many haven't RSVP'd, but we'll fix that. You know the whole town wants to be there. Apparently, something happened on Facebook and no one can see it. It's very odd."

"It's not that, Mom. It's..." Here goes nothing. "There is no engagement."

"Excuse me?"

I look to Barb, whose eyes are abnormally large right now. "The engagement. It's off. Well, it was never on. But it's off."

"Amelia, why are you speaking nonsense?"

"It's more than nonsense, Tammy. It's plain cruel," Barb says. "How dare you joke about something like that!"

"I'm not joking. We're not engaged. We never were. It was a lie."

They both release my hands like it's burning them. I look over to Barb, who seems shocked. Then there's my mom, who looks like she's about to cry.

Fuck, I knew this was going to be bad. But it's my own fault for letting it get this far. Hell, for even suggesting we do this in the first place. These are the consequences of my actions.

"How can it be a lie?" Mom says. "You both are...the way you look at each other..."

"He put a picture of you on his mantel!" Barb yells. "Of course you two are getting married!"

"Because we're *together*," I say. "We aren't getting married, but we are together. Well, at least I think we are."

"What does that mean, Amelia?" Mom asks. "Because I'm all sorts of confused right now."

I pour Mom and Barb each a cup of coffee and explain to them everything. The kiss. The dates. The secret that was only a secret to some. That everything we told them at the diner that day, up to the engagement, was real. Then Paul was told about an engagement and all hell broke loose.

"Paul? As in that good for nothin' ex-son-in-law of mine? This is all because of him?"

"Well, partly," I say.

"Oh, this ought to be good..."

I fill them in on the day that everything started spiraling out of control. As I'm telling them the story, their jaws drop a little more. Then I get to the part of the story at Mona's when things really snowballed, and I'm pretty sure they think I'm making this up.

"Amelia, I know I'm biased in this conversation because I want you, and have always wanted you, to be with my son. But that ex of yours is a real shit stain."

"You're not wrong, Barb," I say through laughter. Cause at this point all I can do is laugh.

"So, you said *partly* earlier," Mom says. "Paul was a big reason. What is the other?"

Oh God is she going to make me say this out loud?

"You. And you, Barb. It was both of you."

There's a second of quiet before Mom yells so loud the dogs two blocks away hear her.

"Us! This whole confounded thing was because of us? Barb! Did you hear her? She's blaming us!"

"Oh, I heard her," Barb says, who is grabbing her cell phone out of her purse. "Where is my son? He has some explaining to do."

"Barb, don't call Shane. Please." I grab her wrist to stop her. "This was my idea. Just like before, going with the secret and the lie, it was my idea. This is my fault."

"Why would you do that?" Mom asks. "Why didn't you tell us?"

"We tried. We tried to stop you that day at Mona's. We told you we had something to say, and you waved us away to start planning the wedding."

"Well, we wouldn't have walked away if we knew it was something big," Mom says dismissively. "You should have told us."

I can't with her right now.

"Mom. We tried. And then I thought, I don't know, that maybe after the excitement calmed down that we could sit down and explain everything."

"Why didn't you?"

I shrug. "I don't know. Partially because it was happening so fast. Then all of a sudden, we were at bridal and wedding appointments. And...well...Shane wanted to. I didn't. I didn't know what to do, and next thing you know I'm sitting in a dressing room with wedding gowns, and I don't know, for half a second I considered going through with it."

I hate admitting that, because that perked them both right up. "You're considering it?"

I shake my head. "No. I told him that I wasn't ready. And I meant that. Every time I thought 'maybe I could,' a voice jumped in, reminding me why we're not ready. We had a huge fight, and we haven't talked since the day we went dress shopping."

"Amelia!" Mom yells. "How could you turn him down after he asked you to marry him?"

"He never asked me!" I stand back up, needing to keep my temper down because I feel it rising again. "He said, 'maybe we should.' That's not a proposal, Mom. And then it hit me—for the second time in my life, I was feeling forced into a marriage I wasn't ready for. Back then it was because I was young and pregnant. Now it's because a comedy of errors forcing my hand. Like hell I'm going to have my second marriage be another one I wasn't ready for just because everyone else wanted me to do it."

"What do you mean, forced?" Mom asked. "Who has ever forced you to get married?"

I stop and stare at her. I don't blink. It has to be at least thirty seconds before I realize she actually has no idea what she did. Granted, I've never talked to her about it. Like many things from that part of my life, I pushed them under the rug. But I can't believe she never saw it.

"You, Mom. It was you."

"I never—"

"Mom, the first thing out of your mouth when I told you I was pregnant was asking if Paul was going to be around and the second was insisting that we needed to get married."

"Well, I wanted to make sure you were going to be taken care of. You know how hard I—"

"I know, Mom. You had it rough because Dad left. And I know you had my best interests at heart. But sometimes marriage isn't the answer. Sometimes it is. But I wanted to be the one to decide that this time. Not you. Not Barb. Not Shane. *Me.* I wanted to make sure me getting married was my decision, no one else's."

My breathing is heavy. I didn't realize how much I needed to get that off my chest. That there is almost seventeen years' worth of emotional buildup released into the atmosphere.

And it feels damn good to be free of that.

"Amelia...I..." I sit back down as she fights back tears. "I'm sorry. I never knew. I just...I just wanted you to be happy. To have it better. I always thought I was helping."

"I know you did, Mom. I know your heart was in the right place. But, how about for now, when it comes to my love life, just let me live it."

She nods. "I'll try."

"We'll try."

I turn to Barb, who reaches for my mom's hand and mine. We all grab onto each other, making a circle I can feel the love pouring through.

"Thank you both," I say. "And I promise, no more secrets."

"And we promise to not meddle."

"Too much," Barb qualifies.

"Until there are more grandbabies."

"Yes, once there are grandbabies, all bets are off. Amelia,

are you off birth control? You know, with your age, maybe you and Shane—"

"Stop!" I yell. "You guys couldn't even go *two minutes*. And did you forget Shane and I are fighting?"

"Oh, well, that's easy enough." Barb goes for her phone again.

"Barb! Stop!"

"Sorry," she says. "Old habits die hard."

I shake my head. "How about this? Breakfast on me. Then we can also tell Mona the news together so that way she doesn't get anything misunderstood."

"Sounds good."

"Do the kids want to come?" Mom asks as we grab our stuff and head toward my front door.

"Luke's at work," I say before yelling up the stairs. "Mariah! We're going to Mona's!"

Usually saying the word *Mona's* is enough to get Mariah running down the stairs. But she doesn't. In fact, I don't hear anything coming from her room.

"Weird," I say, getting out my phone to send a text. "Where is she?"

Just as I'm about to hit send, Mariah comes busting through the door so fast she nearly slams it into Barb. "Hey, Mom."

"Are you okay?"

"Yeah. Sure. Everything's fine."

"Why are you out of breath? Where were you?"

Mariah doesn't answer me and instead turns toward Mom. "Hi, Grandma! Hi, Barb! Where you guys going?"

I narrow my eyes at her. "Mona's. Want to come? Maybe tell me why you're running back in like you snuck out of the house and now you're trying to sneak back in?"

"I wasn't sneaking back in. Well, I was, but not because I was doing something bad. I've been told to give you this."

Mariah hands me a piece of paper, and I don't even have it undone when I start crying.

One night, long ago, a boy kissed a girl because he thought it would be the biggest regret of his life if he didn't. Meet him at that place so he doesn't have to live with another regret.

Chapter 37
Shane

"Where is she?"

I don't know how many times I've walked back and forth along the front porch of Simon's childhood home, but I know it's enough times that I can see my footprints.

"Easy," Simon says as he glides back and forth on the porch swing. "It will take her a few minutes to get here."

I stop and look over to him. "Why are you still out here?"

"Because!" he says. "I've been in this with you since the beginning. Since she was Mary. Do you think I'm about to miss this part? If you do, then you have another thing coming. Plus, these are my decorations. All of those streamers and balloons? Mine. Plus, this is my house."

"Simon, it's not your house anymore. Get in here with everyone else."

The scolding is from Mrs. Banks, and I might be nervous as hell right now, but that doesn't mean I can't laugh at the situation. It reminds me of how she used to yell at him when we were kids.

"Come on, Mom," Simon whines.

"Why do you insist on being the way you are? An instigator. That's what you are." She holds the door open while making eye contact with me. "I'm sorry, Shane. I really tried with this one, but he gets it from his daddy."

"I know, Mrs. Banks," I say. "Thank you again for letting me do this."

She waives me off. "Anything for you boys. And our Amelia."

The sound of a car turning into the long driveway of the Banks house puts me on alert, and I hear Mrs. Banks hiss at Simon again to get inside before she comes out after him.

"Don't fuck this up," he says to me as he passes by. "I *will* punch you."

I don't say anything to Simon as I take in a breath, but don't let it out, as I watch Amelia's car come up the driveway. And if I'm not mistaken, I see Mariah trying to hide in the front seat.

When Oliver said I needed to unpropose, I thought he was crazy. It made zero sense.

Then I thought about it. When was the last time we were happy? And my mind kept going back to Florida. On the motorcycle. Looking at the sunset. We were talking about our future. About a wedding. About forever.

But it was because we wanted it. Just us. Just like Amelia reminded me it should be. Not outside forces making us do something. Not me thinking I could suggest something into existence because it would fix a problem.

Unproposing is perfect. As Oliver explained, it's the best way for Amelia to know I'm doing my best to not only undo the action, but to reverse time. And what better place to reverse time than to go to the place when I first knew, without a shadow of a doubt, that I loved her.

Here goes everything...

"Let me guess, Oliver's back home?"

"Why do you ask that?"

We take a few steps toward each other. "Because only Oliver Price would have given you the idea to tell me to come here. And to decorate."

I shake my head. "The note was his idea. The decorations were Simon. But coming here? That was all me."

"Cunningham. You are a softie."

I reach for her hands, which she gives me. Thank God. "Only for you."

I lead her back to the front porch steps, making sure to sit her down exactly how we were all those years ago.

"First, I need to apologize," I begin. "I don't know what I was thinking. I just...I thought it would fix things. I figured we were headed there, so why not? All I could think about was that talk we had on the beach. That we both wanted to one day be husband and wife. Never did I put together what it would make you feel like. Or how it could give you flashbacks. I'm so, so sorry."

She nods. "Thank you. And I know deep down you meant it from a good place."

"I did. I promise you I did."

"That brings me to my apology," she says. "I'm sorry I made us go through all these hoops. We wouldn't have been here if I wouldn't have been so hell bent on this being a secret."

"I know you needed to say that, so thank you. But in reality, I have a feeling even if we had told everyone right away there still would have been a shit storm. Just a different kind.

"Agree," she says. "Speaking of shit storms, I told our mothers. And I finally told my mother how she made me feel seventeen years ago when she all but forced me to get married."

"Fuck," I groan. "How did it go?"

"About as you imagine. Depending on how this goes

between us, they are demanding a family dinner tomorrow. And every Sunday for the next year."

"That's fair."

I take a breath, because I know what I need to say next. And I need to make sure I say it all.

"Do you remember the night on this porch?"

She smiles. "We were just two young, dumb, and frightened kids."

"We really were."

"Do you remember what you asked me that night?"

She nods and rests her head on my shoulder. "I asked you if you were scared."

"You did. I was scared I'd never see you again. I knew there was a good chance I was going to get sent overseas. I knew if I did, I might not come back. I couldn't imagine a world where I left Rolling Hills not knowing what it was like to kiss you."

"I'm glad you did."

"Really?" This is new.

She sits back up, but takes my hand in hers, lacing our fingers together before clasping it with her other. "Yeah. One, it was a great kiss. Two, I got the satisfaction of knowing I'd kissed you and Emily never did."

We both share a laugh, and I kiss the top of her head. "I was scared that night. Scared to leave. But even worse, when I kissed you, I was scared you'd push me away. That because of one impulsive move, I'd lose my best friend."

I stand up in front of her, keeping our hands joined. "Amelia, I stand here today scared again. I'm scared I messed this up. I'm scared we're over before things even began. I'm scared that I got to taste what forever was going to be like, and I ruined it. So, just like then, I'm going to do something maybe a little reckless, and maybe a little unexpected."

I take a deep breath. Here goes nothing.

"Amelia Evans. Will you do me the honor of not marrying me?"

"Shane—wait, what did you say?"

I chuckle because I can only imagine what that sounded like. "Amelia, I thought about what you said, that we weren't ready. And we aren't. If we're ready to take a step forward, it should be moving in together. Or getting a dog."

"A dog?"

"Yeah, a dog. But not a small dog. Cocker spaniel or bigger."

"Mariah has always wanted a Goldendoodle."

I groan, because of course now I'm going to have to get her one. "Fine. A Goldendoodle. But we need to learn to navigate this. Navigate us. We still haven't even done that, and I know that now. We need to figure out what we want. We should talk to the kids and make sure they're on board. And we can do all of that on our time. Not because we want to stick it to Paul. Not because we want to make our mothers happy. Not because it's the easy fix, but because we love each other and we're ready to spend our lives together. I want to make your dreams come true, but only when you're ready for them."

I stand in front of her, but I don't kneel. No, the day I kneel in front of Amelia, it's going to be for one reason and one reason only.

"Amelia Renee Evans, will you not marry me?"

She laughs and nods her head. "Shane Thomas Cunningham, I will not marry you."

"Yeah, you won't!"

I laugh at Simon's words as I pick Amelia up and kiss her as our studio audience makes their way outside—that being Simon, Oliver, Wes, and Luke.

"I love you," I say.

"I love you more."

"Doubtful."

"You did it!"

I hear Mariah just seconds before she barrels into me, hugging me around my waist. She may be growing up, and talking to boys and using swear words, but she'll always be my Pipsqueak.

"I'm sorry it took me so long," I whisper as I let go of Amelia to hug her.

"I'll forgive you. After you get me my Goldendoodle. Yes, I was eavesdropping."

I laugh as Amelia and I continued to get bombarded by hugs, slaps on the backs, and ear-piercing whistles.

"I can't believe this is happening!" Oliver says through tears, pulling Amelia away to wrap her in a hug. "I've never been so happy for people to not get married."

"Good job," Simon says as he gives me a back-slapping hug. "And I can say that I was a part of the not happily ever after."

I shake my head and roll my eyes. "You're something, you know that?"

We share a knowing smile. If anyone would have told me I'd go through all of this with Amelia, and Simon was going to be the closest one to me during all of it, I would have laughed in their face. Simon, the egotistical, doesn't-believe-in-love asshole, is the one who helped me get, and get back, the love of my life.

I wouldn't believe it if I hadn't lived it.

Then again, I still can't believe I'm with Amelia. Who'd have thought all those years ago, on this very porch, that we'd end up back here.

I sure as hell didn't.

Chapter 38
Amelia

"I still don't know what I'm more upset about, that you guys kept this from me for months. MONTHS! Or that my wife knew and didn't tell me. Or that I missed out on screwing with Paul because I could have taken the engagement story to a whole new level. You know what? No, that's it. That's what I'm most mad about."

We all laugh as Oliver asks to hear the story again with Paul, which of course Simon loves to tell. I take the chance to sit back and look at everyone who came tonight on short notice. Of course, Wes, Betsy, and their kids. Oliver and Izzy. Simon. We've set up shop at the firepit, which is where we tend to gravitate when we're over at Wes's. Then, because we left them out for far too long, we decided to invite our mothers. But let's be real, even if we hadn't invited them, they would have shown up.

So we leaned into it and invited *all* the mothers over. It's been far too long since the five women who raised us were all together. When we were younger, this would be a common occurrence. The five of us getting into trouble somewhere, and the five of them playing cards, or working on some project. Right now, they're currently sitting around one of the tables, laughing and telling stories.

And of course, there is my crew. Emerson and Mariah are doing something on their phones. No surprise there. But then I glance into the pool, where I see Luke, who is with his girl-friend Kylie.

I almost cried when he asked if he could bring her. Not in an overbearing mother kind of way. More like "my baby boy isn't so much a baby anymore" kind of way. It also shows me how serious he is about her. He realizes everyone who's here. He introduced her to his grandmother. Me. Shane. The rest of the crew. And he knows his uncles won't pull any punches if they see any red flags—from him or her. But he just smiled and nodded. He knew. He knows. He said he wanted to introduce her to all the important people in his life.

And I can't be mad. Kylie's a sweet girl. Shy. Cute. Apparently, a hell of an athlete. And from what I can tell in the short time I've known her, the perfect first girlfriend for my son. I don't know what she's saying right now, but my son is all smiles and hearts in his eyes. His arms are around her waist, and I don't think he realizes there is anyone here besides the two of them.

"I know that look," Shane says as he wraps his arms around me. "The boy is smitten."

"Smitten, huh?"

"Yup," he says as he kisses my temples. "He's a goner."

I laugh and look away, wanting to not be the creepy mom who stares at her kid and his girlfriend.

"So, we're all here," Betsy says. "And everyone knows everything, right? No other surprises? Things we forgot to mention?"

"All good here," Wes says. "Football is good. Kids are good. We're good. Everything is good."

"You know about us," Oliver says, wrapping his arm around Izzy. "And now she's back where she belongs. And, we have an announcement."

"You're already engaged, Oliver. And married. You can't keep doing this."

"Shut your face," he says to Simon. "What I was going to say is that we're going to be holding a reception, and a vow renewal, hopefully next month. Of course, I want everyone to be a part of it."

"Hell yeah!" Simon says. "I want to DJ."

Oliver gives him a confused look. "You want to DJ? You can DJ?"

He shrugs. "How hard can it be?"

Everyone just laughs as Izzy leans into Oliver. "Actually, Amelia or Betsy, I need to talk to Whitley. I'd love to hire her to put it together for me."

"Easy enough," I say. "She should be here any minute now. A friend of hers was coming into town tonight because she was going to look at a piece of property tomorrow. Actually! Betsy, it was the caterer from her wedding. You remember her, right? I think her name is Charlie."

It's then that I see Simon stiffen in his chair. I watch him for a second and happen to catch him looking over toward Shane. What the hell is this about?

"Simon?" I ask. "Is everything okay?"

"Yup," he says a little too quick.

"Simon," Shane says, leaning a little closer to him. It's then that I notice the look Shane is giving him. It's his "I know you're full of shit look." He's given it to Simon no less than a thousand times. "Anything you want to share with the group?"

"Nope."

"Nothing at all?"

"I said no."

"So if I say the word 'bug' it isn't going to make you irrationally angry?"

"Wait! Bug!" Wes says. "You mentioned that when we were making sure Shane was alive. Who the hell, or what the hell, is Bug?"

A hush falls over our circle. All eyes are on Simon. What the hell does a bug have to do with anything?

"Simon? Everything okay?"

"Fuck this!" Simon shoots up out of his chair and storms off toward the house. He doesn't pass go. He doesn't collect two hundred dollars. He doesn't even tell his own mother goodbye. A minute later, we hear a car peel out of Wes's driveway.

"What was that about?" Wes asks.

"I've never seen Simon act like that," Oliver says. "And that includes the time he lost a bet to me and had to come read to my first-grade class."

"Oh there's a story," Shane says. "I don't know what it is yet, but I have a feeling it's going to be a doozy."

Everyone starts talking among themselves again, and I lean over to Shane. "What do you know, and why haven't you told me?"

Shane smiles and nods his head, signaling for us to step away.

No one notices that we do as we walk hand-in-hand across Wes's patio toward his house. We step inside, and as soon as we close the door, Shane picks up his speed, nearly dragging me toward...the laundry room?

"What are you doing?" I ask as he slams the door behind me and locks it. "Shane?"

He swallows my words as he dives in for a kiss. He presses

me against the door and lifts me up, my leg wrapping around him as we kiss the daylights out of each other.

"I've missed you," he says as his lips start making their way down the slope of my neck. "I missed you so fucking much."

"I've missed you too."

Shane carries me the few steps to the washing machine, where he sets me down and quickly proceeds to push down the straps of my sundress and the cups of my bra, allowing my breasts to spill over. He catches them and quickly puts one in his mouth, the instant sensation nearly making me cry as I let out a yelp.

"Shh," he says between licks and flicks. "Who knows who could be in the house. But I can't wait another minute to taste you."

I use one hand to hold me up as the other runs through his hair as his mouth takes whatever it wants.

He can. It's his. I'm his. And our forever might not be official yet, but I know it's there.

And I can't wait to get it started.

His mouth doesn't move from my breast as his hands starts gathering up the bottom of my skirt. When it's up my legs, I feel his finger making its way to my center, moving my underwear to the side just enough to so he can insert two fingers into me.

"Shane," I whisper, though I wish I could yell. His movements make me fall into him as I wrap my arms around his shoulders. I'm holding on for dear life as he lets his fingers explore me, landing on that perfect spot that makes my eyes roll back.

"Never again," he says as his finger continues to penetrate. "Never apart again."

"Never," I say, clawing onto his back. "Take me, Shane. Take me now."

He rips his fingers out of me, leaving me heaving as he quickly unbuttons his shorts and pushes them down just enough to free his very big, and very ready, cock.

"Hold on," he says. "And remember, you can't scream."

Easier said than done as he drives into me, which simultaneously makes me lose my breath and want to yell to the heavens. My hands fall back to the top of the washing machine as Shane grabs my hips and pulls me to the front, giving him the perfect angle to take me hard and fast.

Exactly what I need.

"You...are...mine," he grunts as he continues to pound into me. "Now. Forever."

"Yes," I say in a heavy breath as my body shakes from his thrusts. "Forever."

I'm surprised when Shane slips out of me, but before I can figure out what's happening, he's pulling me down so I'm standing and turning me around, bending me over so he can take me from behind. The second he reenters me, I let out a sigh of relief. Every time we're like this—where it's fast and hard, or other times where it's slow and we have all the time in the world—I feel completed. Shane completes me. And I know that's a cheesy line from a movie, but it's true.

And I never understood it until my best friend kissed me.

"Amelia," he says as he wraps his hand around my hair, bringing me up to him where my back is against his chest. "I can't hold on much longer."

"Then don't."

His other hand wraps around my waist, allowing his fingers to access that perfect place on my pussy. It only takes a few flicks and pumps before we're both set into orbit. His grip onto me is so tight I don't think I can breathe. The only thing keeping me standing is my hands on top of the washing machine and Shane's hold.

The two of us both come down from the high, but we don't move. Shane does turn me around, but that's only so he can bring me into his arms, holding me like I might go somewhere.

I get why. This last week has been hard. Emotional. I know he was probably scared. I was too. The longer we were apart, the more I was worried that it was over. That we went too hard, too fast. Add in the secrets and lies, and I was terrified it was maybe too much to come back from.

I should have known better. Because when it comes to me and Shane, we were meant to be. Even if it took me almost two decades to see it.

"I don't want to go back out there."

I laugh as I fix myself and make sure everything is put back into place. "You know we can't stay in the laundry room all night."

"I know," he says. "And it is technically a party for us."

"True," I say, raising onto my tiptoes to give him a quick kiss. "Plus, if we're gone for too long, our mothers are going to come looking for us. And I might be in my thirties, but I do not need my mother—or yours—catching us in the act."

"Fine," he groans. "But only another hour. Max. Then I'm taking you home."

"Sounds perfect."

We safely make our way back outside, and seemingly no one reacts to us returning. Moms are still chatting. Kids are still occupying themselves, and our group is still around the fire.

Look at us, having sneaky stealth sex.

"And where did you two head off to?" Wes asks.

"Just went inside for a bit," I say as I take a seat.

He looks over to Shane. "What room do I need to disinfect?"

I feel the blush coming over my cheeks. I look over to

Shane, who suddenly looks very proud of himself. Considering the orgasm I just had, I'll give him that.

"Laundry room."

"Good choice," Betsy says. "That's one of our favorites, too."

We all start laughing as Wes passes Shane a beer, which they promptly toast each other with. The night continues with talk and laughter. Stories and questions. Soon everyone gathers around the pit.

It's the perfect night.

I take a second to look around, and it takes all I have in me not to get emotional over how many blessings I have in my life.

A meddling mother who I often want to strangle, but loves the best way she knows how.

Two children who, even when so many times I figured I was screwing up, are growing into being the best kind of people.

Friends who have been with me since the beginning. New friends I couldn't imagine my life without. The family that isn't blood related, but I'd die for.

And Shane. The man who saved me in more ways than one. The boy who used to be my best friend. The man I now can't imagine my life without.

The road here was winding. There were bumps. There were times when I for sure thought I was at a dead end. But I'm here now. I've reached the destination.

And that's all that matters. Because I'm with the one I love, surrounded by those who love us.

Epilogue
Simon

"SPEAKING OF REGRETS..." MY WORDS TRAIL OFF AS someone walking past me catches my eye. She doesn't just catch my eye. I do a full double take. It's the caterer. Her face goes out of my sight line and I shake my head. Because no way could that be who I thought it was. "I don't have many. But I do have one, and it's not telling you what a money-hungry bitch Cara was. We all agreed to keep our mouths shut because you seemed happy. Well, guess what? I'm going to speak now. Only this time *you're* being the little bitch."

"What are you saying?" Wes asks.

"I'm saying we didn't do anything to save you from your first wife. But I am going to try and save you from being miserable for the rest of your life. Betsy is it. You're not going to do better than her. If you fuck this up, her future will be fine. It's your future that's going to be alone and miserable."

There. I said what I needed to say to Wes. Now I can get

back to staring at the woman who has a striking resemblance to the girl I knew as Bug.

When she walked past, I could have sworn it was Charlie. I mean, in theory, it could be. Then again, I haven't seen her in fifteen years so what the hell do I know?

I haven't thought about Charlie in ages. But that was by design. She occupied so many of my thoughts when she left out of nowhere that I had to force myself to erase her from my memory. It was the only way I could move on after she just left without a word. Who does that? And who doesn't tell their friends they are leaving?

At least I thought we were friends. Mostly. Yes, we were competitive. Yes, we loved to one up each other. Yes, both of us always wanted to get the last word in. But at the end of the day, we were friends. I actually at the time hoped we could be more than that.

The woman starts walking again, and I swear my mind is fucking with me. Either that or I've had too much to drink.

It can't be Charlie. She doesn't live in Nashville. I mean, she could have moved here from Knoxville. But why? That is just one of the many questions I have if this woman is in fact Bug.

I know I'm staring, but I can't help it. She's exactly what I imagine Charlie would look like more than a decade later. Well, except for the red hair. My Bug was a blonde.

No, this woman is curvy in all the ways that used to drive me crazy whenever I was in her presence. And it wasn't just her body that would drive me crazy. Her boldness was a turn on. Her confidence was sexy. And the way she could verbally spar with me better than anyone I had met? My pants got tight more than once because of that. Take right now. The woman who might or might not be Charlie is at least six inches shorter than every server she is talking to. Yet, standing there in her chef's coat, pointing her finger in all directions, she's commanding the room. Letting them know who's boss.

Even if this woman isn't Charlie, I might have to go introduce myself.

I hear the guys say something to Wes, but I don't know what and I couldn't care less. Because suddenly, the woman turns around and I'm frozen in place.

Because there she is. My Bug.

She's like a ghost of memories from the past. Late nights studying with her random concoction of snacks. The coffee she would make me every day even though I hated coffee. Arguing about who should be on the professional wrestling Mount Rushmore. Dance parties in my dorm room because we were slap happy from pulling all nighters.

The kiss. The one kiss. The last night I saw her.

No woman ever pushed me the way Charlie did. No one ever challenged me like her. Or called me out like she did. No one has ever, outside my immediate circle, made me smile like she could. And no one said no to my offers for dinner or a date more than she did.

She was one of a kind. In every way imaginable.

And she never said goodbye.

I nearly flip the table over as I push away from it and start making a beeline toward her. I'm guessing she hasn't seen me. If she has, she's doing a great job of ignoring me. Which also seems fitting considering the way she left all those years ago.

"Charlie!"

I'm pushing through groups of people without apologizing, which I know is a dick move. But I need to stop her before she disappears.

Again.

My pace picks up as I call out for, but she doesn't turn around.

"Charlie!"

Okay now she has to be ignoring me. I just yelled so loud I think the DJ stopped playing music. And judging by the look on everyone's faces they are hearing me just fine. Yet, she's picking up her speed and not even looking back toward my yelling.

I'm just a few yards away from her when I watch her push the kitchen door open.

"Bug!"

This stops her on a dime.

She slowly turns around. It gives me a chance to take her in. Full curves. Red hair that reminds me of fire, which is sitting wildly on the top of her head in a messy ponytail. Deep blue eyes that I could get lost in so easily.

"Simon?"

"What the fuck Charlie?"

This takes her back. "Nice to see you too."

Did I mention Charlie was sarcastic? The two of us when we were both on our game was a master class in smartass dialog. "Were you really not going to stop?"

"Stop?"

"I was yelling for you."

She slightly shrugs her shoulders. "I didn't hear you."

"Bullshit." She looked up then back down as she shrugged. That's her tell when she's lying. It's subtle. Few ever caught on to it. I was one who could. Good to know that's one more thing that's stayed the same. "What are you doing here?"

"Working."

One word answers. Great. "Can we talk?"

She shakes her head. "I'm working."

"We already ate dinner. I know the bride and groom so if you're worried about not getting paid, I'll take care of it. I think you can sneak away for five minutes. Please. It's been fifteen years and well, I think a talk is the least we can have."

I know I'm begging now, but I don't care. This woman owes me an explanation and I'm not about to have her walk out of my life again without getting one.

She looks back to the kitchen then back to me. And for just a second, her hard demeanor is gone. Her sarcastic shield has been lowered. I only saw this side of Charlie a few times during our years together.

Including the night I thought everything was going to change.

"I'm sorry Simon. I can't."

She turns to walk away and out of reaction, I grab her arm and stop her. She looks down at our connection, then back up to me.

"Bug..." My voice is pleading.

"Please Simon. Just let me go."

She turns and walks back into the kitchen. And for the second time in my life, Charlie has walked away from me without an explanation.

Except I'm not that dumb kid anymore. I have means. I have resources. I have a thorn in my side that's fifteen years old.

Because this time she isn't walking away from me. And I am going to get in the last word.

Thank you for reading Shane and Amelia! I hope you loved their story as much as I did.
*** Now, how about a bonus scene? And not just any bonus scene. Their wedding.***
*** And yes, it's at the beach.***

Also by Chelle Sloan

THE NASHVILLE FURY, PRO FOOTBALL SERIES

Off the Record (A secret relationship, office romance)

Off Track (A surprise pregnancy romance)

Off Season (A second chance romance)

Off Limits (A sibling's best friend, close proximity romance)

NASHVILLE FURY WORLD

Off the Market at Christmas (A childhood friends-to-lovers, opposites attract romance

LOVE ONLINE SERIES

Thirst Trap (A one-night-stand turned more, social media romance)

Match Maker (A female billionaire/blue collar, fake dating romance)

Run Run Rudolph (A celebrity on the run, one bed romance)

ROLLING HILLS

The One I Want (A single dad/nanny, age gap romance)

The One I Need (An opposites attract, accidental marriage romance)

The One I Love (A friends-to-lovers, secret relationship romance)

The One I Hate (An enemies-to-lovers romance - Coming April 2024)

THE SALVATION SOCIETY

Reformation: A Salvation Society Novel (A friend's-to-lovers, redemption romance)

Acknowledgments

When I started plotting this book, I didn't think I had much in common with Amelia. Yes, I was a tomboy who didn't figure out makeup until later in life (oh who am I kidding, I still don't know), but other than that, I didn't think I would relate to her much.

Then I wrote her ex-husband. Because I think many of us have had a Paul in our lives. I have. It was then I realized how much of Amelia was in me. Because a Paul can ruin us. He can make us think that we're not enough. But we are. We are enough.

We are freaking bad ass. And sometimes you have a Shane to help you find that part of you.

Oh Shane...I'm going to be honest, this guy made me nervous. I don't write brood or grump well. It stresses me out. So when people started wanting his book all the way back in The One I Want, I started panicking a little.

How would I do it? Could I do it? Cue the nerves and anxiety...

I hopefully did, because I love this man. I love how he loves. I love how he was with Mariah and Luke. I love the kind of friend he is.

I didn't expect to love these two as much as I do. I hope you do as well...

Now to the things that won't make me cry when I write them...

First and foremost, my parents. As always, you are my biggest cheerleaders even if you still have no idea what I'm doing. You've allowed me to follow my dreams and my path, and for that I am forever grateful.

To my family and friends: Your support has been amazing. Many of you have no clue how I ended up here, but that doesn't mean the support hasn't been there. I love you all.

Kelly, you've been with me on this book journey since day one. Not only are you an amazing alpha reader, but you are an amazing friend. I hope I wrote the Shane you have been begging for.

Amanda, who would have thought when we met nearly ten years ago that one day we'd be here together? Thank you for keeping my life in order. Thank you for reminding me to drink water. And thank you for being my best friend.

Kiezha, thank you for correcting my bad grammar habits and being an amazing editor. Michele: Thank you for dotting the Is and crossing the Ts and your constant cheerleading.

Corinne, I'm here because of you. If you wouldn't have given me a chance I wouldn't have started writing. You forever changed my life.

To the tribe of authors I've been blessed to cultivate over the years: Julia, Georgia, Bella, Mae, Claire, The Nerdy Book Herd, Adriana, and Beck, I love you ladies. Thanks for either the words of encouragement, the laughs, or the help when I start panicking.

To Panera and its Unlimited Sip Club. Thank you for keeping me caffeinated and for my booth that you really need to just start putting a sign at that says it's my seat.

Last but not least: Readers. I love you all. Whether this was your first book by me, or you've been here since Reformation, I'm truly thankful for all of you. There are so many amazing authors you could be reading. I'm humbled that you chose me.

About the Author

Known for her witty sense of humor and TikTok antics, Chelle Sloan is a former sports editor turned romance author. You know, cause you meet someone who has done those jobs every day.

An Ohio native, she's fiercely loyal to Cleveland sports, is the owner of way too many — yet not enough — tumblers and will be a New Kids on the Block fan until the day she dies. She does her best writing at Starbucks, Panera, or anywhere that's not her house.

As for her own happily every after? Maybe one day...

Stay up to date with all things Chelle & join the VIP Squad!